GRACEY JAMES

It's Been Five Years

To my mom & nana who read every word I write... thank you for pushing me to do everything I dream of. This only happened because of you.

&

To my real-life Easton Mills, our friendship throughout our childhood inspires a lot of my art, so... here's to another piece. Maybe in this universe we'll have a happier ending.

Contents

1

Home again

TATE

I was wrong. It's a funny thing to be wrong. Most people dread being wrong so much that they will go to extraordinary lengths to prove that they are right — no matter how much pride it might cost them.

I am most people.

Five years ago, I sat on this very tarmac in the Orlando Airport, only then, I was going and not coming. I made a promise to myself that day that I would never be here again. I've spent years dodging questions from my mother on why I didn't want to come back. I've avoided the people I used to see here like the plague, scared they would ask why I don't visit them anymore. I've kept myself at a distance because, from a distance, things don't hurt as badly as they do on the front lines.

I've made a lot of promises to myself. I will run a mile everyday, and I'll stop eating sour patch kids — but that's the thing about self promises. If you don't say them out loud, the only person that can keep you accountable to sticking to said promise, is yourself. So, I've made lots of promises and most of the ones I've made to myself, I've broken. I'm too stubborn to admit it, but I let myself down more than I ever let others down. It's easier to hurt yourself than it is to hurt others.

The window feels cold against my forehead. I wonder how long I've been staring at the men in bright yellow vests unloading luggage from the bottom of our plane.

If it wasn't for my mother, I wouldn't be here at all.

We sit on the tarmac for so long I begin to get antsy. It might be the anticipation of being back here in Florida, or it might be my mother's leg shaking beside me the whole flight that has my stomach in knots.

She hates flying. Always has. She held my hand during takeoff and during the bumpy landing. She always prays through even the slightest turbulence. I've never known anyone with more stress and faith in the same body. She's passed that along to me, I guess. Though planes don't quite peak my stress levels the way they do hers. My mother is a stubborn woman (I get that from her too). I begged her not to make me come. She's been back a few times, just not with me.

"It's been long enough. You're still living in my house, which means you obey my rules, and that means you're coming with me whether you like it or not," she said this morning as I refused to zip up my suitcase. She's right. Although I just turned eighteen, which makes me a legal adult, I'm still in high school and I still eat her food, and she still pays for my gas. So, I'm here. I've been able to make myself busy in years past when she would randomly decide to come back here, but this time no excuse was good enough to keep her from booking me a ticket.

A place that once felt like a second home to me now feels like a distant memory.

Shockingly, it's not the humid air or massive amounts of bugs, or the disgusting alligators that deter me from Florida. It's not this place or the element. It's a person that has kept me away from this place for so long.

Easton Mills.

Back then, visits to the Mill's house meant being barefoot on the beach, eating ice cream out of coffee mugs, and staying up late in the kitchen talking about everything and nothing at the same time. I used to count down the days til I saw the Mills. I used to see them multiple times a year. But the one constant was two weeks every summer in their house. I counted down the days like it was Christmas.

Back then, everything felt easy. Easton and I were inseparable—best friends who knew each other better than anyone else. Now, I don't even know if he'd recognize me, or worse…if he even cared to.

The seat belt sign dings. I sit up straighter, heart pounding in my chest.

I need to get off this plane.

I don't want to be here.

I want to go home.

✳✳✳

The airport was smaller than I remember. A little dingier too. As a kid, everything was bright and beautiful. Why does the color fade from our eyes as we get older?

I spot Jessie almost instantly. Her big warm smile is hard to miss. She has this way of glowing like she lives on the beach year-round. Which, I guess in a way, she does. She spends every moment she can in the sun. Her skin glows golden like a sunset.

I've always been jealous of her tan.

She starts waving like crazy when our eyes finally meet.

"Tate Knightly!" She calls out, her voice like a a song I didn't realize I had forgotten. It's music to my ears. She is one of two people who call me that. It's reserved for her and my mother only. The two most important women in my life.

My smile widens as I rush toward her.

Her hug is tight and grounding, and for a second, I let myself relax. It's like no time has passed. I didn't realize how much I'd missed her the past five years. Her hug is nostalgic in a way that makes my heart a little sad. It makes me sick to think of how many Jessie hugs I've missed out on since the last time I was here.

"You've grown into such a beauty, sweet girl," she says, pulling back to look at me. My face squished in her hands now. She looks over at my mom, grinning big.

"Look just like your mama in college. Doesn't she Kora?" I laugh as my mom shakes her head in disagreement.

"She's far more beautiful than I ever was. Double as stubborn too," she says.

I've seen pictures of my mom and Jessie from their college days. They were roommates but they had known each other since childhood. They're both from itty bitty towns in Arkansas. They played high school basketball against each other and somehow ended up in the same dorm.

My mom was a stunner, and she still is. Her and Jessie resemble each other a lot actually. Both are tall and athletic and don't need makeup to be pretty. In fact, neither of them ever wear any makeup. Their hair is curly, in a wild sort of way.

As a kid I always prayed that my hair would turn curly like theirs. But apparently God liked my hair the way it is, because nothing every changed. My hair rests somewhere between curly and straight, depending on the day. I guess you could say my beachy brown strands have a mind of their own.

"I've missed you, Jessie," I say after she finally lets me go.

"We both have," my mom battles as she pulls Jessie in for a hug.

They finally embrace like old friends do. They hold each other long and close like the best friends they are.

As we walked toward her car, she fills the silence with updates about Lila, who is currently gone on a mission trip with their church.

Lila is Jessie's only daughter, although she considers me one of her own too. Lila and I grew up more like sisters than friends. She's a year younger than me and Easton is two years older than her, leaving me right in the middle. We were three peas in a pod growing up.

She gives us the run down on their new place, too.

"We're still in the process of moving in," she prefaces. Jessie and Mr. Mills moved into an apartment after Easton started college this year. Lila still lives with them though. The big house I grew up visiting every year felt too empty during the school months for them now. Or at least that's what Jessie says. So, they downsized to an apartment. I loved that house. I never got to say goodbye.

It's weird that we aren't gonna be pulling up there tonight. But if I'm truthful with myself, I don't think it was the house I missed, but the boy inside.

Jessie doesn't mention Easton in her updates, so I don't ask.

I imagine he's off with his friends or working. But he's most likely playing his guitar somewhere. He's always playing his guitar. Easton isn't Easton without his guitar.

I'm staring out the window again, my head, once again up in the clouds. I've started making this a habit. "He's around," Jessie says finally, as if reading my mind. "Working a lot. Three jobs actually. Super busy. But he's staying at a friends this summer. Trying to stay out of our hair, even though he has a room here." I nod, but don't say anything. My stomach twists. That sounds like code for, *he's avoiding you*. I wonder if she even told him I was coming. Why would she? "I didn't tell him you were coming," she says as she reads my mind again. It always bothers me the way she does that. It's one of her many superpowers. Knowing Easton and Lila aren't going to be on the other side of this door makes a lot of things easier, but it also makes some things harder.

Before I know it, I'm standing in front of their blue door. The apartment's on the second floor. I stand in front of the door, just looking at it.

I'm sort of scared to see what's on the other side.

"Well, go on in honey," Jessie yells up at me as she lugs one of my mom's bags up the stairs behind her.

You think after years of coming to see the Mills, my mom would learn she doesn't need to pack her whole closet.

Obeying Jessie, I twist the knob and push open the door, stepping inside. The smell hits me like a wall, sudden and full of memories. Even in a new place, it smells just how I remember. That's the funny thing about people… they tend to bring their scent with them wherever they go. I'm thankful for that when the smell of lemon, vanilla, and old book pages hits my nose. It smells just like my childhood.

It doesn't feel how I hoped it would. It feels better. It doesn't feel like visiting a place. It's like returning to a version of myself I wasn't sure still existed.

Jessie and my mom hurry inside behind me.

I'm handed a fresh glass of lemonade from Jessie before I can even set my bags down.

She runs off quickly to grab bath towels for our rooms. She insists on making sure everything is perfect for us when we come. *The guests get the best,* she always says. She is the most hospitable woman you'll ever meet. I don't think anybody hates Jessie. I don't think that's even possible. If it is, I am most positive it's a sin.

I wander into the kitchen with Jessie's fresh squeezed lemonade in my hand.

The kitchen is completely different than the one I grew up visiting.

It's much smaller, but it has all the same appliances. I burnt my hand on that bright red toaster once. I was seven and Easton was eight. He held ice on my hand for an hour and even kissed the burn before putting a bright pink Hello Kitty band-aid on it. I took the band-aid off and made him replace it with a Marvel themed band-aid instead. I was more of a superhero girl back then. Still am.

I open the cabinets, and they're full of all the same Disney mugs that we used to eat ice cream out of as kids on the kitchen floor.

It isn't all the same. But it also isn't much different. It's still mine in way.

A smirk works its way onto my face as my phone buzzes in my hand, pulling me out of what could easily turn into a storm of memories.

RYDER: Did you make it?

Buddy can't take a hint, I guess.

I really can't deal with this right now.

I take my backpack off, stuffing my phone in the side pocket.

As if Ryder knows I'm ignoring him, my phone rings.

It's him. Jessie's voice cuts through my ringtone. "Are you hungry?" She asks. "Flying always makes me crave popcorn," Jessie says as she dances into the kitchen how she always does.

I unintentionally ignore here due to the mental dilemma of whether I should answer the call or not.

"Is that him?" She asks, but her famous grin has faded a bit.

I guess my mom has filled her in on Ryder.

He's my first boyfriend. Or, was my first boyfriend.

But right now, he's just…a little much.

I nod my head *yes*. "Ryder's…"

"A stage five clinger?" mom suggests, joining us in the kitchen.

"I was gonna say passionate, but yeah, stage five clinger is better," I agree. "He won't leave me alone. This is his fifth call since I left home this morning," I say exhausted.

"Have you told him it's too much?" Jessie asks.

"Yeah. I actually just told him I wanted to take a step back from our relationship. I need a break."

"Ooo, I've used that line before. Let em off easy. Good girl," Jessie spats. She seems proud of me for giving Ryder the boot.

Her smile is painted back on and the sway in her hips is back. She's like a golden retriever in that way. You can always tell exactly how she feels.

"I didn't exactly break up with him," I mutter quietly.

I tried to break up with him, but I felt too guilty for how I was making him feel by the end of it, that I'm not even certain we actually broke up. He sure isn't acting like we ended things.

He's either holding on to hope that I'll let him back in or I really didn't get my point across. Either way, I'm annoyed.

"She doesn't know if she was successful or not," mom giggles as she outs me.

"It's not funny mom," I sigh.

"It's kinda funny," She quips back.

"I agree with Kora. It is a little funny," Jessie says.

I let out a long breath and silence the call. "I'm just glad I'm here. I get to turn this off for the next two weeks. I'm in dire need of a social detox."

Jessie gives me a knowing look as she opens the fridge, pulling out a tub of cookie dough. "Here," she says dipping a spoon into the tub. "Everything feels clearer after a spoonful of this," she says, handing me the spoon. "Best way to start a detox." Mom giggles, "With salmonella?" Jessie sweetly glares at her.

"I forgot you always keep this stuff on hand," I tell her as the cookie dough melts on my tongue.

"Always," she winks.

I take another bite and for a second, the noise in my head fades.

No more ringing phone.

No Ryder.

No guilt.

No thoughts at all.

Just cookie dough and the soft hum of the dishwasher.

Jessie wraps her arms around me. "Don't eat too much now. You can't forget the real reason you came to see me. Your big tournament! I'm so glad I get to watch you play again! It's been years since I've..." she stops herself.

It's sad that that's the real reason I'm back again after five years but it's true.

Beach volleyball has been the most important thing in my life for as long as I can remember, but especially since I stopped coming to Florida. The years have been unreal, competitive, and extremely hard. But I love it... mostly.

The athlete in me loves it.

It's also been my reasonable excuse for getting out of coming back here every summer or seeing the Mills when they came into town. *Sorry, I have practice* or *sorry, I have a tournament* were my blanket excuses, and Jessie knew it. How can one excuse be the reason for ignoring some of the closest people in your life for five years. Even I knew it was a poor excuse as it left my lips every time she called or texted me. But still, I always used it.

I fill the awkward silence as best I can while trying to avoid my cowardliness. "Yeah, college coaches are gonna be there. And with college around the corner, it kind of makes this a big one." I say as I put my spoon in the sink.

This place used to be my escape from the reality of life, but this summer I'm bringing some of the reality here with me. A little competition never hurt anything though.

Right?

"The tournament's only two days. We'll have plenty of time for fun and more cookie dough later," mom reassures us.

My phone rings again. Somehow louder this time, halting the conversation.

"Sweetie, go put your bag up. Get that ringing out of here. We'll play a round of spades when you get back," Jessie says with some sass. I think the ringing is bothering her more than it's bothering me. "Your room is down the hall, right past the bathroom."

I pick up my bag, following her directions. I'm met with two doors. The first door I open is a bathroom, which means the next door is mine. I open the next door which reveals a mid-sized room. The walls are a dark earthy green and it's full of things I remember and stuff I've never seen before.

It doesn't take me long to realize why.

I know whose room this is.

A stack of worn Sherlock paperbacks and old Star Wars comic books sitting on the nightstand give it away. Easton used to underline and annotate like he was trying to dissect the characters instead of just read about them. A guitar leans against the wall near the closet. Mary, I think is what he named her.

A vintage *Star Wars: Empire Strikes Back* poster hangs on the wall by the door, right next to an *Avengers: Age of Ultron* poster. That was our favorite movie growing up. Sitting on the dresser is a framed photo of Easton and Lila. His arms are around her shoulders, and he's flashing that same perfect grin he always flashes when someone points a camera at him. It's sweet the way he hugs her. One of his best qualities is how good of a big brother he is. He's a big brother to everyone. He takes on the responsibility of helping those around him like it's second nature. Because for him, it is.

This isn't just a guest room.

This is Easton's room. I freeze in the middle of the floor, my bag slipping off my shoulder and landing on the ground with a loud thud.

Why would Jessie put me in here? My first instinct is to laugh — or maybe panic. She could have easily put me in Lila's room. She's away on a trip, so I know her room is empty, or I guess now, my mom is occupying it.

I look around again, half-expecting his scent to still linger in the air. It does a little. That familiar mix of salt, cedarwood, and the faintest hint of minty shampoo.

My stomach tightens at the thought of his closeness.

I should've knocked or I should have asked to make sure this was really where she wants me. I feel like an intruder in this room, but I can't move.

But Jessie did say, "Your room is the second door, right past the bathroom," like it was a given. Like this space somehow made sense for me.

And the strangest part? It kind of feels like it does.

Because even though everything feels completely foreign — the records, the hanging chair, the scattered Polaroids on the cork-board. There are pieces of me tucked in here too. A Spider-Man comic book I lent him once sits on the shelf. One of my old hair ties is wrapped around the base of his lamp. I haven't been in a room of Easton's in years. I had forgotten the little things that made it his.

But to my surprise, it hasn't forgotten me.

That makes me smile.

Still, it feels a little intrusive, like I'm trespassing on a part of Easton's life I'm not sure I have access to anymore.

I'm about to move my bag to the foot of the bed when something moves in the doorway behind me.

I turn.

A man stands in the doorway. His tall, tan figure casts a shadow on me. His eyes are curious and bright all at once. It isn't until his teeth show through his small smirk that I realize who I'm looking at.

Easton.

Easton stands there, one eyebrow raised, a towel slung over his shoulder. He looks like he's just come back from the beach.

His hair is messy in a nonchalant way, like he likes it that way. His cheeks have a bit of pink in them like he's spent all day in the sun. He wears that calm, unreadable expression he always wears when he doesn't want you to know what he was thinking. He looks so much different than I remember, but also, he hasn't changed at all. His eyes are the same. They aren't brown and not green. They're a dangerous mix of the two. Hazel, maybe? It's like looking into a time machine.

I feel like a little girl again, looking at him.

He's so much taller. He's always been taller than me but now he towers over me at a good six one or six two. He stands confident in his height. He holds his shoulders back and they have some meat on them, like he's been working out.

He has a confidence that wasn't there before. It's not cocky, it's a newfound steadiness.

What does he notice about me? What's the thing that he noticed first? Is it my hair or my eyes or my chest? I know I've grown a bit in that area since the last time he saw me.

His eyes trail over me, head-to-toe. It doesn't feel intrusive like when a guy on the side of the street does it. It feels like he's supposed to. He's supposed to look at me like this.

He has to notice something, right? I so badly want to know what he's noticing. What's he taking in about my appearance?

"I'd know those freckles anywhere," he says, cutting the silence in half. His voice is low and casual.

His eyes don't leave my face as he says it, like he's trying to find something on it.

Freckles cover my face, especially my nose. *Maybe he's counting them?* For a moment, I worry something might actually be on my face.

My mouth opens but words don't come out right away. "Jessie told me it was past the bathroom. I didn't know this was…yours," I finally say.

He looks around at all of his old room decor. I know it's not a good excuse and so does he. But it's true. I didn't know it was his room until I walked in.

"I get it. Place is huge. Easy to get lost," he smirks, with his usual dose of sarcasm.

Oh, how I missed his sarcasm.

"I didn't know you'd be here," I defend.

Part of me hoped he would be. Even just for a moment, I wanted to see him. I wanted to remember what it felt like to be looked at by him.

He has this way of looking at me like I'm one of a kind. Like if he looks away, he'll never see me again. It's like he has to soak up every detail just in case he doesn't get the opportunity to look at me again. His eyes make me feel special. They always have. Even when we were just kids, they made me feel like the only girl in the world.

My stomach turns, no, it hurts. I feel sick. My stomach turns and turns.

I was worried it wouldn't anymore. But my worry has taken a seat by the wayside as the butterflies in my stomach remind me that he still holds the same power over me as he did when we were kids.

These butterflies haven't flown in a while. But now, they are in full flight.

Great.

"Yeah, well I guess today is full of surprises for both of us," he says, sharp. It's not mad, just assertive.

He really didn't know I was coming.

"I'll take the couch," he says, running a hand through his hair that's still wet from the ocean.

Still, I hesitate. "You're staying?" I ask.

"Is that alright with you?" He asks even though I know he isn't really looking for my approval.

I nod, "Well, do you want your room?" I offer.

He shakes his head *no*. "No…" his eyes staying on me a little too long. "The room likes you better anyways," he says with a wink. "Besides. Guests get the best, right?" He recites.

He is his mother's son. We both knew he was gonna let me have the bed. He's always been chivalrous in that way, even with the little things. But it still felt right of me to offer.

"Right. Well, thank you," I say with a little grin working its way onto my face.

He flashes his cheesy grin at me. It's the first time I've seen his real adult smile in person. Five years ago, he had braces.

Ugh.

I always loved his smile, even with the braces, but this smile… it's perfectly straight, teasing, and somehow still familiar.

It makes my stomach ache.

He pushes off the door frame. "Let me know if you need anything. Just don't mess with Mary."

"I'll try to resist."

And just like that, he's gone.

The door clicks shut behind him, and I stand there in the middle of his room, heart sitting in my stomach, wondering what the hell just happened.

I walk into the bathroom to splash water on my face. The hope is that this somehow cools me down and brings me back down to earth.

I can't believe Easton's here.

I can't believe I just saw him.

I can't believe he still makes me feel the way he did back then.

I can't believe he still makes my face flush like this. Even after everything that happened that last summer.

I take a deep breath, attempting to let everything roll off my back. I wasn't ready to see him, even if I did have five years to prepare.

My reflection stares back at me with tired eyes and flushed cheeks. I haven't even been here a full hour, and I already feel… different. Like the version of me I spent years trying to bury is starting to unravel. I thought I packed her away in my suitcase when I left that last summer, but the girl looking back at me isn't the girl I've been seeing recently.

I almost recognize her.

I smile, liking the version of myself that's starting to come back. I shake my head, almost annoyed that the light in my eyes has come back so quickly. I thought I buried that spark a little deeper than this.

But once again, I guess I'm wrong.

Voices echo from the kitchen. Laughter. Jessie's definitely, and my mom's too. They're already dealing cards for spades I bet.

Jessie always likes being my partner because she says we share the same brain when it comes to reading peoples tells.

I look at my phone one last time before leaving. Ryder's name glares up at me from the lock screen like a neon sign I can't ignore. Three missed calls. Two texts. One voicemail. He's sweet, but it's too much for me right now.

I don't listen to the voicemail. Instead, I turn my phone off, leaving it on the counter.

I check myself in the mirror one last time and take a deep breath. I let the bathroom door creak a little as I open it, so they'll hear me coming.

"Took you long enough superstar," Jessie mocks. She loves calling me things like that. From anyone else, I would hate such a nickname. But from Jessie, it's sweet.

My mom is dealing the cards.

Jessie hands me my stack like it's a sacred ritual.

Mom does the same with Easton. Just like old times.

"Your spades game better still be good. Don't let me down," mom says to Easton as she sorts the cards in her hand.

Easton smirks, "Wouldn't dream of it."

And for the first time in a while, I feel at peace.

I'm not running toward anything. I'm not running from anything. I'm just here.

The Mills have always been my home away from home. And right now, I feel at home.

Maybe this won't be so bad after all.

Because it's feeling good to be home again.

Even if it is just for two weeks.

2

Promise?

TATE

The sun slips through the blinds, casting golden streaks across the dark green walls. I blink against the light, disoriented for a second by the softness of the mattress and the strange mix of familiarity and the unknown dancing in the air. Then I remember where I am.

Easton's room.

I sit up slowly, pushing the comforter off my skin. The scent of saltwater and linen lingers in the air, and for a moment, I wonder if this was how he wakes up every morning. Not that I needed to be thinking about that, but I can't help my mind from wandering there.

The house is quiet, except for the distant sound of someone humming from another room. I know a Jessie hum when I hear it. It's happy and full of rhythm.

Jessie is always humming or singing, often turning her sentences into little songs. Her kids get their love of music from her. In college she used to write music and make little homemade tracks and music videos with her friends. When my mom wasn't at practice or on an away trip with the volleyball or basketball team, she'd be the one behind the camera helping Jessie. One summer she let us all watch one of her music videos. It was surreal seeing a much younger version of her playing the guitar and singing. She dreamed of having an album and such, but once she started a family, that dream got pushed to the side. We became her favorite audience. She'd often sing with Lila and Easton around the campfire or when we were really little, she'd sing us all to sleep. She sings the greatest lullabies.

My stomach flips. Another thing I've forgotten so much about Jessie, it makes me feel sick. I'm not sure if it's the guilt or my own hunger that's making me feel unwell, but either way, coffee is bound to help.

I slide my feet into a pair of slippers and grab my phone off the nightstand. No missed calls. No texts. Maybe Ryder has finally given up — for now. I slip my phone into my hoodie pocket and make my way into the hallway. The faint smell of vanilla and cinnamon hit my nose instantly. Jessie's famous cinnamon rolls. She spoils me when I'm here.

"Good morning sunshine," Jessie chirps as I round the corner. She's standing at the stove, flipping cinnamon rolls out of a cast iron skillet onto a tray — her apron dotted with flour and her normal amount of spunk.

"Morning," I say, rubbing my eyes and attempting to suppress a yawn. I got a full eight hours of sleep last night, but after a long trip, it's still somehow not enough.

"Coffee's already brewed," she adds, pointing toward the freshly brewed pot of coffee with her icing covered spatula. There is nothing in this world that makes me as happy as coffee does in the morning. "Your mom ran out to grab tea bags. You know she can't survive a beach day without her stash of iced sweet tea. I can't believe I forgot to grab them for her."

I can't help but hear the disappointment in her voice over the fact that she's forgotten something so simple about my mom, but it isn't her fault. It's mine. Sure, my mom has been back for a day or two here and there and she talks to Jessie on the phone almost every day, but we haven't been back for a normal summer visit like this because I wouldn't ever join her. My mom and I are a team in that way. She spends her summers with me and if I didn't come back, then neither did she. A wave of guilt washes over me. The reason my mom hasn't been back here in years is because of me. I don't like how acquainted me and guilt are getting.

Mom and Jessie always spend the first day of every summer visit out on the beach. Mom has to get that base layer burn so that her tan can officially start. She's always determined to try and catch up to Jessie, even though that's an impossible goal. I chuckle at the thought of her complaining about how it hurts to move tomorrow because of red she most definitely will get today. It's inevitable. I'll be helping her find the aloe later.

I grab the cabinet door handle to get a coffee mug, and to my surprise, all the Disney mugs are here. Out of habit, I reach for the chipped Captain America one on the top shelf. It's been mine for as long as I can remember.

"I can't believe this made it through the move," I say.

"Some things are sacred," Jessie says, after taking a sip of her own coffee. It's a cream and blue Starbucks mug from a Starbucks in Taiwan. My mom got it for her as a souvenir on her college mission trip. It's been her favorite mug ever since. "You don't mess with a girl's mug hierarchy."

She's right, you don't.

I pour my coffee, adding four spoonfuls of sugar and a dash of cream. I like a little coffee with my cream and sugar. I think about my dad as I stir my coffee. My dad always gives me a hard time for making my coffee this way. *You can't even taste the coffee,* he usually says as he sips his plain black coffee. I give him a hard time for how he drinks his coffee, but if I worked as many early mornings and late nights as he did, I'd probably end up drinking it the same way he does. If you drink a pot of coffee a day, you can't afford to drink it the way I do. Not unless you want diabetes.

My dad's working right now, like he usually is in the summer. I miss him. Sometimes he'll pop in on a weekend if he gets a break from the demanding life of Hollywood. Being a filmmaker has its perks, but it also means you work weird hours and weird times.

I settle on a stool at the counter with my mug heating my hands. I watch Jessie drizzle icing over the second batch of steaming cinnamon rolls.

"Smells like summer in here," I say.

Jessie gives me a proud little shrug. "That's the goal. I want you to have the perfect visit sweet girl and cinnamon rolls are the only way to start. Helps with jet leg and even complicated feelings."

I raise a brow. "What makes you think I have complicated feelings?"

She gives me a look that says, *baby please*. "You're eighteen, babe. I remember being your age. It's full of complicated feelings. It's part of being young." Fair point.

She slides a plate in front of me and leans against the counter. "Lila hates that you're here while she's gone."

"Where is she exactly?" I question.

"Arkansas."

I was expecting something more… global, than that answer, but I guess people need Jesus everywhere, even Arkansas. "Oh," I remark. "Did she go with the church?"

The Mills have always been very involved with their church. They're the family that's always around the church just helping with whatever needs to be done. Benefits, local outreaches, helping the homeless, and anything else to serve the community. They are just those kind of people. Kind, loving, selfless people. Lila sings for the worship team. That's her special way of serving. Her voice is angelic, and it has been since we were kids. She takes after Jessie. Easton plays keys occasionally for the worship team too and loves helping out with the kid's ministry on Wednesday nights. Mr. Mills leads a father and son program that helps dads bond with their middle school sons. They go on Boy Scout type adventures, teaching the boys manly life skills and such. It's sweet. Jessie whips up casseroles and sweet treats for all of the church events and always helps watch the staff members babies when they need it. She always loves the babysitting gig most.

Lila joined the worship team a few years back. She didn't tell me, but I saw it on her Instagram. She's always posting with this girl who sings beside her on stage. The girl is about Lila's height with jet-black hair that falls right past her shoulders. She's far paler than Lila and Lila is the palest of the Mills, that's really saying something. I don't know her name, but she seems close to Lila. Although Lila never tags her in her posts, which I've always thought was a bit odd.

"Yeah, the church sent the worship team and youth volunteers to this camp your mom and I used to go to, and Annie convinced Lila to go with her last minute. She tends to do that," Jessie explains, trying to keep her voice neutral. Though there was something in her voice when she mentioned Annie. I can't quiet pinpoint what it is though.

"I'm sure she just likes having Lila with her. I know I always do," I say trying to brighten the mood.

Jessie smiles, "Yeah. Who wouldn't want my sweet Lila around?"

It's true. Lila is beautiful. She has deep blue eyes and bright blonde hair. She carries more of Mr Mill's genes, but she definitely has Jessie's smile. It's big and bright and lights up the room. It's basically impossible to not be happy around Lila. Happiness just seeps out of her. She's pure joy walking around in human form. Anybody is lucky to be her friend. I know growing up, I always was.

She's an easy person to miss and I've missed her loads, but if I'm honest… I kinda feel like she hasn't missed me. I know she has a life here and friends I don't know about, but it always stings a little to see that her life goes on so well without me. I take a quick bite of the cinnamon roll Jessie set in front of me in attempt to eat away at my selfish thoughts. It tastes sweet but not as sweet as normal. It's because I know I don't deserve it. I should have called Lila or at least told her why I didn't come back. She was only twelve when I left. For all she knows, her best friend just abandoned her.

I am a terrible friend.

I'm glad Lila has a friend like the girl on Instagram… Annie, even if she is my replacement.

"She's a sweet girl, Annie," Jessie continues but her tone doesn't match her words. There's something there. Something unspoken and a little hesitant beneath her usual warmth. She moves past it quickly, motioning to the couch. "I was surprised to see Easton last night. He must have sensed your presence." I laugh awkwardly.

What does that mean?

"Did y'all get to catch up?" She asks before I can say anything.

"I don't know if I'd call it catching up, but I saw him and he said *hi* and stuff," I tell her.

She chuckles to herself, "He's grown a bit huh?" *You can say that again.*

"He's taller for sure, yeah."

"You are too. You've matured so much. Becoming a woman before my eyes." She shakes her head in disbelief. I know she's thinking about all the time lost and milestones she's missed as she takes in my new, older self. "Still gorgeous though. And even more freckles than last time," she jokes. But it's true. I do have more freckles. For me, more time in the sun equals more freckles.

"Yeah, playing an outdoor sport is helpful with that. I don't tan like you, I just freckle," I tease as I rest my face in my hand, leaning on the counter.

I catch a glimpse of Easton sleeping on the couch. His new muscly body pokes out from under the covers. I can't help but stare.

"He is knocked out," Jessie says with a chuckle, lowering her voice a bit. She checks her watch and I look at the stove clock behind her. *10:45.* "Almost eleven" She clicks her tongue a couple times, in a judging manner. "He was probably up late watching a movie. You know how he is."

I do. I do know how he is. Or at least I used to.

Movies were our thing back then. We loved them. All of them. Rom-coms, action, comedy… but especially superhero movies. It was one of our many ways of bonding. We were tiny little movie critics, always obsessing over the latest Avenger movie or cult classic. We spoke in movie quotes and references, and nobody got them but us. It was like we had our own language.

Sometimes I wonder if we can still speak it.

I smirk into my coffee as I think about all the times we stayed up all night, just bingeing our favorite movies, even if we'd already seen them thousands of times. We never got tired of watching them. Not if we were together.

As if he heard us talking about him, the couch in the living room creaks from Easton's sudden movement. His ears must have been burning. I turn slightly to see Easton pushing himself upright, rubbing his eyes like he's still half in a dream. "Talking about me already?" He asks. His morning voice makes him sound older than the nineteen year-old boy that he is. But more importantly, it does something to my stomach. I suddenly feel like I'm being warmed from the inside out. All because of his scratchy, deep, sexy morning voice.

His gaze finally lands on me, then shifts to Jessie, then back to me again.

Jessie comes up with something to say, "I'm happy you decided to stay last night. Are you gonna stay for the whole…"

Easton interrupts, "What happened to good morning," he says, voice tough and sleep heavy.

OK, he needs to wake up. I can't take much more of this morning voice.

I take a swig of my coffee to hide my smile and cheeks that are most definitely turning red. My body is deceiving me.

We're mad at him, remember? I try to remind myself.

"Morning, sleepyhead," Jessie says brightly, already reaching for another plate.

Easton runs a hand through his messy brown curls like he's in an Abercrombie and Fitch commercial. Can't he do things in a slightly less attractive manner. I would much appreciate it at this moment.

"Didn't mean to interrupt your girl time," he says walking into the kitchen with slow, easy steps. His joggers sit low on his waist, exposing his toned midsection and tan skin.

He's trying to kill me.

"That's alright," I say quickly. Maybe too quickly.

His eyes linger on me for half a second longer than they need to. I hope he's taking in my new adult figure and my more defined jaw and my longer, prettier hair. I hope I don't look like the little thirteen-year-old girl who left him here five years ago. I hope he sees the woman I've grown into. Something passes between us — acknowledgment, recognition, something soft and old. It's almost like we both accept that we don't know the version of the other person standing in front of us. We used to know each other. But not anymore.

"I've missed mornings here," I say to cover my previous eagerness and my wandering mind.

Jessie's smile takes up half her face as she says, "They've missed you more." She makes a plate for Easton with a fresh cinnamon roll placed in the middle. She slides it right beside me on the counter, in front of the only open seat in the kitchen. "Eat and shower. You look like you slept on the beach," she says to him.

He smirks, pulling out the stool next to mine. And just like that, we're sitting next to each other for the first time in what feels like centuries. I can't even count the amount of meals eaten together sitting next to each other just like this. Even when we were little, it was always us sitting right next to each other. I'd sit between Lila and Easton so I could talk to both. But without Lila here, there's this silence in the air that we haven't felt in years. It's tense and suspenseful, like a held breath. Easton and I sit side by side at the island, both pretending we aren't doing the very thing we're doing... glancing sideways, studying each other, testing the air for familiarity.

His leg keeps grazing mine as he swivels back and forth in the spinning bar stool chair. It's driving me crazy, but I don't even think he knows he's doing it. Which somehow makes it worse.

"I'm headed to the beach to meet Kora for a few hours. We need our catch-up time. Easton, you should take Tatey to Disney today. It's the perfect day for it," Jessie offers.

"Oh, we don't have to..." I begin.

"That's a good idea mom. How's that sound?" he asks looking at me with big eager eyes. I'm shocked to see he's so excited to spend one-on-one time with me. I fear that once we're alone he'll ask me why I haven't come back. Or maybe that's exactly why he wants to get me alone.

"Sounds like old times," I say with a smile.

Jessie grabs her beach bag and towel as she heads for the door with a quick *love you* to both of us as the door closes behind her, leaving just me and Easton alone.

He takes a bite of his cinnamon roll and lets out a low groan. "Okay. I forgot how good these are."

"You don't have them all the time?" I ask.

"She only makes them when you're here," he says without looking at me.

Oh.

"You're still special around here," he adds.

I look at him full-on for the first time since last night. Same jawline, a little sharper now. Hair still unruly, just longer. His eyes have deepened into something quieter, older, more mature than the last time I saw him. Like he's seen things in the last five years that I don't know about. But that spark that lives in his eyes is still there. And his smile… that perfect smile that used to knock the breath out of me is still there. It's the same as I remember it — soft, comforting, and genuine. "And you still eat like an unsupervised raccoon," I say, nudging his elbow.

He smirks. "You've missed me."

No. No I haven't. Is it that obvious? I straighten up and raise an eyebrow. "You wish."

He shrugs. "I don't need to wish. You're here."

"Don't flatter yourself. I came for the cinnamon rolls and the tournament," I say more harsh than I want to. It wasn't my intention, but it all comes off a bit defensive.

"Sure. Came all this way for pastries and sand. Because you can't get that anywhere else," he says with his typical sarcasm.

"Exactly."

"Totally not for me," he says looking over at me.

"I didn't even know you'd be here," I remark. I had hoped he'd be here a little bit. As much as I didn't want to see him, I couldn't help but hope that I'd at least see him once. Now I'm not so glad I'm seeing him. I don't like the way he's teasing me. It wasn't this way before. He used to tease me in a joking manner but right now it feels real, like he means it. Like maybe he really thinks I came back for *him.*

"Yeah, well I didn't really expect you to be here either," he says quietly, just above a whisper.

Last night, when I saw him in the doorway of his room, he did look surprised to see me. I guess, maybe that's part of what he wanted me to feel. Like I don't have the power to shake him. But maybe, maybe I do.

"Stop taking everything so seriously," he jabs. He's grinning again, wider this time, leaning back in his stool.

"I'm not serious," I say.

He scans my face. "You're a lot more serious than you used to be."

I don't think I'm more serious than I was the last time he saw me. More mature? Sure. Older? Yes. Maybe a bit more realistic, but since when did that hurt anybody? I would never consider myself serious about anything other than beach volleyball. But that's always been the case. I take my dreams seriously, but I always have. So, he can't be talking about that.

"You're meaner now too," he says interrupting my thoughts.

I take a sip of my coffee, attempting to hide my face.

"I've said an eighth of my thoughts," I stutter.

"Exactly."

There it is — that rhythm. That light back-and-forth, the instinctive jabs and shared memories sliding back into place like puzzle pieces between us. It feels normal to be this playful with him. We've always had this comfortability with each other and we're starting to slip back into it. Time makes things awkward sometimes. They say time can help you heal or forget, but I haven't forgotten him. No matter how much time has passed or how hard I try to push the memories of him down, they always just resurface. It's hard to forget someone you knew so well at one point. Especially when you knew them as a kid. It's like you slip back into the version of yourself that did know them. It's dangerous, because we didn't just know each other. We loved each other, long ago. Or at least I think that's what it was. I don't need to learn him again. I just need to remember.

No. I need to forget. I need to ignore. I've spent five summers keeping my distance from him. I won't let two weeks back unravel all that, no matter how I feel when I'm around him now.

Sitting this close to him isn't safe. It's feels wrong, even though everything about it feels right at the same time.

He confuses me and makes everything clearer all at once. It makes me want to scream. Five years is a long time, but it also feels like I was just here yesterday. *Ugh.*

"Remember that time we built a fort in the backyard at the old house, and we tried to sleep out there, but you bailed halfway through because you swore you saw an alligator?" He says in between laughs.

"There was an alligator. The house was right next to a pond. You know they lived in there," I say defending myself.

"It was a squirrel."

"It was not. Lila saw it too."

"Lila agreed with anything you said back then," he says.

"Well, at least then she talked to me," I say before thinking. His face softens in a way that makes me feel bad for saying what I said. I quickly cover it up. "You left us out there anyway."

"I came back," he says with reassuring eyes.

"Yeah, you always came back," I say holding his gaze.

The truth is, the night he left us out there was more of joke to make us girls upset more than anything. He isn't a leaver. Lila and I both knew that. The silence hangs in the air — heavy. He clears his throat but doesn't move.

"So… this tournament… it's a big deal, I take it?"

"Yeah, lots of college coaches will be scouting," I say proudly.

He nods, watching me. "That's wild." He shakes his head in disbelief. "I still remember you practicing in the backyard, serving balls into a laundry basket."

"Yeah, that was a long time ago."

"Tate Knightly, beach volleyball college commit," he says moving his hand across the air like he's picturing the words on a non-existent banner in front of him. "It has a nice ring to it."

I smile. "Yeah, well, I need to actually commit somewhere before we decide if it has a nice ring to it or not. So please don't jinx anything."

"I can't jinx anything. You don't believe in luck anyways."

He's right. I don't. I believe in hard work and prayer like my mom. The truth is, I do believe I'll commit somewhere; I just worry about where I'll commit a little too much these days. I want to go to a school where I'll fit in and have fun and get to play. The biggest and most daunting part is that I need to go somewhere that's going to largely cover my expenses. Unfortunately, I don't come from money.

"You'll get an offer. The crazy part is that you're gonna be a freshman in college next year. Time flies," he says confidently.

I shake my head, not knowing what to say.

Easton is tall and fit but he was never much of an athlete. Playing guitar and piano were more his thing. He even dabbled in songwriting. He keeps those close to his chest, but he's let me hear a couple over the years. But, when it comes to sports, he always thinks I'm the best.

"I was your biggest fan back then. Still am," he says to fill the silence, and I know he means it.

That stops me.

How can he still be my biggest fan if we haven't as much as exchanged words in five years?

My cheeks flush, but I hold his gaze until I have to break it. I grab our plates and walk over to the sink, putting some much needed distance between us. I start rinsing off our plates then ask the only question I can think of that will put some stiffness in the air. "So, who is Annie?" I ask. I'm glad I can't see him. I'm too scared to see his face when he responds.

He doesn't answer immediately. The hesitation in his voice makes me anxious for some reason. "What do you mean?" He finally asks. "She's a friend from church. She's with Lila right now on a mission trip or church camp or something."

"They're close? Her and Lila?" I ask as I put our dishes in the dishwasher.

"Yeah," he says slowly.

"What about you guys?" I ask. "Me and her?" He questions.

"Yeah."

He hesitates again. "She's… a friend." Just a second too long of a pause. Just enough uncertainty to stir something unsettling in my stomach. I wasn't expecting his hesitation in that answer.

Before I can question him anymore, my phone starts ringing. It's sitting on the counter next to him. I'm thankful it rings. I don't know how the rest of that conversation was gonna go. Saved by the bell, I guess.

Easton picks up my phone, looking at the caller ID.

"Ryder?" Easton says with more curiosity than I think he wants me to hear. And when his eyes meet mine, he reaches his hand out, offering my phone to me.

I don't want to answer Ryder, but I want to take the phone from Easton. Normally, I'd silence any phone call just to talk to Easton. My days were always numbered here at the Mills. Just two weeks, so I wouldn't let anyone get in the way of even a minute with Easton, but something in his eyes dares me to answer or begs me not to.

That look alone gives me my answer. I take the phone from him, confidently. "I'll just be a minute," I say.

I slide the answer button across my screen, putting the phone to my ear.

"Hey babe!" Ryder says.

Ugh. Why did I answer again?

I hang up the phone almost as quickly as I answered. Ryder went on and on about how much he misses me. Which sounds nice, and I know he means it but for some reason I just want to get back to Easton.

***

By noon the sun is already high and hot, and the quiet hum of the house has turned into the shuffle of sandals and sunscreen. Easton leans against the door frame, twirling his car keys on one finger, a smirk tugging at the corner of his mouth.

"So," he says, "Want to go to the happiest place on earth?"

I look at him, secretly a bit excited at the the thought of running around Disney with him again. "Should we?" I say.

He tilts his head. "It's Disney. Of course we should."

"Good point," I laugh.

His dad still works at Disney, just like he did when we were little. He's an Imagineer. Pretty sick job if you ask me. It's the kind of job kids dream about. Imagine waking up every morning, making a cup of coffee, driving to your office where the Cinderella castle is right outside your window. It's turkey legs for lunch, caramel apple treats, and VIP access to everything. It doesn't get much better than that.

Mr. Mills has the kindest soul, which makes him perfect for the job. The job keeps him busy though. But he comes home happy every day, always grateful. He's a hard worker, and his family loves him for it.

It's the kind of job that comes with perks — like backdoor access to parks, fast passes, and free tickets we never had to think twice about. Easton and I had basically grown up at all the parks. Our favorite parks have always been Magic Kingdom and Hollywood Studios. We know every shortcut, every dole whip station, and exactly which bathrooms have the best air conditioning. We could give tours of the place better than the employees that work there. I swear I can still get you anywhere in the park with my eyes closed.

For me, Disney is the place I always end up at in my dreams. Corny, I know. But it's always magical. Nothing can ever go wrong when you're at Disney.

Getting to go for free was a nice perk during our visits. But it wasn't the part of the summer that I looked most forward to. You would think that having the blessing of going to "the happiest place on earth" any time we wanted would be a kid's favorite thing, but my favorite memories were always spent outside of Disney. Easton and Lila were what I looked forward to every visit. Just being around them — playing cards, singing karaoke, or laying in the grass looking up at the stars with them beat any day we ever spent at Disney. I hope they know that.

Now we're driving, windows down, in Easton's car... flying down I-4. He drives a 1998 silver mustang. I never really pictured him driving a car like this but somehow it suits him. The Star Wars Han Solo dice hanging from the rear view mirror is a nice touch. It adds a splash of Easton to the car, really making it his. It adds that little hint of nerd that I've always adored about him.

Before today, I've only driven with Easton one other time. That last summer my family came to Florida, he had just gotten his permit, and it was only a quick drive around the block. He wanted to show off. My mom was scared out of her mind, but she let me go. Nothing bad could happen if we were together, or at least that's what I thought at thirteen.

Part of me still feels that way. I feel safe with him. Just like I do now.

Easton queued up one of our old playlists the second we got in the car. It's the one we made the summer I was thirteen and he was fourteen. It was filled with Disney movie soundtracks and early 2010 hits. We both knew every word to every song that played. We sang our hearts out, both trying not to look at the other as we sang the words.

I groan at the first notes of "Call me Maybe" by Carly Ray Jepsen. I haven't heard it in ages. Easton, Lila, and I used to scream this song around the house at the top of our lungs. It was sort of a joke, sort of not. As stupid as it is, I loved this song. It's highly overplayed but to me it holds sentimental value. During the five years of missing them, I stopped listening to it or any other song that reminded me of here. It hurt too much to listen to them. Not seeing them was hard enough to deal with. I didn't need to rub it in my own face.

"You still listen to this?" I ask.

"It's a classic," he says with pride.

There was a time when I didn't have Spotify, and my family couldn't really afford to get me my own account, so Easton sent me his login, and he let me listen whenever I wanted. We shared the account like that for about two years, until I got my own.

We both feel the memories the song holds as it blares through his speakers. But neither of us say anything. It was always that way with Easton. So many unspoken thoughts just lingering in the air around us. *I need it to go away.*

I don't want to let the past cloud my judgment of him, but I also don't want him to think that things are different now or that he's off the hook somehow for how he treated me that last summer. We're different people than we were five years ago, but I still feel the pit in my stomach every time I think about what he said to me that made me never want to come back.

I'm sure he feels differently for me now than he did then. Because even if I don't want to, I feel a mixture of old and new feelings flying through the air around us. Like my hair in the wind, I can't control it.

***

When we get to the park, everything smells like candy and sunscreen and nostalgia. Magic Kingdom has a way of making you feel like a kid no matter how old you are.

That feeling never gets old.

I had forgotten how much I loved this place. But the second we step in the gates; everything falls back into place. The way my body instinctively moves through the crowds, turning left where everyone else turns right, avoiding long lines like a pro. I fit right back in, like I never left.

For most people Disney is a notorious tourist attraction. But to us, it was always a jungle gym. We don't even bother with the big rides at first. An expert knows you wander around the park in the daylight and see everything you want to see and eat everything you want to eat while the lines are super long and then, when the sun starts to set, you ride every ride possible. AS MANY TIMES AS POSSIBLE. That's the key.

First thing, we grab our Mickey Mouse pretzels and walk through Adventureland, weaving in and out of the spots we used to hide in when we wanted to escape our parents.

As we walk by Space Mountain I'm thrown back into my childhood. This was always the ride that scared me the most, because it's pitch black on the inside. "Remember when I threw up after riding Space Mountain three times in a row?" I say as I lick salt off my fingers from the pretzel.

Easton chuckles. "You blamed it on the turkey leg, but *I* think it was just the consequence of trying to prove a point. No sane person rides Space Mountain *three* times in a row." "I was twelve!" I say defending myself.

"You were reckless. You still are."

I roll my eyes. "You loved it."

He looks at me sideways, his voice quieter now. "I did."

"How do you know I'm still reckless? It's been a while.

I could have changed, you know," I jab back.

He thinks for a moment, taking the new version of me in front of him in. "Your eyes. They still have this… this sparkle to them. It's a bit wild. They haven't changed a bit."

He grabs the trash out of my hand, cutting the moment.

I didn't realize he paid that close of attention to me now, let alone back then. I always wanted him to tell me how he felt, but that's just not Easton. And I'm not one to ask, or pry, or beg someone to love me. I never have been.

Either you do or you don't.

Maybe I had too much pride or maybe he had too many nerves. Whatever it was, it made for a bad mix and a lot of miscommunication.

We start to wander into Fantasyland like we always did near sunset, when the crowds get softer and the sky starts turning a beautiful combo of burnt orange and cotton candy pink.

We don't talk as much now. Just walk. Sometimes, quiet is its own kind of language. Occasionally our hands brush against one another as we stroll around. I am painfully aware of how close he is or isn't, and I hate it.

Right outside the carousel, we sit down on a bench. Easton walks to the cart near us and buys us a churro, because it's a tradition to eat a churro every time we enter the Magic Kingdom. Quite a fattening tradition but we partake none-the-less. We share one without thinking about it, because we always do.

"You know," he says after a moment, "This feels weird." *Oh.*

Here I am thinking that this is a sweet moment and he's thinking the whole thing is weird.

I turn to him. "Weird how?"

"Like… it's the same, but I know it's not. You and me, I mean. Just being here together… again."

I nod slowly. "I was thinking the same thing," I lie. I was thinking it was nice to be back here. But I know we've both been walking around the elephant in the room.

Why didn't I come back?

That's the question hanging in the air. Neither of us wants to address it. Or at least, I know I don't want to. I know he's wondering why I avoided him. I can see it all over his face. He wants to ask me.

"But it's also kind of nice," he adds. "Like, I didn't realize how much I missed this. Or missed us, I guess. Until today."

I glance down at our hands. Not touching, but close. Closer than strangers. Closer than old friends.

"Me too," I say softly.

I have the same question to ask him.

Why didn't you reach out when I didn't come back? Why didn't you text me on my birthday? Why didn't you ask if something was wrong? Why didn't you ever say sorry?

Selfishly, I want to put the blame on him, but I know we're both at fault, even if I don't want to admit that to myself. I think he knows it too.

So, we just sit here, both at a loss for words, both lost in thought. We were so close for years. It's a strange thing to sit next to someone you used to know. The worst part is that your mind tries to convince you that you still know them.

But five years does a lot to a person.

His phone buzzes. He checks it briefly, thumb hovering over the screen before flipping it face-down on the bench again. I caught a glimpse of the contact before he flipped it.

Annie.

I look away, pretending not to notice, but something tightens in my stomach anyway.

He doesn't explain. I don't really want him to. I don't want anything to disrupt this moment between just us. He leans back against the bench, watching the castle as it lights up for the evening fireworks show. We have the perfect spot, like always.

"Promise me something?" He asks, voice almost lost in the chatter of the growing crowd.

"What's that?"

"That no matter what happens… we get one day like this every summer. Just one."

I think about how nice that sounds. I would relive today any day if given the chance, but is that realistic?

He's had five years to rekindle our friendship or explain why he never reached out and now he's acting like it just never even happened. He's just moved on from it like it didn't hurt him, or me. Like the last five years didn't happen.

I weigh the pros and cons. Even if I only got to see him for one day every year for the rest of my life, it would be worth it. He won't remember he made this promise anyway, so I agree.

"Deal," I say, holding out my pinky out of habit. I've always taken pinky promises pretty seriously.

He grins, hooking his pinky with mine like we're little kids again. He kisses his hand, and I kiss mine — sealing the deal. Our faces are close, and I like it.

I pull away first, shutting off my brain from any wandering thoughts.

I wonder if he has these too? Probably not. He would have kissed me back then if he had wanted to and, well… he never as much as held my hand.

I always wondered what it would feel like to kiss Easton Mills. That pinky promise might be the closest I'll ever get.

I lean back on the bench and for the first time in a long time, I feel like we're good. Even without the apology I want or the conversation we probably should have. It feels good again.

I hope this feeling lasts.

***

Back at the house, the sky is dark and glittering with stars, it's the kind of clear night that makes you feel like summer can last forever. My skin is covered in dried sweat and leftover churro sugar dust, and my legs ache from walking what had to have been at least twelve miles.

Easton yawns as we step inside the apartment, rubbing the back of his neck."That was a good day," he says.

"It really was," I agree.

He smiles, but there's something behind it — an emotion I can't name. Something soft. Something maybe a little scared.

Instead of saying whatever is behind his smile, he says,

"Night, Tate."

"Night, Easton." I say softly.

He closes the distance between us, wrapping me in a hug. I would be ecstatic if this wasn't so normal for us. Or for the old us, I guess. Our families are huggers. We always hug goodnight.

He breaks the hug and walks toward the living room where he is still sleeping on the couch, and I walk toward his room, a little lighter than I was before the hug. I pass the bathroom as I debate on a shower. I decide I'm too tired. I just need to sleep. The bigger debate I'm having is whether or not to talk about what happened between us. Or whatever happened five years ago, that is. It feels good between us right now.

But how long can we go on with the elephant sitting in the room?

How long can we keep pretending?

How long can pretending last?

3

BA?

TATE

I collapse onto the bed, exhausted and too full from all the Disney snacks. I just barely have the energy to plug in my phone. I set it on the nightstand, when suddenly, it buzzes. I roll my eyes, expecting a notification from Ryder, but it isn't him.

It's Easton.

EASTON: question of the night: favorite animal?

I smile, already knowing my answer. I don't wait to type back. There is no point in doing that with Easton.

ME: a tiger. Or a lioness.

EASTON: that fits. BA choice.

BA?

Ohhhh. Bad Ass.

Oh. He thinks I'm badass.

ME: same question.

EASTON: For me, toss up between an elephant or tiger.

Two minutes later, another text comes in.

EASTON: yeah, the more I think about it, your passion and drive make those choices make total sense.

I stare at his words for a long time. The kind of long where you don't realize you're smiling until your cheeks hurt. The kind of long where your heart feels like it's stretching and shrinking at the same time.

I click my phone screen off, rolling onto my side, and pulling the blanket up to my chin.

Everything feels like it's falling back into place.

Even if I don't know where it's all going yet, I know one thing for sure… This summer is going to change everything.

4

The Last Summer

TATE

(The summer I was 13 & he was 14)

I t was the last Friday night of the last summer at the old house. The air smelled like salt and barbecue smoke that had drifted from somewhere down the beach all the way up to the Mill's front porch.

Jessie left the porch door cracked, the screen creaking every now and then when the wind blew by. It broke up the noise of cicadas humming and the distant crash of waves.

Inside, the house was warm and loud, as it always was.

Lila was curled up on the couch with her head in Jessie's lap, half-asleep after begging to watch a princess movie she didn't have the stamina to finish. Mr. Mills had nodded off in his armchair, half a root beer sweating on the side table. My mom and Jessie were making plans for next summer over the noise of the princess movie. They always make plans for the next summer on our last night. Easton and I were outside, sitting on the old wooden steps that led down to the sand. It was our own little tradition. We tried to ignore the fact that we were parting ways in the morning like our lives depended on it.

I remember our knees were touching. We always sat like that back then — so close you could feel the heat radiate off the other.

He was fiddling with his phone, thumb brushing over the cracked screen, hair falling into his eyes. He'd grown his hair longer that year, letting his curls become a bit unruly. I thought it made him look older. He liked it and I liked it too — not that I ever admitted that out loud.

I was talking about nothing. Just telling him how next year I'd be trying out for the high school volleyball team despite my young age, my level of skill allowed me to play with the older girls. I wanted him to know because I wanted him to be impressed. I went on and on about it eventually telling him how my mom promised she'd find the money to buy me a new backpack. He was nodding, but he wasn't really listening. I could tell. I knew Easton's listening face — he'd tilt his head just a little, eyes on my lips or my hands as I spoke. But in that moment, his eyes kept glancing back to the glow of his phone.

"Who are you texting?" I asked, nudging his shoulder with mine, playfully.

He didn't look at me when he said, "No one."

I rolled my eyes. "Liar."

He huffed out a half-laugh, then locked the screen and shoved the phone into his sweatshirt pocket. "Just someone from school. Doesn't matter."

He didn't say her name, but I already knew who it was.

Izzy.

She'd been around all summer — older, fifteen, maybe sixteen. She'd come by on her bike sometimes, parking it crooked in the driveway. I'd watch them from the window. Easton would lean in too close, Izzy would push her long brown ponytail over her shoulder like it was nothing, but she was doing it to look cute. She was putting some kind of spell on Easton all summer. Needless to say, I didn't much like her.

I hated how I noticed every detail. I hated that I noticed her at all, but that summer Easton made it impossible to ignore her.

I hated that I cared.

"Are you gonna see her tonight?" I asked before I could stop myself. I didn't say her name either. It felt like a bad word in my mouth.

He shrugged, but I saw the grin tugging at the corner of his lips. "Maybe."

Ouch. I could throw up.

I pushed my knee harder into his, trying to get him to look at me. "You promised me we'd watch Age of Ultron tonight. You said you'd stay."

He leaned back on his elbows; head tilted toward the stars that hadn't quite come out yet. He smelled like coconut sunscreen and remnants of the bonfire from earlier. We had spent all day together at the beach, so I'm sure we both smelled that way. But on him, it was different.

"I didn't promise. I said, *maybe.*"

"That's basically a promise, and I'm pretty sure there were pinkies involved," I told him trying my hardest to not sound like I was annoyed. I hated how small my voice came out. I tried to laugh, but it cracked halfway up my throat.

He didn't answer right away. He looked at me, then really looked. And for a second, he was still my Easton — the boy who stayed up late reading comics with a flashlight under the covers with me and Lila. He was still the Easton who taught me how to body surf when I was scared of the waves. He was still the Easton who played me his songs on guitar.

I'll never forget the way he looked at me that night.

His eyes softened, mouth opening like he was about to say something important, then his phone buzzed again. The moment was gone as quick as it came. He sat up, pulling it out so fast I almost laughed, but it wasn't funny.

"Geez, Easton," I snapped. "She's not even that pretty." The words flew out of my mouth without warning, mean and harsh, before I could stuff them back down. I didn't mean it. She was pretty and taller and more mature, and she wore mascara and she didn't still wear a training bra.

She was pretty and I could see it, but I would never admit it.

I bit the inside of my cheek, regretting the hurtful words that I just let slip. I wasn't trying to be mean. I never said mean things, ever. It wasn't in my nature.

I'm just sitting there waiting for him to tease me, or to playfully push me like he usually does when I got moody. But he didn't. He just laughed. It was a sharp, humorless sound that's burned into my brain. It hurt more than if he had yelled at me or gotten mad. Which he never did, but he also *never* laughed at me.

"You don't know anything about her," he said, eyes back on the screen. "She's different." "Different how?" I asked.

He pushed himself to his feet, brushing the nonexistent sand off his swim trunks. "Well, she doesn't act like a kid all the time."

The words landed between us like a slap. I felt my face get hot — from the inside out, a burn that reached the tip of my ears. He was looking past me now, down the dark stretch of beach where the older kids always met by the lifeguard tower. It's where they'd sneak beer and talk about things we were still too young to do.

He shifted his weight, glancing at the house behind us and the flicker of the TV light against the curtains. For a heartbeat I thought he'd cave. I thought he'd say he was sorry for what he said and that he didn't mean it. I thought he'd tell me he'd watch the movie with me because he doesn't ever break his promises. I thought he'd grab my hand and pull me into the house and we'd both forget everything that was just said. I thought he would because he always caved for me.

Then his phone buzzed again. He didn't even look at me this time when he said, "Cover for me, okay?"

I stood up as he hustled down the porch steps. I had stood up too fast and my head spun. "Cover for you?

What am I supposed to say? That you ditched me to go make out with what's her name?" I said louder than I wanted.

He looked me dead in the eye, begging me to stop. His voice is harsh in a way I'd never heard before. "Tate, grow up."

I opened my mouth to argue back, like I normally would but he was already in the sand. He didn't look back. He didn't even slow down. I stood there, heart pounding in my ears, watching him become a shadow the further he got away from me.

Something in me knew that whatever friendship I thought we had was dying. The Easton I knew would never have ditched me for anyone, let alone a girl. The air got suddenly thick making it hard to swallow, and my eyes began to burn. I swallowed hard, begging my eyes to keep the tears inside. I didn't want him to have that kind of power over me.

But the truth is, he did.

I sat down on the steps again and pulled my knees to my chest. I waited there until Jessie called me inside.

When she asked me where Easton was, I lied for him like he wanted me to. I said something like… his Boy Scout friend wanted to meet him for ice cream or something.

She bought it without a second thought. Before I knew it, she had picked up the conversation about next summer with my mom.

I sat next to Lila on the couch, making her shift on Jessie's lap. She moved around like the sleepy angel she was and she mumbled something in her sleep like she always did. The weight of me sitting down on the couch woke her up just enough to notice it was me sitting next to her. She sleepily rubbed her eyes as she sat up. She wrapped her arm around me in her in sleepy state, like she knew I needed the comfort.

As much as I didn't want it to happen, it did. The second her arms were around me, the tears left my eyes. Tears silently crawled down my face one at a time and I felt each one. I cried quietly for what felt like an eternity as I hid my face from the moms. I couldn't let them see me like this. I couldn't tell them who made me feel like this.

That night, I cried the first tears I ever cried for Easton Mills.

In that moment, I swore to myself that they'd be the last.

5

Kilby Girl

TATE

Who doesn't love the beach? I mean, I play beach volleyball after all. It would make sense that I'd love a good beach day where I wasn't expected to keep a ball off the sand repeatedly for hours, but honestly, going to the beach just to be there has never really been my thing. We've spent most of today at the beach against my better suggestion to stay in and have a movie marathon. It was just the mom's and their first born — Easton and I.

It's nostalgic but it's also HOT.

I brought a book to read to help pass the time while I bake in the sun. I've never understood the concept of tanning. It's like being baked in an oven for hours. I feel like a rotisserie chicken the whole time. I always end up sweating more than when I play beach volleyball and something about that has never sat right with me. People tan for the result, not for the enjoyment, that's for sure. But no matter how hard I try, I can never get as tan as Jessie or Easton.

My mom and Jessie sip their iced sweet tea like it's a cocktail, but neither one of them drink. Although, by the sound of their laughs, you would think the tea was spiked. They don't need alcohol to have a good time. They bring the party with them.

Easton sits beside me, knees bent, elbows resting lazily on top of them. He has on navy swim trunks. They're frayed a little on the edges, probably because he spends a lot of time at the beach. Resting on the pillow of his curls is a pair of old sunglasses that might've been mine at some point in middle school. They're old school black shades that look a bit familiar, but I don't say anything. They look better on him anyway. He's just looking out at the waves, but his mind is turning. I can tell.

Maybe he's thinking about the conversation we need to have. The elephant is getting larger by the second. It's like one of those foam capsules you put in water as a kid that turns into an animal, and this capsule is an elephant and it's taking up the the whole bathtub. He hasn't said much since we got to the beach. Someone's gotta say something.

"Did you bring a book?" I ask, mostly just to say something. Maybe if I distract him, I can hold off on this uncomfortable conversation for a bit longer.

My own book is face-down in the sand beside me, collecting heat and sadness from being ignored. I always try to read at the beach, but the sun makes the pages too bright, and I end up getting overstimulated. Plus, the beach is the last place I should be stressed. So, just like today, I end up just setting it down.

Easton glances over at me. "Nah, I figured people watching would be more entertaining." He always has a way of making doing nothing fun somehow.

I raise a brow. "And? Were you right?"

He smirks, nodding toward a group of college-aged guys playing spike-ball way too competitively. "So far, yeah. That dude's taken three dives and still hasn't made contact with the ball," he chuckles.

I laugh, watching the chaos with him for a moment.

"Spike-ball guys are the worst. No game, all ego," I add.

"You just described half my college," Easton says.

"Do they go to your school?" I ask.

Easton just finished his freshman year. Studying business and hospitality at a local junior college or at least that's what Jessie told me he was doing. She also said he works three jobs. He's interning at Disney, waiting tables, and serving at the church. He's a hard worker, but he never talks about it. You have to pull information out of him.

"I've seen em around," he answers.

Jessie looks over from her chair. "Y'all better not be making fun of the locals again!"

"Never," Easton calls back innocently, but Jessie knows better than that.

My mom leans toward Jessie, "They're back to their old ways," she whispers, but I hear her. I think we both do.

It does feel like old times. Like a version of myself I haven't seen in years is being revealed as layers get slowly pulled back, allowing my old self to show up again. Underneath all the layers is a girl who doesn't worry about timelines or other people's opinions. That version of myself just lives in the moment and doesn't have to take a deep breath every time her phone rings.

I glance at it now, face down on my towel. I haven't really touched it all day. Ryder has chilled on the texting after my *I need space* text last night. That should hold him off for a while... I hope.

"You, okay?" Easton asks.

I blink. "Yeah. Just thinking."

He nods, looking out at the ocean again. "Thinking can be dangerous."

"Then you must be safe," I tease.

He turns his head toward me with a grin. "Ouch."

I smile, letting the silence settle between us. I've never once thought Easton was dumb. Quite the opposite actually. There has never been a problem that Easton can't fix. His brain just works like that. It can fire at all times as quickly as needed to figure out any situation. He is book smart and street smart — a deadly combo in a dumb world. But little does he know, I do think he's safe. He's always been a safe spot for me to land. Or at least he used to be.

"The waves are good today," he states. "I think I'm gonna go out."

"Since when did you surf?" I say shocked.

"You've been gone a long time Tate. I've changed," he gets up quickly, leaving me speechless.

Easton is talking to the college spike-ball boys now. I thought maybe he was gonna ask to play with them but then I realize they probably have a board that he wants to use.

Something about him surfing doesn't fit to me. I really thought he was joking. It isn't until he comes back from the parking lot carrying a board that I realize he's being serious about the whole thing.

His tan skin and curly brown hair does make him look beachy, but I've never known him to be the surfer type. Before I know it, he's in the water. It's only a couple minutes before he catches a wave. It's surprisingly easy for him.

I wonder who taught him?

* * *

I step out of the car, adjusting the straps of my tank top. I decided on a navy tube top and a short jean skirt paired with my black Birks. It's one of the three more "dressy" outfits I packed for the two weeks I'm here.

My mom says navy brings out my freckles after a day in the sun.

I only got dressed up because I felt like it. My favorite part about a beach day is that little slot of time in-between laying on the beach and dinner. There's something about that shower after being in the sun and sand all day. Just lazily getting ready with the music echoing in the bathroom while throwing on something comfortable enough to chill in but cute enough to post on Instagram. It's at moments like this that I'm thankful to be a girl. A low maintenance one at that. No makeup or hair styling necessary.

In fact, my hair is still wet and tucked behind my ears as we walk into Four Rivers, the Mill's favorite BBQ joint. Jessie said they just built the place, but it's quickly become a regular dining spot.

Smoke from the grill fills the air as it dances with the ocean breeze as we walk into the back part of the restaurant. The whole thing is tucked beneath a canopy of string lights and driftwood signage. *Four Rivers.* It's the kind of place you'd miss if you blinked, but Jessie swears by their ribs and watermelon sweet tea like it's scripture written on her heart.

Easton and I follow them toward the patio, where picnic tables and laughter spill out in every direction. The moms go order while Easton and I walk around the place trying to find Mr. Mills, who's been saving us a table. He came straight from work.

I hear him before I see him. "Tate," Mr. Mills calls out as soon as he spots me, waving from a table under one of the string lights. He stands as we approach. "Look at you, so grown up," he says with that same warm smile. He's wearing jeans, and his hair has gone fully white, but everything else about him is as familiar as the porch swing that used to creak outside their old house.

"Mr. Mills!" I give him a quick hug, his aftershave unchanged and nostalgic.

Easton gives him a pat on the back and then slips away, but I don't see where he goes.

He pulls back to look at me. "You're still playing volleyball I hear? Jessie says you're playing in some big tournament this week." He isn't really a sports guy. Deceiving considering his 6'3" stature. "Yeah, it's a recruiting event. College coaches and all that," I answer. He nods like he's genuinely impressed. "That sounds big. I hope they give you a scholarship and then some. What about your brother? How's Nate? What's he up to?"

I smile sweetly. "Nate's still figuring things out. He's had a rough year. Been bouncing between schools. We just want him to graduate in one piece. Then he'll start making movies like dad."

The moms walk up, joining us at the table.

"Ah, your dad," he says with a meaningful nod, turning to my mom. "Still in the Hollywood biz?"

Mom shrugs like it's nothing. "Always. He's in pre-production on a spy thriller now. More explosions than he's used to, but he loves it."

They all laugh. I smile, but my eyes are scanning the place for Easton. I try not to make it obvious. He didn't say much in the car. Just sat with one arm out the window like the breeze might carry away whatever it was he wasn't saying. We haven't really talked since yesterday's whole day at Disney, other than for a moment at the beach. I don't mind sitting in silence with him though. I don't ever feel like I have to force a conversation. So, in the car, I just let him be. It's what felt right at the time.

I see a few eyes turn as my mom starts to talk about my dad's latest movies. That's something I don't think I'll ever get used to. Dad lives a different life than us with long days on set, celebrities, directors, wrap parties, movie screenings, and red carpets. I know he does fun things and that it sounds big and glamorous to everyone, but I never think about those things when I'm with my dad. He's just dad. I love him just like that. So, when people's heads turn at the sound of what he does for a living, it always makes me chuckle a bit. Because, of course dad makes movies.

That's what he does.

A waiter passes by with a tray full of brisket and corn on the cob and my stomach growls on cue. It smells heavenly. Mom and Mr. Mill's catch-up conversation washes over me like a wave.

I can't stop thinking about where Easton might have slipped away too. Or maybe I'm more concerned of who he might be slipping away to.

My thought is put in the grave when Easton slides into the seat beside me. He tosses his phone on the table, stealing a piece of cornbread quickly. He doesn't look at me directly, but I can feel the heat of his presence like sunlight through a glass window — warm, soft, all encompassing. His phone screen pops on, and something sticks out to me.

His wallpaper. It's of a girl.

My heart sinks to my feet.

Annie.

She has long black hair, paired with a quite pale complexion. It's the girl from Lila's posts. The one on the worship team with her. The one he told me was just a friend the other morning in the kitchen.

I want to swallow it down, but it just sits in my throat. I'm disappointed. Disappointed that he didn't trust me enough to be honest with me when I asked about her the other day, and disappointed that I care so much.

I'm sort of dating someone anyway. Well, not anymore actually but it's all for the best, I guess.

Something in me aches anyways. I'm jealous. Not of her. But that she gets to have Lila. And now she has Easton too.

Easton clocks me and immediately knows something's wrong.

I shake my head *no* before he can ask me if I'm OK. The last thing I want is to talk about it. I don't even want to think about it, but that ship has long left the harbor.

The concern on his face remains.

Jessie passes me a mason jar of watermelon sweet tea. "This place has live music after sunset," she says. "Usually high school kids or local college kids who think they're the next Ed Sheeran. It's either a super hit or a super miss but I've got a feeling about tonight. I think it's gonna be good," she says with a big smile.

I nod, sipping slowly, silently thanking Jessie for saving me from having to answer Easton and his curious eyes. The tea is cold and syrupy, making it super sweet — the kind of sweet that hurts your teeth a bit. I know it's bad, but I like that feeling.

Under the table Easton's leg presses firmly against mine. He turns to face me when he talks, making sure I feel included since I'm at the end of the table. When he tells a joke or I make him laugh he gently places his hand on my leg under the table, just above my knee. It's only for a second, but that second does something to me. I hate it as much as I love it.

I don't want him to act any different than he is right now but *shouldn't* he if he's dating the girl on his wallpaper. Would he act like this if Annie sat across from us? Part of me wants to believe that he would treat me the same. He's known me longer than her. Maybe he would be the same.

Maybe this is just who we are — friends who secretly want a little more but are too chicken to own up to it. Or maybe we're just this close and I'm reading into it.

Whatever it is though, it's sickening.

Ugh.

I don't move my leg, and I don't tell him to stop.

Because I can't.

* * *

The sky has turned the color of a ripe clementine and the air is buzzing with cicadas and the smell of brisket floats through the air as I walk back from the bathroom. We have all eaten and are just visiting now. Everyone's chatting. Jessie is deep into a story about a church bake sale gone wrong and my mom can't stop giggling. Mr. Mills just joined in with some dad-joke commentary that actually lands, making both the moms laugh.

But Easton's not at the table. He's gone. Again.

I scan the place. His seat is empty and his plate is completely clean. He was here when I left.

I don't join the parents. I wander around looking for Easton. I make my way toward the edge of the little outdoor yard we were sitting in, but before I can wander too far, someone calls out. "Looking for tall, dark, and brooding?" A voice I don't recognize calls out.

I turn to see a tall, toe-headed boy. By the looks of him I'd guess he's in college, but if you told me he was younger I would believe it. He has piercing blue eyes and beach blonde messy curls, he's very California. The blonde is almost white. His necklace chain is in his mouth — a nervous tick I'm assuming. He's holding drumsticks.

Kind of an odd accessory for a BBQ joint.

I look at him, but don't say anything.

"I'm Walter. Walter Hughes. You must be Tate Knightly," he says matter of fact, like I'm a celebrity he just spotted out in the wild. I've never seen this boy a day in my life, but he seems to know me somehow.

How does he know my name?

"Easton said you were beautiful, but wow," he says as his eyes trail my body up and down as he takes me in.

Easton's friend, I'm guessing.

"You know Easton?" I question, completely ignoring his compliment.

"I'm his drummer," he says, trying to help me put together the pieces but it's not working. "I'm also his best friend."

"Oh, sorry. I just didn't know he had a band," I say, and I can feel the confusion popping up on my face. I know it can't be a pretty sight.

I knew Easton played instruments, but I didn't know he performed, other than the keys at church occasionally.

That was always Lila's thing.

"Do you carry those with you everywhere?" I motion to the drumsticks in his hands. He clings to them like a security blanket.

A very goofy laugh falls from his lips. It's cute though.

"Usually, yeah," he assures me.

"Have you seen Easton?" I ask with a little bit of haste.

"The wind whispered that he's around here. Mysterious type. You know how it is," he says like it's a piece of poetry. I'm starting to think he was just smoking something. What he said didn't answer my question at all.

"Walter," I say in hopes of sobering him up from whatever he is high on.

He tilts his head. "Look, I didn't say anything… but I also didn't not say anything either. Just…stay close.

Something is happenin'." And with that cryptic nonsense, he winks at me and jogs toward the makeshift stage behind him. He twirls the drumstick in his hands like he's heading into a sword fight.

I stand there for a second, heart weirdly racing as I watch him. A few more people gather near the small stage under the string lights now. The moms are waving me over, and Mr. Mills catches my eye, gesturing toward an empty chair beside him. "You alright, kiddo?" He asks when I reach the table.

I nod. "Yeah, just a bit tired," I lie.

He just smiles, leaning back in his chair, the lines on his face are catching the fading light and I realize how much older he's gotten since the last time I saw him. He's not just older, he's wiser and he wears it well.

The first few strums of a guitar ring out, soft like background music as it breaks the silence in the air.

My eyes snap toward the small stage.

Easton is stepping up to the mic, hair a little messy from the breeze, guitar slung over his shoulder and his eyes scan the crowd like he isn't looking for anyone and he's looking for exactly one person all at once. My breath catches.

He's performing?

He adjusts the mic with the kind of ease that only comes from doing something in private a hundred times before sharing it. He's rehearsed this moment. His fingers pick at the guitar strings, then settle.

"Uh…" he starts, then clears his throat awkwardly.

"Hey, everyone. I'm Easton. And this is my buddy, Walter."

Walter plays a fast drum combo as a way to say *hi* to the crowd.

"And we're *Two Boys in a Band*. We hope you like this," he says the last part looking at me. My heart isn't even in my chest anymore. It's jumped and crawled out of my throat.

A few people clap. Jessie lets out an enthusiastic, "That's my boy!" from the picnic table. Mr. Mills raises his cup like a silent cheer and my mom smiles softly next to him.

I don't move. How can I? I'm still trying to catch my breath from just seeing him up there.

As a kid, he always struggled to perform songs for the family. We'd all sit around the living room or around the campfire in their backyard and listen to him play. He'd always forget a lyric or sing slightly out of key. Not because he didn't know the right words — he just had stage fright when it came to singing. He has no reason to have it. His voice is beautiful in a raspy sort of way, and he's beyond talented on any instrument. Back then, he'd play songs for just me if I begged him. He always put up a fight, but he always caved… eventually. He never messed up when it was just us. He sounded his best singing just for me.

But now, he's standing in front of a lot more than just me. More than just our families.

Easton's eyes flicker across the small crowd. For one second, for one single heartbeat, his gaze meets mine. His eyes say something I can't read.

"This one's called *Kilby Girl*. If you know it, sing along," he says. He doesn't specify, but I know it's not one of his originals. I'd know if it was.

He starts simple. No back track. Just the sound of his guitar and Walter's slow drumming and the grain in his voice.

"*We're both throwing smoke into the night… It's raining, I suppose you need a ride… She said I've got nothin' to do and neither do you… There's a place down the road we can waste the whole afternoon*" he starts off singing and then the instruments come in stronger. "*I overheard that she was nineteen… she's got a fake ID and a nose ring… those kinda girls tend to know things… better than I do. And I'm dying, to figure out what she's hiding. She's playing it cool but she's lying better than I do.*"

Then he steps away from the mic playing the guitar facing Walter now. He's so into it and it's amazing.

He's killing it. He sounds even better than I remember.

I'm overwhelmed with feelings. It's like someone just threw a rock into the still water of my entire stomach. I can feel every ripple. I can literally feel my heartbeat in my ears.

I'm so proud of him.

He sounds different than he used to. More mature. More confident. It's a good look on him. All of this is a side of him I've never truly seen.

Easton, the performer.

"She's playing it cool but she's lying... better than I do." He sings as the last note lingers longer than the rest through the electric air of the restaurant.

He steps back from the mic, his hands falling to his sides.

People clap — lightly at first, then louder. Jessie stands to cheer, and my mom joins her. "Oh, Kora, he did such a good job didn't he?" Jessie asks my mom.

"He really did," my mom says with a proud grin.

Walter taps the cymbal gently, giving a slow *that was legit* nod.

Easton gives a half-smile and a quick *thank you* to the crowd, then jumps off the stage joining us at the table. Jessie and my mom walk around the table, bombarding him with hugs. "You sounded amazing, Easton!!" Jessie says squeezing him so tight he can't respond.

"You did good kid," my mom says.

"I'm impressed," Mr. Mills says from his seat. That means a lot coming from him, and I know Easton appreciates such a compliment from his dad.

Easton makes his way to me, so I hug him. "Maybe you have changed," I say just loud enough for him to hear. He pulls away wearing a cute little smirk, as if he's saying something else. His face says, *you have no idea.*

I can't tell if that's a good thing or a not so good thing.

What I do know, is that I so badly want to know. I want to know how else he's changed. It feels desperate how badly I want to know all the ways he's evolved over the years.

But the truth is, I know he'll show me… eventually.

I just have to be patient.

Which is gonna be a lot harder than it sounds.

Especially with Annie.

6

Firsts

TATE

I wasn't allowed to have a boyfriend growing up. My parents said I had to be eighteen before making that kind of decision. If I could enlist in the army and choose whether smoking cigarettes is a smart decision or not then I guess I'm old enough to choose a mate — or at least start the process. That was their philosophy.

So, at the ripe age of eighteen, toward the end my junior year of high school, I started dating the first guy who showed any interest in me — Ryder. He's a sweet guy, or at least to me he is. We grew up together actually. We went to the same church and our parents were in the same small group Bible study. We'd have play dates and go to the water park together, but we weren't best friends or anything — just family friends.

We didn't grow up together the way I grew up with the Mill's. I didn't grow up with him the way I grew up with Easton.

Ryder has a rough exterior, and a soft teddy bear inside. He has good intentions, but he doesn't really know what to do in a relationship. It's not really his fault though, and I know that. The one thing he knows a lot about is football. He's got a pretty one-track mind. His interests are mainly football, basketball, and his favorite rapper. But that's it.

He has one really close friend and a few acquaintances. He doesn't really fit in at his preppy private school. That's one of my favorite things about him. You would think because of his strong six foot three stature and strong religious beliefs that he would fit in at the preppy Christian school he goes to, but he just doesn't.

I hadn't seen him in years until last year when our moms bumped into each other at the grocery store. Next thing I know we're eating dinner together. Both families at one table. After years of only seeing them on Instagram.

It was really nice. Now that we're all grown and in high school, we all have a great time. His younger sister is my brother's age so Nate got a friend out of it too. It was a bit awkward at first, but it got better. After a few meet ups it started to feel normal.

Ryder and I hung out once last summer with a bunch of church friends and he just kind of followed me around. Whatever I did, he did. I guess that was his way of letting me know that he liked me. And sadly, it worked. I loved being adored, and Ryder adored me. I didn't know any better at the time though. I was just dying to know what it was like to have someone. *Desperate, I know.* I always wanted to know what that was like. Even though my mother cautioned me to wait for the right person, I didn't.

Ryder was my first kiss.

I'll never forget it. We sat on a picnic table at the park near my house — both our butts on the tabletop with our feet on the bench with our legs fully touching.

The picnic table was painted green, and it was peeling. I was nervous it would stick to my legs when I stood up. The table was under a wooden cabana. I'd only ever been down there a few times since moving into the neighborhood. Each time I went it was to watch the kids I babysat from down the street play on the swing set. They loved the swings.

Ryder and I had wandered down there one night to carve our names into the wooded siding of the cabana. I don't remember where that idea came from. It doesn't really sound like something I'd suggest, so I guess it was his idea. Thinking back now, I see that it was an excuse to get me alone. He just wanted a moment, just us.

We carved our names into the wooden post using a broken tree twig. *TKS...* Tate Knightly Sellars, I carved in a boxy shaped font. *RBL...* Ryder Brody Lawson, he carved beside mine. Before he put the twig down, he looked at our initials carefully with a tilted head, like he was thinking something.

"What?" I asked.

"It's missing something," he whispered as he brought the twig back up to the post. Before I could question him anymore, he had carved a heart around our initials. He looked so proud of himself. It was a sweet gesture.

We sat down on the picnic tabletop, both facing forward and there was this weird silence in the air. Not tension, not build up, just silence. I looked over at him to say something to fill the awkward quiet. But before words could leave my lips, he was on them. We were kissing.

I kissed him back eventually, but I wasn't really sure why.

It wasn't what I expected at all. I kept waiting for him to pull away, but he didn't. He just kept kissing me. I wasn't even sure I was doing it right. I wasn't really doing much at all. It had been longer than I wanted, and I wondered if this was kissing?

This is what I had been missing out on? Eventually he pulled away, and he looked... happy. Really happy. It made me smile the way he grinned so big. His cheeks must have hurt from how big his grin was. He really was a sweet guy. And that was it. A kiss. Multiple kisses all at once? Whatever it was… it was over.

I had just had my first kiss.

Something twinged in my chest on our walk back to my house. I had been saving that moment for someone else. For Easton. I had always hoped Easton would be my first kiss. But I knew that wasn't realistic. It was a dream. Easton was always just a dream. Real for a moment, but then when you wake. Gone.

7

Tattoos?

TATE

The house is quiet in the way it only gets late at night. It's so peaceful just sitting here on my own. No one to bother me, other than my own thoughts. My journal lays on top of the counter as I doodle away inside the already full pages with nothing but a ballpoint pen. I've been drawing for so long that my hand begins to ache.

Drawing always calms my brain when it's going a million miles an hour. It's like that first deep breath after a long run. It slowly takes the weight off my chest, lightening the emotional load.

I'm not great at drawing by any means, in fact, I don't dare show my work to anyone other than the anonymous Instagram account I post to. I have no followers, and I follow no one. It's not about that. Posting makes it final to me. That's why I do it. If I don't post a picture of the drawing, I'd keep adding lines here and there, never truly being finished with it. Posting makes me move on to another drawing, because I have to.

My mom's giggle floats faintly down the hall. She disappeared into

Jessie's room over an hour ago. They're having a sleepover. That's what the mom's relationship is — childish in all the ways that are still good. They're in their forties, but a sleepover isn't weird for them somehow. It is silly, but I love them for it.

The best part is that Mr. Mills happily sleeps in the office on nights like these so they can have their girl time. Every year. He knows it's a sacred time for them. Living far away from your best friend isn't easy, and he knows that. He respects Jessie enough to give her her space when she wants or needs it. It takes a good man to do something like that. It takes a secure man to not feel threatened. When a real man loves his wife, he understands her wants and desires. I've always admired that about him.

Mom and Jessie offered to let me join them tonight, but as much as I would like to put on a face mask and jump in the massage line to watch *10 Things I Hate About You* while stuffing my face with chocolate covered caramels… I'm still too caught up on the events of what happened at dinner to properly enjoy a girl's night the way it is supposed to be enjoyed. I fear that if I sit with both of them for that long they'll read me like a book. And at this point, I don't even know what they would be reading because I don't even really know how I feel.

I'm barefoot standing at the sink, sipping water from a glass when Easton walks in, his voice low and playful. "Not joining mom and Kora tonight?" He asks as he grabs a soda from the fridge. I haven't seen Easton since dinner.

He stayed after to help Walter pack up their gear. I turn slowly to face him, shaking my head *no*.

I have so many questions circling in my mind.

Why didn't he tell me he was seeing someone? Why do I feel like I deserve to be told that kind of information? Does he think she's gorgeous? How long have they been dating? Is she his girlfriend? Why didn't Jessie tell me they were dating? Does my mom know about them? Is that why Lila stopped talking to me?

Because Annie was her best friend now? Is everything I felt for him growing up real? Did he feel the same? Does he feel the same? Does it matter? Does he love her? Does he love her? Does. He. Love. her?

"No. Didn't feel like it," I say sharply, attempting to calm the thoughts begging to crawl out of my brain and roll off my tongue.

The air isn't as warm and flirty as it usually is. It's cold, tense, rough. He feels it to. His eyebrows furrow together, subtly asking me if I'm telling the truth. I don't answer. I don't know how to.

"What are you gonna do then?" He asks.

Anything but be around you. Think of something. Hurry. "Uh… I was gonna start the new season of Ted Lasso. Have you seen it?" I make up. *Did I just invite him to watch with me? Ugh, I'm too nice.* I do plan on watching the new season, but I have no real intention of watching it tonight. Something has his attention. He's studying something on the bar… *Oh shit, my journal.* I bolt over and grab my journal, swiftly shutting it before he can grab it.

"I didn't know you were an artist?" He says.

I laugh awkwardly but he doesn't laugh with me. *Is he being serious?*

"Why are you drawing a butterfly?" He questions.

I immediately regret everything. I should have joined the moms. I should have never brought my journal out. I should have never gotten up to get water. I should have never even come here. I can't believe he saw my drawings, even for a second. They're not meant to be seen.

"I don't know," I say lying through my teeth. He won't care why I'm drawing it anyways.

Thankfully he senses my uncomfortable feelings toward this topic of conversation and changes the subject.

"The Jason Sudeikis TV show? The one on Apple?" He asks me

successfully shifting the subject back to something more comfortable.

I piqued his curiosity. *Great.*

"Yeah, that's the one," I say leaning back on the counter, slightly defeated.

"Well, I have a proposition for you. Feel free to say no. It sounds like you've got a great night planned, but would you wanna run to Publix with me, real quick? I'm craving ice cream," he says tapping his stomach with a smirk.

When is he not craving ice cream?

Publix runs for ice cream were very normal with our families during the summers. But I had never gone with just him. It was always with Lila and always with my mom and Jessie.

I don't want to go. Being alone with him isn't a good idea, but I can't help but feel like I should. I love the idea of being with him, but I know it's a recipe for disaster.

The biggest battle you'll ever fight is the battle between you brain and your heart. There are eighteen inches between them but right now it feels like they're having a fist fight.

He must sense my internal battle because he adds, "Your pick." As if he knows that letting me choose the flavor of ice cream we get is gonna win me over.

Screw it.

"OK, but I get the aux," I say smiling at him.

Five minutes later, we're in his car.

The windows are down, and the wind cuts through my long brown hair so much it flips into my face. I probably should put it up in a knot. It would keep it out of my face.

But I feel prettier with my hair down, so, I'll pay the price — which today is mouth full of hair.

I didn't really expect him to give me the aux. I said it as a joke, because he's always the DJ.

Music is one of the ways we connect. Our taste in artists and playlists is so similar that it never matters which phone we use to play music. They're almost identical.

He hands me his phone without question.

I hesitate before opening it. I don't want to see the picture of Annie again. I get over myself and turn his phone on. There she is. I slide the home screen, now faced with his four-digit code. Without even thinking, I punch it in.

0-3-1-8. His birthday.

It unlocks with ease, and Easton doesn't even bat an eye, like I'm just supposed to just know those things. It's expected that I know his password, because it's me.

It won't matter what song I play. He'll vibe to whatever I put on. I can feel him glancing over at me as I scroll through his Spotify, looking for a playlist. This feeling of being watched by him is addicting. I need it. I want it to last as long as possible. The plus side to picking the music is that I get to feel him watching me.

Truthfully, I always play songs I know he'll like. I love getting to see his face light up when he likes the song I pick. I swipe over playlists with weird names and even weirder pictures. He's always been a goofball, but it seems like his humor has increased, and I like it. My thumb freezes over a playlist with a picture of me on it. I've never seen this picture, nor do I have any recollection of it being taken. Its playlist title is just "HER." I click on the playlist and hit play. Suddenly, the speakers of his old silver mustang are playing the song I had just heard him play in front of a small restaurant crowd — *Kilby Girl* by the Backseat Lovers.

It's the song him and Walter performed.

I didn't know who the Backseat Lovers were until now. But now I think they're my favorite band. His head leans back against the head rest as he pulls into the Publix parking lot. His arm is straight out holding the steering wheel as he turns. Relaxed. Calm. Cool. He makes everything look so easy.

He parks the car, but he doesn't get out. I don't move, because he doesn't. His head doesn't leave the head rest as he tilts his head toward me. The lyrics of the song buzzing through the air. His smirk is evident, even in the dark of night surrounding us, I can see it. It's different somehow too. But I can't place why. His eyes are dark and mysterious. *"I've been carrying you since you left my roooom,"* He sings out at me without breaking eye contact.

My soul leaves my body.

Nothing in me can break the eye contact, even if I wanted to… I just can't do it.

He chuckles to himself then adds, "Had you heard it before tonight?"

"No," I answer quickly. He wants me to compliment him on his performance, and normally I would. But right now, I won't let myself.

"It's a good song. I like them," I say, complimenting the band. I'm not lying. They do sound amazing.

"Yeah, yeah. They're great. *Olivia*'s a good song of theirs too. You should queue it up for the ride back," He covers himself well, but I know it stings a little bit. It stings that I don't say anything about his performance at dinner. It stings that I don't compliment him. It stings that I don't even mention it. But that's what I want… isn't it?

We stumble inside not really saying much. It's not that he needs the validation of me telling him he did a good job. It's that he wants it. It's that we've always been each other's biggest fans. That was the kind of friendship we *had*. Past tense. It's not that way anymore. Right now, we can feel the five years of separation between us.

At the freezer aisle, he steps aside and holds the door open for me with a teasing grin. "Your destiny awaits," he says with a not-so-great British accent.

I scan the ice cream row. Strawberry sounds heavenly. But so does chocolate. And then my eyes land on one I haven't had since the last summer I was here. I grab it out of the freezer. "Mint chip. Classic." He says, putting up no objections.

He grabs some chocolate syrup for good measure on our way to the cashier.

He pays. I knew he would, but part of me wondered if he'd be weird about paying for it. Ryder is weird about that stuff sometimes. Easton doesn't even hesitate pulling out his wallet. I didn't even have to pretend like I wanted to pay for it.

Something about standing next to him at the register while he swipes his card makes me feel weird. Or maybe it's the fact that I don't feel weird that makes me feel weird…

YIKES.

I have always pictured us doing this someday. Making dinner together, traveling together, living together, even grocery shopping. It feels right.

The lady cashier who scanned the ice cream and syrup looks at us like we might be there as more than just friends.

I know we aren't, but it's nice to feel like for even just a second that I'm his.

For the first time out of any of the summers I've been coming to Florida, I feel fully grown. It hits me that Easton is nineteen and I'm eighteen. We're adults. Baby adults, but adults none-the-less.

As we walk out of the automatic sliding Publix doors, it hit me like the wind on my face. I'm acting like a child by avoiding my issues. I may have been a kid the last time I was here, but now, I'm not. I need to start acting like it.

Back at the apartment, the tub of ice cream is slowly starting to sweat into the plastic Publix bag in the back seat. Florida isn't the best environment for ice cream.

We should head up, but for some reason we both just sit there in the silence of the car. No music. No noise. No talking. Just us.

"You ever think about getting a tattoo?" He asks me randomly, eyes still focused forward.

I look at him, surprised. "Yeah, actually."

"Me too," he adds quietly. "My grandparents would kill me if they saw ink anywhere on my body but, I think about it."

"Is that the only thing keeping you from getting one?" I ask curiously.

I've never really pictured Easton with tattoos. His parents don't have any. I don't think they're necessarily against them, but they also aren't outwardly for them.

"Mostly," he says. "You thinking about getting that butterfly? He adds, turning his head to look at me. "The one you were drawing up there." He says referencing the doodle from my journal.

I feel caught. Because, yes, I was planning on getting it for my nineteenth birthday.

How'd he know?

"Yeah, but smaller. I'd want to be able to cover it if I needed to."I state as I try and think about the tattoo and where I'd want to put it.

Both my parents have tattoos. My mom has four or five and my dad has six or so. All pretty small. My favorite of their tattoos is on both their left ring fingers. My dad has "KORA" tattooed on the top, right under where his wedding band sits. And my mom has the same for my dad, "CHRIS" on the same finger but on the underside of her finger — closer to her palm. It's a marking on them both that they wear proudly. It sort-of says, *I love you, forever* in a small simple way. I desire a love like that — true, loyal, and real. If I ever find it, I'll get the same tattoo.

But maybe just the first letter of my person's name. I like dainty tattoos.

So, I guess you could say my parents are a bit more open to the idea of tattoos than Jessie and Mr. Mills. They'd never say it, but we just kind of know they don't like them.

"What's the point in getting one then? If you're just gonna cover it up." Easton remarks with a bit of sass. Easton is like this — always kind, but he carries a bit of attitude in his back pocket, and he only uses it on special occasions.

Most occasions involve me.

"I didn't say I would cover it up. I just want to be able to if I need to for a job or whatever," I say, backing myself up.

"Like for modeling?" He asks.

"And acting," I confirm.

I've always wanted to try my hand at acting, but my dad didn't want me to end up like a lot of kid actors — drug addicted and lonely. So he didn't let me start pursuing it til I was almost twelve. By that age I was already very competitive in beach volleyball. I was playing almost every weekend and traveling all over the country to compete. I only got a few jobs every so often when I had the time. I did some modeling for Dillard's and a few commercials, that was at the peak of my preteen cuteness, when having crooked teeth and a silly smile was still adorable and unique.

Thank God for Invisalign. That wonky smile needed correcting.

"As much as I want to pursue that world, I don't think I'll get the chance til I'm done with college. Not til I'm done with volleyball," I add.

"That makes sense," he says. "I forget how thought out with things you are. You already know what you want to do in college and after and you probably have your 10-year plan mapped out in a google doc somewhere." He doesn't say it mockingly. He's admiring my ambition. "I can't even pick a major I like," his voice drops a bit.

I don't want to talk about either of our futures. That's not what summer is for. For as much as I think about the future, summer is for being in the moment. Summer is for living in the now.

"What would you get? If you got a tattoo? No regrets." I ask, attempting to change the topic back to something lighter.

He thinks for a moment. "Probably a lightsaber." I chuckle, but I believe him fully.

"Probably just the handle though. And then I'd have the lightsaber be done in glow in the dark ink," he adds confidently.

"What color lightsaber?" I inquire.

"Purple. Mace Windu all the way," he says with a huge laugh. It's the first real laugh I've heard from him since being back. My stomach sinks at the sound of it. I missed that sound.

He always throws his head back like a little boy when he laughs really hard — only when something is really funny. His own tattoo idea has sent him into a giggle fit.

For a moment, I remember why I had been in love with him all those years ago.

This is why.

8

Package Deal

TATE
(The summer I was 8 & he was 9)

There were some perks to Mr. Mills being a Disney World employee. We got to hop parks as many times as we wanted, he had the employee discount, and he knew all the Disney characters that walked around the parks. But when we were really little, my favorite perk was the Disney Cast Store. It's like a Disney goodwill. It had shelves filled with Disney clothes, character plushies, Christmas ornaments, books, posters, pins, Mickey ears — all of it. But the catch was, all of it had something a little bit wrong with it. The t-shirts might not have sold well or had something wrong with the printing. The Christmas ornament might have been chipped, or the Mickey ears were a character not many people liked. Everything was marked down like 80-90% off.

It sounds boring, or maybe even lame but to us, it was wonderland. All of my favorite souvenirs came from this store. I liked that everything had a quirk. It made each item cooler to me. It gave it character.

74

The summer I was eight was the first time all of us kids were old enough to all go to the store together with the moms. Easton was nine, Lila was seven, and the youngest was Nate. He was five, but still small enough to be picked up by my mom. He was an active little boy, — so in my mom's arms he stayed.

The rest of us, however, ran around like kids in a candy store. Lila and I found princess dresses. I grabbed a Belle dress, and she grabbed the Cinderella one.

We tried to convince Easton to try on a Prince Eric costume, but he refused. He was more into superhero's than being a prince.

I remember how badly I wanted him to be my prince. In a lot of ways, he was.

He would hold my hand when we crossed the street, and he would get the stool for me to stand on in the hall bathroom so I could wash my hands when we came in from outside. One time, he even gave me the last clementine when we were waiting in line for Splash Mountain.

He was perfect in my eyes back then. He could do no wrong.

Me and Lila wandered around the store for about half an hour while the mom's looked at Christmas ornaments.

I hadn't seen Easton in a while, until I heard him… "TK! Come over here!" he yelled a bit too loud.

I started running around the store trying to find him. I went down all the aisles trying to follow the sound of his voice.

When I finally found him, he was standing on an aisle filled with dishes.

The first thing I saw was a Ms. Potts tea pot and I thought of how perfect it would go with the Belle dress I just tried on. But before I could think about grabbing it, Easton pulled me toward the other end of the aisle.

"Look, TK!" He said with more enthusiasm than I had ever seen come from him.

When we came to a stop he pointed at the shelf in front of us. Right in the middle of the shelf sat a big blue coffee mug. The mug was so big, if it hadn't had a handle I would have thought it was a bowl. It was the kind of mug you eat soup out of. It had a Captain America shield right on the front.

I didn't care much for superheroes. They were cool, in like a dinosaur sort of way. I liked the idea of them, but they weren't real.

He was so giddy to show me, that I acted as excited as he was, just to make him happy.

"Captain America?!" I said, "You have to get it!!" I added.

"You haven't even seen the best part yet." He said turning around to the other shelf. He grabbed a mug from the shelf and set it next to the Captain America one. The new mug was dark grey and had a red star in the middle. I had no idea who that character was supposed to be. I wasn't sure how to react.

"It's a Bucky Barnes mug. He's the Winter Soldier.

Captain America's best friend." He informed me.

"Oh, that's so cool!" I said, still unsure why it was really so cool.

"It's like us." He said looking at me. "In the movie, Captain America and Bucky have this saying. 'I'm with you, till the end of the line'," he says.

"What does that mean?" I asked him.

"It means no matter what happens, they always have each others backs. Like you and me," he said grabbing my hand.

I would have kissed him right there, but at the time I thought that's how babies were made, so I decided it was better not to.

So, I just stood there holding his hand until he let go and grabbed the mugs.

"They're seventy percent off. Let's ask our mom's if we can get them!" He said running off.

The big blue mug is heavy in my hand. I rest my thumb in the little chip on the handle. I love it.

I thought I was the Winter Soldier in this scenario, but he handed me the Captain America mug.

I'd never had coffee, but I could picture myself drinking it out of this mug on the porch one day when I'm older with Easton.

Another thing I could imagine my future self doing with him.

With a bit of begging from Easton, our mom's agreed to buy the mugs. He was ecstatic as we walked out of the store. We begged Jessie to make chicken noodle soup for dinner so we could try out our new mugs.

She agreed.

So that night Easton and I sat on the couch and watched *Captain America: The Winter Soldier* with our matching mugs and I was in heaven.

Chapter 9: Package Deal.
  Pt. 2

9

Package Deal pt. 2

TATE

Mr. Mills is out like a light in his office when we walk back into the apartment. His latest murder mystery is held open by his thumb, seconds from falling onto the floor. He's always a little tired because of his commute to and from work. He loves his job at Disney and Jessie loves the beach. He happily lives over an hour away from work just so his bride gets to see the beach every day.

After we chuckled at his snoring, Easton walks into his office, putting Mr. Mill's book on the desk, covering him up with his blanket.

This is the part of him that I missed. This is the part of him I coveted. He isn't helping his dad to look kind to his dad or to me. That's just his natural instinct.

Most boys would just walk past their sleeping dad and let his book fall on the floor but that's just not Easton. He's kind and genuine. No matter how adult he becomes, he's still that little boy who held my hand to cross the street.

He's just older now.

78

It's dark in the kitchen when we walk in. The only light is coming from the freezer light I'm currently standing in and the TV light peaking out from under Jessie's bedroom door. A little laugh echoes from behind their door every now and then.

It's past midnight and I can't stop thinking about everything I want to ask Easton. He walks in when I close the freezer door.

"You wanna watch that show you were talking about?

While the ice cream refreezes?" he asks me.

That sounds like a valid excuse to avoid having the deeper, more meaningful conversation I know I need to have with him, so I agree. "Let's do it."

He walks into the living room searching for the remote.

They got a new couch with the move. Something that fit the apartment a bit better. It's light brown leather and kind of a "c" shape. It looked like something you'd see in a game room. I plop down onto the cushions, sinking in. I wasn't expecting it to be this comfortable. No wonder Easton doesn't mind sleeping out here. It's almost more comfortable than his bed. His pillow is on the opposite side of the couch and the blanket he uses sits next to it. I'm not cold but I have the urge to grab it. He must see me looking at it, because he says, "You cold?", as he grabs it and offers it to me.

"Thanks." I say with a big grin.

He turns the TV on and sits right next to me.

I'm not sure what I expected to happen, but it wasn't this.

This couch has eight cushions, and he chose to sit on the one directly next to mine.

I put the blanket over my legs, positioning myself in a criss-cross position as he finds the show. I throw the blanket over both our legs without thinking much about it.

"Have you seen any of the seasons?" I ask him.

"Nope, I've heard great things though." He says. "Well, let's start from the beginning then," I say.

He eyes me. "Are you sure? They're like hour episodes."

"Ahhh, I see. Can't pull all-nighters like we used to huh?" I say looking deep into his dark brown eyes. It's a challenge I know he'll accept.

He looks at me, and something in his face shifts. But the look is gone as quickly as it came. He starts the show and leans back. He shimmies himself further into the couch, closer to me. His leg skims mine and then settles next to mine. Something about it feels purposeful. "Buckle up. We've got three seasons to binge." It's gonna be a long night.

We've made it through half the first season of *Ted Lasso* now.

Being an athlete myself, I love this show. I wondered if Easton was gonna like it because he's not really a sports guy. He played basketball when he was younger but, it wasn't really his thing. Easton's always been more of an arts guy. He plays the guitar, piano, sings, and even did a few plays back in middle school — but sports… that was my thing.

His boyish laugh came out every few minutes, chuckling at something on the screen which told me he was enjoying it.

I wasn't really watching the show all that much, for two reasons. One, I have already seen the first two seasons a couple of times through. Two, I've been studying every minor move Easton makes like my life depends on it.

Maybe I'm crazy but, every time he laughs I swear his body gets closer to mine.

I can feel the heat radiating off his body. I can't tell if it's that or my nerves making me sweat, but either way, I'm sweating.

I frantically pull the blanket off my body and stand up.

He looks at me like I just told him I was Spider-Man or something.

"You OK, TK?" He asks me, confused.

TK.

That nickname sends shivers down my spine. No one calls me that in anymore. No one calls me that at all, actually.

Only Easton Mills.

He coined it, years ago.

It was his.

It only sounds right leaving his lips.

"That ice cream isn't gonna eat itself." I say walking myself into the kitchen.

"Oh yeah," he says as he follows closely behind me.

My palms are sweating along with the rest of my body. I need this ice cream to cool me off from the inside out.

I stick my hands in the freezer, silently begging the cold air to cool me down.

I don't know what's come over me.

After grabbing the ice cream, I turn around to see Easton standing in front of two mugs, holding an ice cream scooper.

They weren't just any mugs; they were our mugs.

"I can't believe Jessie kept those," I say with a little bit of shock in my voice.

"I wouldn't let her get rid of em." Oh.

"Why? They're so old and chipped," I say as I put the ice cream down on the granite counter. I open the lid, trying to avoid his eyes as he responds.

"They were old and chipped when we got them," he says. "And I like them."

"So, you still use it?" I question.

"Of course not."

My eyes pop, meeting his.

"They're a package deal. You know that," he says with a chuckle as he scoops ice cream into our mugs.

The mugs are a package deal. Even though when Easton found the mugs they were on opposite sides of the aisle, we knew they went together.

If only I could say that about us.

"I guess I just thought eventually you'd pack them up and put em away," I say grabbing the ice cream scooper and adding another scoop to my mug.

"You don't pack away good memories, TK. That's how you forget them."

His words hit my chest as he walks away toward the couch. Good memories.

We did have a lot of good memories. I can only really think of one bad one.

As I sit down beside him on the couch, I sit a bit further away than I was before. I fear he'll smell my guilt if I sit too close.

Unlike Easton, I *have* packed all my memories of him away. All the shirts of his I stole, all the pictures of us, all the trinkets and toys that reminded me of him are put away in a big box that I have hidden in the back of my closet. I put my luggage right on top it, so I won't even see the box. I didn't want to see it. I didn't want to think about him. So, for me, that was the only way to keep the memories good. I had to forget them.

But it's obvious he didn't want to forget me. If he had wanted to, he would have let Jessie sell our mugs at the garage sale she probably had before the big move. But he didn't. He made sure to keep them.

And right now, I'm glad he did. No other dish in this apartment was big enough to hold the amount of ice cream I needed to eat right now.

Easton starts the show back up, but not without noticing my distance. He takes slow bites of his ice cream, with long breaks in between each bite. It was annoying me thinking about his ice cream melting in his mug. I hate when ice cream melts. There's a reason you buy it in the freezer section. It's meant to be eaten cold. Which means, that even if you get brain freeze while eating your ice cream you must eat it as fast as possible, while it's still holding it's scoop like shape.

"Am I bothering you?" He asks.

"Don't ask questions you know the answers to

Easton." I say.

"I like the way it melts in the bottom. Then I can actually sip it at the end."

"Sipping is for cereal milk, not ice cream," I say with a bit of sass.

"It's the way I do it," he remarks.

"Shhh, I can't hear Ted Lasso," I say as I put my mug down on the wood floor. I sit back up, grabbing Easton's pillow and putting it in between me and him. I get the pillow as close to his legs as possible, then I lay my head down.

I try with all my might not to look up at him, but I can't help myself. When I look up, he's already looking down at me.

His eyes move from my face to my hair. That's when I realize my hair is all over him. I start to sit up, "Sorry, my hair."

He interrupts, "No. No, it's OK. Don't move." So

I don't.

I stay exactly where I am.

10

My Tate Knightly

EASTON

You know after a run, when you finally stop and you take that first big breath? When you rest your hands on your knees and you can feel your heart beating so hard that you feel the beat more in your left toe than in your chest?

That's what it feels like when she looks up at me. She put my pillow in between us and rested her head on it. I'm worried she can feel my heart pounding through my leg as it radiates through the pillow

Surely not.

No matter how much I try to tell my heart to slow down, it won't. Not when I'm around her.

Tate Knightly, in all her beauty.

I wasn't expecting her this summer. Although, even if I had known she was coming, I don't think there would have been a way to prepare myself.

It's been five years since I've seen her in the flesh. In fact, I stopped following her on social media a few years ago. It's what was best for me. I didn't want to see her, if I couldn't have her. She didn't want anything to do with me.

When she left all those years ago, I knew I had lost her forever. Or, maybe, ninety-nine percent of me knew she wouldn't come back. That one percent though… that one percent was hope.

Her long brown hair is all over my legs, and I can't help myself from wanting to run my hands through it. I'm not sure how Tate would respond to such an action. She might think it's weird.

So, I settle with running the tips of her hair in between my fingers. She won't even notice. I can't help but hope she does notice. I shake my head, releasing the thought.

She doesn't like me like that, no matter how much I wish she did.

She tried to move, but I asked her to stay just the way she is. She's comfortable and sweet and everything I've been missing. She isn't bothering me. She couldn't possibly.

I love having her this close. I've missed having her this close. It's been too long.

We're on the season 1 finale of Ted Lasso. I'm hoping she doesn't ask me how I liked the show because after we got ice cream I sorta stopped watching it. How could I with her laying right there, basically in my lap.

Tate watches the screen with such intensity. I wonder if it's because she loves sports or because she loves film. It might be a mix of both. Watching movies and shows with Tate has always been one of my favorite things to do with her. Maybe it's because her dad is in the industry or maybe it's because she wants to go into the industry, but she brings this creative opinion to things we watch. She sees things I don't see. She hyper-fixates on the shot choice, and the coloring, and the symbolism.

Watching things with her is fun, but talking about them after is what I look forward to most. Usually, I can bring something interesting to the table, but today, I'm too distracted.

She responds to things the same way she used to.

She still giggles at the awkward moments, and her face still softens when something is sad. She truly feels what the characters feel. My favorite of all her little reactions is when she pulls the blanket up to her nose, attempting to hide her face. The only time she does this is when two characters look like they're about to kiss.

When two characters begin to kiss on the screen her cheeks get all pink and she pulls the edge of the blanket up to her face. It's resting on the bridge of her nose. Her big, beautiful hazel eyes glisten in the TV light. I've always wondered what she looks like under that blanket.

She looks up at me again, with the blanket still covering part of her face.

I've never met someone with eyes like hers. They dare me to do things I would normally never consider. They tempt me and torture me in ways she'll never understand.

She puts me under some sort of spell. I'd do anything for Tate Knightly. She could ask me to jump out of a plane with her tomorrow, and I'd do it.

She knew it back then. She knew I would move heaven and earth for her to be happy. I couldn't help but want her to be happy. So, when she decided not to come back after that summer, I figured it was because she didn't want to.

It was because she didn't want me in her life anymore.

I thought about calling her. Every summer that rolled around I debated on making the call to ask why she won't come back. But I always chickened out. I was always wildly afraid of the answer. Deep down I think I know why she never came back.

It's me. She's been avoiding me.

For the life of me, I don't know why… but I think deep in my bones I know that I'm the reason for her absence. I even thought about texting her happy birthday every year but that seemed kind of pathetic. Plus, it's not like she texted me either. I thought about telling her *sorry*, even though I didn't know what for. But what good is apologizing if I don't even know what I did?

I thought about all of it though.

I loved her back then. I might have had an odd way of showing it at times, but I did. I always did. I thought she knew that. But when she never came back, I realized maybe all the love I felt was one sided. Maybe it was just me who felt my heart beat out of my chest when I was around her.

Maybe it was just me.

I've been letting myself believe that maybe it's different this summer. Maybe she'll feel something this time. I might have to let her know I like her a bit more obviously than I have in the past. A corny joke, or kiss on the cheek isn't gonna work right now. Not like it used to.

Think. Think. Think.

I can't do what I would normally do with other girls.

Whatever made Izzy or Ryan like me isn't gonna work on Tate.

Tate is… different.

She won't fall for all the *classic* guy moves I have stored up my sleeve. I can't push her hair out of her face and tuck it behind her ear. She'd slap my hand. I can't compliment her looks because Tate doesn't like that kind of thing. Even though she's beautiful and the prettiest girl I've ever known, I wouldn't be caught dead calling her pretty.

She hates that.

I called her pretty one time when I was twelve. It was a risky move at the time. I thought she would be flattered, but then she went on this long tangent about how flowers and princesses are pretty. She and Lila were beautiful, she told me, with her little eleven-year-old attitude. "Like art and the sky at sunset".

That was my favorite thing about Tate.

She knew exactly who she was. Exactly what she liked and what she didn't. She knew what she wanted and where she was going. And she didn't let anyone tell her any different.

I can't just ask her friends to find out if she's interested in me either, because I don't know her friends and none of them are here. It's just us.

The idea hits me like a smack on the back of the head. *I'll rest my hand on her back.* It's not my greatest idea, but it's definitely not my worst. I'll stretch and then lay my hand on her back. Super natural.

When we were younger, she'd lay with her head on my shoulder or her legs over mine. Our hands never really touched or were placed in such a "touchy" way before. It would be normal and new all at the same time.

This is a stupid idea.

Even though it kills me, I break eye contact with her.

I gotta do this quick if it's gonna work. I stretch my arms wide in the air, causing us to shift slightly. I feel like an idiot the whole time

She turns again to face the TV, still resting on the pillow. The pillow got closer to me as I stretched. She's more on top of me now than she was a minute ago, but it doesn't seem to faze her.

That's a positive sign, right?

When I bring my arms down, I put my right one in my lap, where it was before and when I bring my left one down, I lay it gently behind her on the couch. I rest my hand on the cushion. The way she's turned, her t-shirt is bundled up toward the top of her back, exposing her lower back. I let my hand sit as close to her skin as possible without touching her.

This is still safe. This isn't crossing the line of friends. *Right?*

When we were kids, we'd lay like this all the time. I'd hold her hand to cross the street. I'd kiss her cheek when we played house with Lila. I was always the dad, and Tate was always the mom, and Lila was always our little princess.

Being this close isn't abnormal for us, or, for the old us that is.

But now, it's different for some reason and I like it. I guess time does change things. We haven't been this close in years, but everything in me knows it's what's been missing. It takes everything in me not to rest my hand on her back. I want to. I'm feeling reckless. I want to test the waters.

What is there to lose?

I move my hand a millimeter forward and chicken out. I grab the hem of her t-shirt instead, like a coward.

Breathe dude. Breathe. This is Tate. It's just Tate.

Just as I muster up the courage to move my hand forward again, she shimmies back a little. I moved my hand back like a reflex, out of respect for her.

What am I doing? That was my in!! Stop being such a nice guy, Easton.

With a deep breath, I start to move my hand toward her back but then before anything can happen, Tate sits up and stretches like I had just done a moment ago, but she adds a little yawn.

Ugh.

I had an entire season of Ted Lasso to make a move, and I did nothing!!

I'm mentally punching myself for moving at the speed of a tortoise. I thought the saying was, "Good things come to those who wait?" *Well, that's bullshit.*

"So good right?!" She asks me enthusiastically, looking at me with those big hazel eyes.

I shake my head *yes*. "I really liked it," I add.

She leans forward, picking up her mug and then reaches for mine.

"Don't you just love Ted? He's so funny," she says as I stop her from grabbing my mug.

"Wait. We're not done with these yet," I say.

I've got the perfect thing to help me loosen up. I just need some liquid courage.

I walk to the fridge and pull out my dad's secret stash. My dad keeps it in the back of the fridge behind the Costco sized orange juice. He barely ever drinks but when he does, he drinks vodka.

I hold up the bottle with a shrug, looking at her face in the fridge light. The bottle is cold in my hand. It's almost frozen from touching the very back of the fridge wall. I love when it's this chilled.

"I didn't know you drank," she says dryly.

Crap. She's not into it.

"I don't, most of the time," I say taking off the lid. "But on nights I have ice cream, I have just a little bit."

I walk toward her pulling both mugs toward me on the counter and pour a little bit of the vodka into both our mugs. The mint chocolate chip immediately fizzes and melts. I love that sound.

I take a sip. "You've drank before, right?" I ask her.

She shakes her head *no.*

Great, so now I'm a terrible influence.

"Oh, well you don't have to…"

She cuts me off. "I'll be OK. I'm just worried about the flavor. Mint chip and vodka? Sounds kinda gross."

"Nothing to worry about. It makes it sweet," I say, taking a sip.

I turn, leaning beside her against the counter now — so close our shoulders graze against each other.

"Tell me something about you I don't know, TK," I say after taking another sip from my mug.

She blinks, looking at me like I offended her. "You really think I've changed that much?"

"You look like you've changed," I say a bit snarky.

She slaps my shoulder and moves away from me.

I should have seen that coming.

I wasn't lying. She has changed a lot. For starters, her hair is lighter than it used to be. It's still long, like really long. It has a natural glow to it now. It's not like highlights or whatever girls do to their hair. It's glowy like it's the sun's work. I bet it's brightened up because she plays beach volleyball in the sun all the time. She hasn't touched her hair; it's cut straight across the bottom like she might cut it herself.

Knowing her, she probably does.

When she was little the freckles populated on her nose and on her cheeks right under her eyes but now her face is covered in them. I search her body, head-to-toe. There are freckles other places too — her arms, her neck, her collar bone.

I'm overwhelmed with the desire to find them all and kiss each one.

She's obviously grown up. She was more mature in every sense of the word, it was hard not to notice. So much has changed about her, except for two things.

1. Her eyes. They're exactly the same. Big, bright, and beautiful.
2. Her nose. It's still cute and petite, like it always has been.

I used to joke when we were kids that she looked like a bunny. I meant it as a compliment, although I don't think Tate ever took it that way. It's the most perfect little nose.

She's grown up now, but she's still my Tate Knightly.

IT'S BEEN FIVE YEARS

92

11

People Like You

I know I've matured but I don't think I look *that* different. The way he's staring at me makes me wonder if I really have changed a whole lot. I'm taller now and my teeth are straighter, but other than that, I'm just me. I'm not one of those girls who does a lot of… extra. In the mornings I wash my face and put a few drops of argan oil on and call it a day. A hint of blush and a swab of mascara if I'm feeling dressy, neither of which I'm wearing now.

"That's rude, Easton," I say firmly.

"No, no. I didn't mean it negatively. You—," he stutters. "You grew up well, he finishes. *Is that a compliment?*

"It's a good thing to change. We all change. Otherwise, what's the point, right?" he smiles, taking another sip.

I join him and take my first sip. It's sweet at first, but then it burns a bit. "Ugh, you actually like this?" I ask, changing the subject.

"I do," he laughs, "You don't?"

"Not particularly, no," I answer as I slide my mug across the counter to him. "All yours."

I don't like the idea of alcohol. People who drink it usually have something to numb. Being numb is my least favorite feeling. Being drunk would be a nightmare. I lied to Easton though. I have tried alcohol before. A beer once, at a family cookout back in Arkansas, when I still lived there. I hated it, but I drank the whole thing just to do it.

I don't like the way it makes my stomach expand and I hate that warm fuzzy feeling. And my least favorite part of the experience is the spaciness in my head that comes after a couple sips. I can tell what's going on, but everything feels kind of spaced out or slowed down.

I have no desire to feel that way again. Especially not in front of Easton.

How have I changed? What's something he wouldn't know?

"Okay. Something you don't know…" I trail off. "It can be anything," he says.

"Okay. Something you don't know…" I chew my bottom lip as I ponder his question. "I almost quit volleyball last year," I add.

He looks up, surprised. "What? Why?"

"Burnout. Pressure. College scouts. I didn't feel like I was playing for me anymore."

"Who were you playing for?" he asks quietly. "It's not like that. It's not like I was playing for anyone other than me. It's just like… my heart wasn't in it as much. I don't know," I tell him.

"Are you playing for yourself now?" He asks, eyes genuine and soft.

"I think so." I say, meeting his eyes. "This tournament. It could change everything."

"He nods, like he understands more than he's saying. "Well, for what it's worth, I've always thought you played like you mean it. When you're playing, it's obvious you love it."

A pause.

"What about you?" I ask. "Tell me something I don't know."

He looks down, thoughtful. "I want to move to Nashville." *Whoa.*
I shake my head in disbelief. "Seriously?"
"Yeah. I've been writing music and stuff. It's hard for me to sing in front of people. I never show anyone the stuff I write —" He takes a sip from my mug this time. "I guess no one other than you. But I've written some new stuff since then."
"You sang in front of everyone at dinner. It was great." I say.
"That was a cover. Not an original. It means so much more when you've written the words. People are more judgmental you know?" he says looking away in between each sentence.
"What are you scared of?" I ask.
"Oh, I don't know… being rejected, letting my parents down, failing, no one listening to my stuff," he rambles on until I interrupt.
"I'll listen to your stuff and so will my mom, and Jessie, and Lila and your friend… uh, Walter. And I'm sure
Annie will too."
His face falls like he just remembered something important. Like mentioning Annie's name somehow pulled him back down to earth.
"Yeah, I know they will," he says.
"Then what's stopping you?" I say pushing his shoulder playfully.
He smiles and then his face softens. He's wearing an emotion I can't quite read. "You remember my originals?" He asks with wide eyes that are now staring into my soul. "Of course I remember. Every single one of them," I say confidently.
Easton smiles, but there's something vulnerable about. it. "It's scary. I don't know if I'm good enough. Or if I'll ever be as successful as… you know, people like you." I tilt my head. "People like me?" I say confused.
"You're going somewhere, Tate. I've always known that.
We all have." His voice drops a little. "And I love that about you."
He does?
The air thickens. He moves closer to me, closing the space between

us. I'm awkwardly aware of how close my back is to the counter. I can't scoot any further away from him even if I wanted to. Which I don't. I'm stuck. But I'm not mad about it.

He rests his hand on the counter beside me, leaning toward me a bit. I don't know what to do with my body.

His eyes are looking straight into mine. My heart drops so low into my stomach, making me look away. The silence between us is loud, but not uncomfortable. It's familiar.

Too familiar.

He smells like pine and sea salt and his breath smells faintly of sugar from the mint chocolate ice cream.

He shifts a little closer. "I missed this," he says.

"Me too," I say without thinking.

We're toeing the edge of something. We're dancing into a space we've never been before. This is uncharted territory. If he leans in an inch more, I'll meet him halfway. But instead of meeting him like my pounding heart wants… I stand up straight, backing away from him.

Annie.

One of us has to think of her.

"I should head to bed. Big week," I say quickly avoiding his eye line.

"Wait!" he calls out in a whispery yell.

He grabs my hand and pulls me toward him. I don't know if it's the vodka giving him this confidence or if this is just him now. His arm wraps around my waist. Our faces are so close I have to hold my breath so our noses won't touch. I don't know what to do with my hands, so I just lay them against his chest.

"What?" I say nervously.

"Have you been kissed before?" he asks me.

I don't know how to respond to such a question. I don't know why he's asking such a question. *Yes, but I wished it was you.*

"Yes," I say instead.

His eyes are piercing my soul like daggers. He closes them tightly like by closing them it somehow helps him hold something back.

In this moment I wish I had never been kissed. I wish I would have been able to answer *No, I waited for you.*

But I can't. I gave that piece of me away.

He nodded, standing up fully, letting me go. He takes a step back. I didn't realize how warm his body was keeping me until it's gone.

"He's a lucky guy," he says looking at me, with a sad forced smile.

I awkwardly take a step back, looking at him. Still shocked by the moment we just shared. Still stunned from our sudden closeness. "Goodnight Easton."

"Goodnight TK," he says, walking toward the couch.

For the first time ever, we don't hug before bed.

We've already been close enough.

I walk into the bathroom, closing the door behind me quietly. I stop in front of the mirror, looking at myself with disbelief. The girl looking back at me is shocked. I bring my hands to my lips — they've never felt so cold.

My hand drops down to my heart as I check for a pulse.

I'm alive, barely.

What. Just. Happened.

I change into my oversized tee and flop onto Easton's bed, my heart's still thudding like I just finished working out.

Right as I put my phone down on the bedside table, it buzzes.

It's Easton.

When I look, it's not a message. It's just an image. I click the notification, enlarging the image on my screen.

It's a picture of a tattoo, but not just any tattoo. It's the ugliest tattoo I have ever seen. It's a thumb in the shape of a head and there's a man's face on the head. He's angry, yelling almost. It looks like a character from an old propaganda poster. The thumb is holding a baseball bat, wound back like he's ready to hit something. A message comes in after I observed the disturbing image.

EASTON: should I get this before or after the lightsaber tattoo?

I can't help but laugh, but I don't respond. I can't stop thinking about the events of the night. How he was so close to me. How he looked at me when I told him I had already been kissed. How his hands felt around my waist. My head gets dizzy at the thoughts running through my head.

Why did he even ask me if I had been kissed? Why does it matter?

I want to believe that whatever just happened isn't going to make the rest of the trip weird between us but how could it not?

We almost kissed? Didn't we?

He looked like he wanted to kiss me… so why didn't he?

12

The Monorail

TATE

(The summer I was 9 & he was 10)

I must've been around nine. Old enough to roll my eyes, but still young enough to secretly believe that the princesses at Disney were real and that they actually all lived in the castle at Magic Kingdom.

I'll never forget it. We were on the monorail at Disney, riding the loop between parks. The sun dipped behind Cinderella's castle, painting the windows in gold. I sat between Jessie and my mom, my arms holding onto a lanyard full of Disney pins — that was my thing. Easton had introduced me to pin trading the previous summer. This was the first summer I actually had pins to trade and I was so excited. My nana bought Nate and I a whole bag of them and gave them to us before we left on our trip. Every cast member wore a lanyard around their neck or pin patch that hung from their belt, full of Disney pins. It was a special part of the Disney World experience. You could run up to the cast members and ask to trade pins with them if you found one you liked.

Easton sat across from us with his head pressed to the glass, lost in thought like he normally was.

Nate was dozing off with his face smushed against my shoulder as he sat on my lap. His long curly blonde hair stuck to his face from the sweat. He was tired and cranky, but he was so much fun at that age. Lila was braiding her own hair like she was in a Disney princess montage. Rapunzel had just been added to the Disney Park and that was her current obsession. We'd always find her out in the yard sticking flowers in her hair.

Jessie leaned in close to my ear and whispered like she was telling me the biggest secret in the world, "You'd be the very best daughter-in-law, you know. You could be Lila's sister!"

I shook my head confused. "What? How?" I asked. She gave me this sly smile, the kind only Jessie could wear without looking ridiculous. "You and Easton. You just fit. Like peanut butter and jelly. Or Mickey and Minnie."

I didn't like peanut butter and jelly, but Mickey and Minnie were cool.

My mom, sitting beside me, whispered to Jessie, "Maybe one day, but they're way too young to think about that now."

"I'm just saying," Jessie sang in a quiet whisper, eyes sparkling. "They'd be cute," she adds.

Easton definitely overheard the whispers and started to look embarrassed, like he wanted to deny everything Jessie said, but he didn't. I watched the corners of his mouth twitch like he thought about saying something… but he didn't. I watched him for a while, his eyebrows furrowing like he was thinking deeply about something. I could feel heat rise to my cheeks as I watched him. I looked away, resting my head against Nate's messy curls. "We would not," I mumbled to Jessie.

"Y'all totally would," Lila chimed in, not even looking up from her braid. "He gets weird around you, which means he has a crush," she adds.

"You guys are weird. Tate's my best friend," Easton said suddenly, not looking away from the window. "I just—I just love hanging out with her. She's just… Tate," Easton insisted, still not looking at me.

That sentence hung in the air for a beat too long. It's the very first time Easton Mills called me his best friend. I'll never forget that monorail ride.

I didn't say anything. But for the rest of the ride, I couldn't stop glancing at his reflection.

I didn't know what it meant to be a daughter-in-law at the time, but I hung on to those words of Jessie's for years.

I wanted nothing more than to be a part of her family. Having her as a second mom would be the dream scenario.

Maybe that's where it all started. My love for Easton.

Jessie was to blame.

Or maybe I was, for believing that what she said could really happen.

13

Game Buffet

TATE

As we got older, we stopped going to Disney as much as we did when we were little. It's not that the magic died, because at a place like Disney — the magic never dies. It's just that the magic moved to other parts of our lives. The magic became each other. We didn't grow out of Disney. We just grew up.

The last summer in Florida we spent every waking moment together. Easton, Lila, and I that is. We made a good group as we got older. All so close in age. It was nice. We only went to Disney for one day out of the whole trip because that was all we needed. We made everything we did fun. Especially game night.

This summer, in particular, we became more and more competitive. Everything was a competition. We raced everywhere from the house to the beach. From the car to the house. Down the grocery aisles. On the beach. From the beach to the house. Everywhere. But this summer we started to play board games. We played every board game. If you could think of a game, we played it. If it had a board, we played it. If it was cards, we played it. If it was a riddle game, we played it. Monopoly was always a favorite. Easton was the dog, and Lila was the boot. I was always the thimble and the banker.

We also played the card game War all the time and we played it everywhere. In the living room, by the pool, in the backyard, in the lines at Disney, in the car — you name it. This summer we played a game of War for five hours straight. It was the longest most terrible game of my life. I thought I was gonna win like twenty-five times, but one of them always crept back in. After that game, as a group, we swore to never play the game of War again. We'd already wasted enough hours of our lives on it.

One night right after Easton had ditched me for Izzy and her friends that last summer, He came to us with an idea. Despite my efforts to ignore him, I let him tell us his grand idea. He wanted each of us to each pick the game we wanted to play, and we would all play each game together, in one night — *Game Buffet* he called it.

I was still angry with him for ditching me for Izzy a few nights prior. But the reality of the situation was that my family and I were leaving tomorrow morning. So I told myself to enjoy the last night I'd ever have at the Mill's house. I acted like everything was normal and I went along with his plan.

In past summers, on the last night of my visits we'd lay in the backyard on the trampoline. We'd look up at the stars, talking about the year to come. I would always pray in my head that I would get to come back the next summer, and we would all just pick back up right where we left off. It worked every summer, until it didn't. But tonight, I'm not praying to come back. Tonight, I'm praying that by next summer, I won't even think about Easton Mills. I'm praying to forget him.

Because of that, I was glad that we weren't laying on the trampoline like normal.

The tradition will already be broken. So, I accepted it for what it was. This was the beginning of change.

Game Buffet ended up being extremely fun. Lila chose *What Do You Meme?*, I chose *The Game of Life*, and Easton chose *Risk*. Lila's game went by quick. My game took a while, but when we're all together we never really cared about the time. We always got lost in it. Time always felt endless at their house. During *The Game of Life* Easton made a comment about how he wished the little pink piece he put into his car had big hazel eyes and freckles that covered it's face. My cheeks still get flush when I think about it. Back then my eyes were still too big for my face, and I had more freckles than I have now. He was trying to hint at me. It was obvious, but a lot of what Easton did back then was obvious. I just couldn't see it at the time.

But the other night he chose Izzy.

That's all I needed to know, so I continued to remind myself of that. No matter how hard it was.

This was the summer all our feelings became real. We became conscious of the fact that we liked each other, although neither of us said anything. We were just too young to act on it. Or at least that's what I though until he willingly walked away from me to see Izzy. He treated me like a kid. To him, I guess that's all I was. No matter how much he might make me feel otherwise. That was what he said, and I know he meant it.

Easton won *The Game of Life.* I didn't like losing but there were worse people to lose to. Like Izzy. I was losing to her in my actual life because she gets to see Easton whenever she wants. She lives in the same state as him and goes to school with him and goes to youth group with him — and for that I'm jealous.

After *The Game of Life*, I tried to convince Easton for a solid twenty minutes that we should just watch a Marvel movie instead of playing Risk, but there was no convincing him. When Easton has his mind made up, there's nothing you can say that will stop him.

Never have I ever played a game of *Risk* that took less that three hours. This night, I didn't last much past two hours before I started drifting to sleep. Lila bailed on us an hour in. She was never as much of a night owl like us. That was always Easton and I. Staying up into the late hours of the night was our thing. Whether it was playing games in his room, watching a movie on the couch, or eating ice cream in the kitchen — the nighttime hangs with Easton were one of the things I missed most in the summers to follow.

I had been falling asleep for fifteen minutes, in and out, before my eyes officially shut. I was laying on the floor right by the *Risk* board. I had no chance of winning, which is probably why I lost interest. Easton took *Risk* very seriously and to be honest, I never really saw the appeal. It was long and drawn out. "A game of strategy" he'd say. But to me, it was just boring. It was fun the first time, but only the first time.

He didn't try to wake me. He wasn't going to disturb me. He could have just packed up the game and left me there, but he didn't. I started to wake when he grabbed my arm. He had bent down in front of me and scooped both my legs up into one of his arms. He threw one of my arms over his shoulder— holding me bridal style. The way he threw my arm over his shoulder woke me a bit, but I kept my eyes closed. I didn't want to ruin the moment.

Until this moment, we had never really touched. Other than the hugs he gave me at night before bed, but everyone got those. The closest thing would have been the hugs he gave me when I got out of the car for the first time every summer and before I got back in the car to leave to go back home. Those hugs were longer and sweeter.

That was the closest we ever got. We never even held hands — unless you count him grabbing my hand to pull me around Disney when I was walking too slow or to help me cross the street safely.

Somehow this moment felt different than those. It wasn't obligatory. He didn't have to pick me up. He could have just woken me up and said goodnight or could have just left me there to sleep on the floor, but instead he chose to pick me up. I was suddenly very aware of how many girl scout cookies I ate during **Game Buffet**.

This summer I was staying in his room, and he slept in Lila's room with her, because their Meemaw was in one of the guest bedrooms and my parents were in the other.

He was taller than me, but he was still scrawny. I was shocked at how strong he was. It felt nice to be carried. He laid me down on his bed, gently. He was a little too old to have Star Wars sheets, but he had them none-the-less. "They're vintage," he would say when I poked fun at him about it. They were vintage, the original ones too. I secretly liked them. I loved Star Wars and not just because he liked it. I liked it for me… and because of Anakin Skywalker. But I am just a girl.

He put his old, worn-out sheets and comforter over me, tucking me in. He just looked at me for a moment and then he pushed the hair covering my eyes behind my ear and kissed my forehead. At this point in time, I had never been kissed. The only time he'd kissed me was on the cheek, back when we still played house. But we were little then, and it didn't count.

I'd always wanted Easton to kiss me, but I was never going to ask and frankly I thought I was too young. But this kiss on the forehead made my whole-body tingle. I had goosebumps everywhere, instantly. I was warm on the inside. I had butterflies in my stomach I didn't know were living there.

"Goodnight, TK. I miss you already," he said in the sweetest voice I had ever heard leave his lips. I thought I was dreaming.

He turned the light off and walked out of the room. I sat up in bed, pinched myself and slapped my own cheek just to make sure I wasn't sleeping. I'd dreamt something similar before, but it had never felt this way. I felt my hand hit my cheek and realized I was, in fact awake - and the moment was real. Easton had picked me up and tucked me into bed, and he had, in fact, kissed me on the forehead!!

* * *

After that night of sleep, I woke up the happiest I'd ever been. I woke up in a pure bliss. Maybe Easton had felt for me what I felt for him, and he just had a funny way of showing it. It was more than just flirting this time.

Maybe, he really felt it too.

Today was the day that I dreaded most.

The day I go home.

The day I leave the Mills.

It's especially hard this time because I'd already convinced myself I wasn't going to come back. After last night, I've been rethinking things. I mean, it seemed like he really cared for me. Just because he thought I was a kid and that I needed to grow up doesn't mean that he hates me… right? I had been writing a pros and con's list in my head all morning.

Maybe the other night when Easton left to go see Izzy wasn't that bad? Maybe I could forgive him and just come back?

I was riding on such a high from last night that I was leaning more toward the "I can come back next summer plan" vs. the "I'll never speak to him again plan." I was riding in the back seat of Jessie's car, next to Lila when

Easton put *Call Me Maybe* by Carly Rae Jepsen on from the passenger's seat. He was trying to brighten the airport drive that we all dread, and it worked. Us kids all eyed each other. This was our song. We sang it at the top of our lungs and Jessie smiled along, loving the sight of us happy.

Easton kept glancing at me through the rearview mirror. There are those butterflies again. We're becoming acquainted, me and these butterflies.

The song ended and Easton said, "Mom, you should hear Izzy sing this song. She's amazing."

My heart hit the ground and sunk through the car floor. I think I actually felt my heart drop to my toes — each inch was excruciating. "What?" I asked before thinking.

"Izzy is Easton's crush," Lila said in a tattle-tell way.

Maybe I didn't lose my heart because now it's in my throat.

"Oh, sheesh, Lil," Jessie said looking back at Lila and then to me, with worry in her eyes. "Easton is too young to have a crush," she added but it didn't make me feel any better. The last time I heard Jessie mention a crush of Easton's, I was the crush.

I'm gonna be sick.

We weren't too young for crushes either. Easton was fourteen and I was thirteen. A lot of girls my age had already had two boyfriends. And boys Easton's age had already been to second base, or worse.

"Mom, she's not a crush. Izzy's my girlfriend. You've got to accept it at some point," Easton said annoyed with

Jessie.

Oh. I guess he really was old enough. Or at least he was for Izzy.

I'm nauseous now. I could have hurled right there, but I kept it in. If I hurled, my pride would have gone with it. That was all I had right now, so I held on strong. I didn't need any more embarrassment. Jessie's eyes darted at me in the rearview mirror again. Pity, it covered her face like poorly applied makeup. She knew my heart, and she knew Easton had it. I had never wanted to leave Florida more than I did in that moment.

When they finally dropped us off at the airport, I hugged them all, but I didn't hug Easton the way I normally would have. I couldn't, so I hugged him quick. If

I hugged him normally, he'd feel my heart racing against his chest. It was over before it even really started. It felt a bit harsh, but it was earned.

"See you soon, TK!" He said as I pulled my suitcase through the doors of the airport.

I didn't respond, or look back, or even wave.

He didn't deserve it.

"Are you OK honey?" My mom asked as we walked up to the ticket counter. Her and my dad had driven with Mr. Mills in his truck. They didn't hear anything Easton said. I couldn't explain to my mom what had just happened.

There was too much and too little to explain. Everything and nothing. How does one explain that. The nausea began to eat at me, crawling up my throat.

I needed to find a bathroom.

14

Think You'll Remember This?

TATE

The air outside is sticky and warm, a leftover blanket from today's heat. The sky above the courtyard is deep navy, scattered with stars. I haven't seen stars like this in such a long time. I almost gasp at them. Crickets hum in the bushes covering the sound of our heavy breathing as we race to the pool.

It's quiet and the night is still. It feels like the whole world is in a deep sleep. Except us.

It always felt this way as kids when we would sneak out. Even if it was in the light of day. Nothing else mattered when we were together. All other parts of life just fade away when we're together. No school, no friends, no struggle matters when it's just me, Easton, and summer.

Easton pushes the gate open with his foot. The latch clanks softly behind us. The water glows pale blue under the pool lights as they activate from the motion of our bodies as we rush through the gate.

This pool is different from the one we grew up with. This pool is nice, and big in a country club kind of way. There are nice new pool chairs with shiny metal legs surrounding the pool. The whole area is fancy. The pool is shaped like a rectangle, about nine feet deep in the middle and is big enough that you can swim laps in it if you so desire. The part that's most different from their old neighborhood is the hot tub that sits at the end of the huge pool. Their old neighborhood pool had nothing of the sort. It was small and usually had bugs floating around in the water. I can see the steam rolling off the hot tub that sits directly in front of the main pool. It's big enough to be considered a pool itself. I've never seen anything like it.

The pool is nice, but it makes me miss the old neighborhood they lived in. It was cozy and calm. Most the houses were filled with older couples who were retired or younger couples who were newly married without kids. So it was always just us at their neighborhood pool — kinda like it is now.

Easton drops our towels on one of the fancy pool chairs and glances back at me, his smile a bit crooked.

"Last one in has to spill a messy truth?" He exclaims as he runs toward the pool at full speed.

"Not fair," I shoot back with a groan.

As much as I don't want to share a messy truth, I have no shot at winning. He's halfway to the pool by the time I even get to the pool chair.

He takes his shirt off as he runs, tossing it off onto the concrete when he's at the edge of the pool. I try not to stare but I can't help myself. He canon balls into the pool like a little kid, making a big splash.

He catches me looking at him, but still, I can't look away.

He's bigger in every sense of the word. He gently brushes his wet hair back, out of his face. His biceps are big, like he's been working out. His shoulders are strong and sturdy. Growing up I never really noticed things like this, but now I can't help but notice. He lays back in the water, floating on his back. He has no care in the world, or maybe he does and he's just trying to show off. My eyes are drawn to his torso. It's defined. He has abs — six of them to be exact.

Growing up, Easton was always soft. Sports were never his thing, so when we were little, he just looked... normal. Average. Nothing super special other than his million-dollar smile, which he's flashing at me now, teasing me. He knows he's won. I want to wipe that smirky smile right off of his face.

I finally look away as I tug off my shorts and sweatshirt, leaving me in my blue bikini. This is the nicest bikini I own. My mom says it makes me look older.

Probably just because it pushes my boobs up and together. I love the way I feel in it. More confident. More beautiful. More me.

I would never compete in this bikini due to the fear of something falling out. If I was active in this, there would most definitely be... spillage. What a horror that would be.

Part of me hopes Easton will say something about my new bikini or even better my new body. But I know he won't. If I was ever lucky enough to receive a compliment from Easton, it was never about my physical appearance. Unless he was complimenting the Marvel or Star Wars shirt that I was wearing. His compliments were always focused on who I was.

I don't run into the water to join him. I walk slowly, holding eye contact with Easton. He watches my every move like I'm his favorite movie. I've missed being looked at like this. He's the only boy who ever looks at me like this.

I've efficiently wiped the smile off his face. His lips fell and his eyes grow wider and wider with each step closer I get to the water.

His eyes are soft, full of something I want to untangle.

He's my calm and my storm. He's the love and the hate.

He's the bitter and the sweet. He's mine. My brain wants to forget him, but my bones won't let me. That's the pain that comes with your childhood best friend. Forgetting is rewriting the memories that made you. Our friendship is something that made me. No matter if I hated it or not, I can't change it. The sickest part about Easton is that he isn't just my childhood best friend. He's my first love.

Every fiber of my childhood self adored him. Wanted him. Loved him. I can deny it all I want, but my body knows the truth.

He doesn't deserve me. If he did, he would have called to check in on me or asked what happened, but he never did. That was my answer.

With a deep breath, I pull myself back down to reality.

It's been five years since I felt that way. I don't feel that way now.

I repeat that over and over again to myself in my head as I stand at the edge of the pool as he watches me, silently.

I jump in, attempting to canon-ball, but I know mine won't be as good as Easton's. They never are.

It's warmer than I expected it to be, the water wraps around me like a blanket. I pop up, hair stuck to the back of my neck, laughing. Nothing makes you feel more like a kid than the swimming pool.

Easton swims closer, his grin wide, water dripping into his eyes from his hair. We are the only two people in the world right now — just like we used to be.

"You cheated," I say, splashing water on his face as I start swimming backwards, attempting to put some space between us.

"You're slow," he teases, splashing water back at me.

I flick water back at him, and he laughs. I've just started a war I don't know if I'm capable of finishing. I splash back none-the-less. We chase each other in slow circles, our laughter echoing off the apartment walls. I know all his neighbors hate us right now because we are being anything but quiet.

Eventually, we both cease fire and call it a tie. I float onto my back, as Easton drifts closer, resting his arm on the edge of the pool, watching me like he's memorizing something.

"You know the rules. You owe me a messy truth," he pushes.

"Are we really still doing that?" I say back, trying to act unbothered.

Messy truths are a tradition that Easton and I started back in middle school. You have to admit something to the other person that normally you'd be embarrassed to admit to anybody else. It's usually the form of punishment for losing something. Occasionally though, it's used as a safe place to admit something you want to get off your chest.

Usually that happens over ice cream on the kitchen floor.

The pool is no place for messy truths.

I stand up in the pool, facing him. Silently begging him not to make me say anything.

"Come on, it's been a long time, Tate. You have to have some good messy truths by now"

I don't want to play this game, but I know he won't give up until I say something.

"Tate, it's just a silly game. It can be anything," he adds.

"I'm embarrassed of my first kiss," I say frantically as I back away from him.

He looks me dead in the eyes, his face has dropped from light and happy to something sadder. He takes an imaginary dagger and pushes it into his chest, acting hurt. "Ouch," he says.

"Don't feel bad for the guy, you don't know him," I say jokingly as I spin around playfully, trying to keep the moment lighthearted like it was before.

When I turn my head toward him, his eyes are so dark they almost swallow the blue out of the pool lights.

"You're kidding right?" he asks seriously.

"You're telling me you know Ryder Lawson?"

"Ryder? What… no. He wasn't your first kiss," he argues matter-of-fact.

What is he talking about? He just asked me if I had ever been kissed the other night in the kitchen. He knew someone had kissed me.

"I was your first kiss," he says. Shocked

I say, "you?"

"Yes me, geez don't sound so disgusted," he says with a nervous laugh.

"I'm not, it's just you weren't my first kiss Easton," I say sternly. "Why did you ask me the other night then? If I had been kissed before?"

"Because I wanted to know if you remembered," he defends.

"We haven't kissed, Easton! I would remember," I say.

The heat is rising in my face and I feel it everywhere, but mostly in the tips of my ears. I'm angry. How can he think we've kissed?

Easton is stubborn and sarcastic and loves a good joke, but there is one thing Easton Mills is not. A lair.

"Tate, we have. It's a fact."

"When? Where?" I ask him frantically. I don't believe him. He's messing with me. He has to be. A kiss with Easton Mills is not something you forget.

He stares at me, looking past my eyes. He's looking somewhere deeper, for something deeper.

"Don't look at me like that, Easton. Answer me," I insist. The words are coming out of my mouth before I can even let myself process that I'm thinking them.

"June 14th, 2008. In Arkansas. It was the summer our moms took those pictures of us in the daffodil field. You were wearing a blue long sleeve shirt, and I was wearing that Star Wars t-shirt that I wore til it got holes in it, remember?

The flowers were yellow, and Nate tried to eat one." I've seen those pictures of us in the daffodil field, but I have no recollection of a kiss.

"In the back of the car, I helped you put your seat belt on and when I was leaning over, you kissed me, right on the lips."

Oh. I do remember that.

I was so embarrassed at the time. I was little and scared and Easton was helping me and I wanted to tell him thank you. But when he wiped his lips and sat down without a word after I pecked his lips, I thought I had done something terribly wrong. I thought I'd get in trouble.

I guess I forced myself to forget.

Easton's right. He was my first kiss all those years ago.

I swallow the memory.

I swim away from him, pulling myself up on the ledge, getting out of the water.

"That didn't happen. I don't remember that," I lie.

I can't let him know he was right. I can't let him have that. I don't even remember, so it doesn't count.

He follows me. "Tate? Come, one. You really think I'd lie?" He asks, slightly offended.

"I don't remember that Easton, so it didn't happen. Ryder was my first kiss. As much as I don't like that he was, I can't change it. It doesn't count when you're that little anyways." *Right?*

Easton follows slightly behind me as I get fully out of the pool, walking back toward the apartment. I didn't even bother to grab a towel. I'll air dry.

"Is it really that bad that I was your first kiss? Why is this such a big deal?" He says behind me but I don't turn around.

"Yes, Easton, it is that bad. This whole time you've been thinking I was your first kiss, or you were my first kiss when you really weren't."

He grabs my wrist, finally catching up to me. "Why does it matter what I think? Especially if it's the truth, I mean, I remember it."

"Well, you know what I remember?" I say turning to look at him.

I remember how you never called me. I remember how you picked Izzy over me. I remember how you called me a kid and told me to grow up. I remember how you picked me up and put me in your bed and kissed my forehead and then find out you had a girlfriend. I remember feeling second best. I remember every feeling. I remember how you made me feel, Easton.

When my eyes meet his, I can't say what I want to. I yank my wrist from his grasp. "I would remember if we kissed. That's not something you just forget," I say instead.

I take off walking up the apartment stairs toward the door.

"I know, that's why I'm telling you it happened. I remember it clearly."

I turn at the top of the stairs, looking down at him. He's a few steps below me.

"Well, I don't. I don't remember it, so can we just drop it, please?" I plead as I push open the apartment door softly despite my angered state. The mom's will be fast asleep by now and Mr. Mills is still in his office fast asleep.

"I can't just drop it. This is something we need to figure out. You think it didn't happen and I do. Let's talk it out," he says as we enter the kitchen.

"There's nothing to talk about. It didn't happen!" I say in a whisper scream. "It couldn't have. A first kiss is something you remember and I don't remember it," I lie again — a half truth really.

I remember it happening now that he's explained it a bit, but I can't remember how it went or how it felt to be that close to him. I wish I could remember. "A kiss is something you remember and I don't remember how it felt, or any of it, I don't remember. I don't remember." Easton looks at me, brows furrowed, not angry but confused. He walks right up to me and we're suddenly the closest we've ever been to each other since the last time we were in the kitchen. Nose to nose almost, but it feels different. I'm upset and he's upset. We aren't seeing eye to eye, despite our current stance which figuratively begs to differ.

"You really don't remember?" He asks me again.

Gosh, how many times do I have to say it?

I shake my head *no* and then before I can say anything he grabs my waist, pulling me into him. He grabs my face, guiding me toward him.

Our lips touch and it's soft and gentle. I can't stay frozen in my anger anymore the way I once was. I melt into him, like I'm supposed to. Like two puzzle pieces fitting together. His lips move against mine and I don't stop him. He tastes just how I imagined. Like honey and mint. My mind wants to pull away, but my heart won't let me. His tongue slips into my mouth meeting mine. I let out a little gasp I didn't know I was holding onto.

I had no idea kissing felt like this. Whatever I had done with Ryder was nothing like this. This is warm and relaxing and sending shivers down my spine. I don't want it to stop. Our skin is touching — his torso to my torso, both still in our swimsuits. We're as close as you possibly can be while standing up. I grab the back of his head and pull him closer to me, wanting to close the remaining gap — if there even is one. *What am I doing?*

I can't control myself.

Yes, I can. Just pull away.

I drop my hand from his neck. I ease off his lips, for a breath, to think. I can't possibly think with his lips on mine like this.

His hand, that was resting on my jaw, is now on the back of my neck, pulling me back in, closer to him than I already was somehow.

Just accept it, Tate, you're trapped. And you like it. Admit you like it.

I grab his sides, pulling at his back connecting our skin again. I've spent five years miles and miles away from him, trying to get him out of my head and now all I want is for him to be closer. To hold me tighter. To kiss me longer. To never let me go.

I feel like I don't need anything other than this. Not water, not air, not food, not sleep. Just this. Just him.

What about Annie? We can't both forget Annie. I can't forget what he did to me five summers ago, like it was nothing. No. This has to stop.

I push him away, it's gentler than I want it to be. I want to push him as far away as I can, but I don't. I need to put the counter in between us, a door maybe, a state or two. I can't think when he's this close, but I can't move. I stand close enough to him that I could still kiss him if I so desired. He's still right in front of me. We're both breathless.

Every word I had planned to say to him is gone, vanished — poof, right out the window.

I stare at the little scar on his chin, that he got when he saved me from a dog as kid. I've always loved that scar — he got it for me.

"Think you'll remember that?" He says, just above a whisper, a bit breathless, and then walks away.

So, he was just proving a point? That's why he kissed me. *GREAT.* The greatest kiss of my life was a pity kiss. A kiss to prove me wrong. *UGH.*

What is this feeling in my chest? I'm happy but I'm angry like before, I want to push him, but I also want him to kiss me again. I want to feel him again but I also want to yell at him too.

"You've got some nerve," I say.

"You're just now figuring that out?" He says without skipping a beat. He's a little too nonchalant for the kiss we just had.

Maybe I just don't know what a normal kiss feels like.

Maybe that's how all good kisses are supposed to feel.

"I'm being serious."

"You wanna be serious. Let's be serious. Why'd you stop coming every summer?"

Cut right to it, Easton. Geez.

How could he ask such dumb question?

I step away from him, putting the much needed space between us so that we can have this conversation.

What? What does he mean, "why did I stop coming every summer?"

Doesn't he know?

"What?" I say, unaware of how to properly respond to him.

"Well, I know beach volleyball picked up for you, and you train in the summers, and you were really busy. But I don't know, I guess I kind of thought you would always come back to see us. Even if it was just for a week or a couple days. But you just didn't," he says with his eyes anywhere but on me now. He moves his hands by his side, a nervous tick.

"Easton, I stopped coming back because you didn't want me back," I say confidently. A weight releases from my chest as the words rolled off my tongue. Finally, it's all in the air.

"What?" His voice is small, hurt, offended. "Tate, of course I wanted you back. Why would you even think otherwise?"

The air has shifted. It isn't warm and fuzzy like it was moments ago when we hung from each others' lips.

"The better question is why you stopped calling? I left that last summer and we were the closest we'd ever been and then nothing. Not even as much as a 'I had fun this summer 'text or 'did you make it home? 'Nothing. For a year. Why?" I say defensively, and I can hear the anger in my voice.

"Tate," he says like my question is unfair. Like I've wronged him.

"No, Easton, for an entire year I got nothing from you. Not so much as a happy birthday. Do you know how bad that hurt? Don't sit here and make me feel like the bad person for not coming back. Because I made the hardest decision I ever had to make that summer. Mom begged me to come back, and I did everything in my power to say *no*. I couldn't bear to see you because, because you chose... you chose *her*."

His brow furrows when I say *her*, like he's trying to figure out who. I continue none-the-less. "Izzy. You chose
Izzy. I was always your first choice until she came around.
You broke my heart that summer."

"We were kids, Tate," he defends. His face hardens, like he's mad. *What right does he have to be mad with me?*

"That doesn't mean it didn't hurt. That doesn't mean it wasn't real,"

I say as my lip quivers against my want to look fearless and confident in this conversation. Tears well up in my eyes. They're threatening to fall, but I won't let them.

The air is thick and heavy, and I can't bear the silence any longer. He just stares at me, his eyes heavy with something he won't express. They haven't moved from my face. I've made him speechless. No quippy comment. No sarcastic facial expression. No running. No hugging me. He just stands there. I want him to tell me I misread the situation and that he missed me and it was all a misunderstanding, but he doesn't. He just stands there, staring into my soul. His silence tells me all I need to know… I'm right and I'm not the only one at fault here. He is too. For not calling, for not asking why I didn't come back that next summer, for not trying to mend whatever it was we were back then. This feeling of being right, is hell.

My heart falls to the floor again, like it always does when he hurts me. I want to walk away and leave him. I want to pack my bags and get on a plane. I want to leave right now and never turn back. But what good did that do the first time? I still ended up right back here, in front of him again.

"I thought we were best friends," I say breaking the silence. A tear falls down my cheek, onto my lips. I bring my bottom lip in between by teeth — biting down gently, attempting to keep any other tears from falling. I can taste the salt on my lips, wiping away any remnant of Easton I had left on my taste buds.

Regret covers his face, but still, he's motionless.

"That's not fair," he finally says. "You know that's not fair. Tate, you know I…" he stops, catching the rest of his sentence before the words spill out.

You what?

"Even back then I… I…" he tries again.

Whatever he wants to say, I don't let him. "Don't say something you'll regret." I say, my face hard and cold.

"Annie wouldn't want you to." I blurt out finally.

His eyes are wide. He looks… caught, because he is.

"What, Tate. It's…" he starts, but I don't let him finish.

"Your words don't matter, Easton. I learned that a long time ago. Nothing you say is gonna make this better. I saw your lock screen the other day. You're with her and that's fine, but that's it. You're with her. Just because she's gone doesn't mean you get to kiss me and make me feel…" I stop. Now I'm the one who's caught.

His eyes stare straight into my soul. He's daring me to say it. To admit it. That I feel something for him. He wants me to admit that I can't help but feel this way around him. It takes everything in me to not finish that sentence. My bones are crying out to tell him, but I can't. I won't rather. "Don't say something you might regret," he says grabbing his keys, turning and walking out the front door without even looking back.

His words hit my chest. I'm the one speechless now.

He didn't say it angry. He said it, like he was making a point.

That we both did something wrong by letting what just happened, happen. Him kissing me was wrong. But so was me letting him.

By the time I muster up the courage to say what I should have said, he's long gone.

* * *

I've never felt this empty.

I lay in Easton's room, clinging to his pillow. My head is pounding from everything I just said. Regret is flooding over me like a tsunami as I play back what just happened in the kitchen.

122

I've been lying here for two hours. I'm wide awake. I keep hoping I'll hear him come in the front door, but I don't. I know what he's doing. He's driving around the apartment complex in circles. He wouldn't drive on the highway with such heightened emotions. I don't know if he's upset with me or himself more. But either way, I know he didn't go far. He just needs to clear his head.

I'm trying to do the same. Lying here in bed, staring at the ceiling wondering why I let him kiss me. I was angry at him after all. There are more good reasons to make sure he never got anywhere near my lips than they're are bad ones, and yet I let it happen.

I feel guilty, about Annie mostly. I keep reminding myself of what I overheard Easton and Walter say earlier, about him and Annie not being anything. But deep down I know that can't be true. Not if she was on his lock screen.

It has to mean something. Even if it's just a little something.

But I just can't bare the thought. He can say whatever he wants about how he forgets everyone when I'm around but that's just it.

What happens when I'm the one not around? What happens when I'm the one who's gone, and Annie is the one standing in the kitchen with him? I'm sick at the thought.

It's an unrealistic Disney fairy tale that I have let myself believe for years. This idea that true love exists and soulmates are real and that Easton is both of those things and more. The truth hits, and when it hits — it hits hard, like a ton of bricks. The truth hits me in the face and mocks me while I lay on the floor bleeding. The truth for me is the same as it has been for the past five years. He forgets me.

He'll always forget me.

Deep down I know that's the truth and seeing him awestruck in front of me today made my darkest fear come to life.

I'm not as important to him as he is to me.

15

That Third Set

TATE

It's been two days since whatever happened in the kitchen with Easton. If I didn't know any better, I would think he was actively avoiding me. He had a full day of work yesterday and he wasn't on the couch this morning when I woke up.

We haven't had a chance to talk about what happened, but I can't say that I'm upset about that. Everything we've said to each other this summer has been light and airy. I don't know what talking on that deep of a level would cause for us. I like that I we haven't talked about it yet, but I also know deep in my bones that a heart-to-heart conversation with him is unavoidable. No matter how much we try it's inevitable.

I can't think about that right now. Not the other night. Not the almost kiss. Not even Easton. The last one is getting harder to avoid by the minute.

Easton and Jessie came to the tournament today to watch me play. They always make an effort to watch me when I come to town.

I keep taking quick glances back at him. I'm half expecting him to be bored and looking at his phone, but he isn't. His phone is in the pocket of his chair and he's all eyes on me, talking to mom and Jessie about whatever it is they're talking about.

It's the second day of competition in Tavares, Florida.

The competition is sick. Everyone here is good. The teams come from all over — Texas, Arkansas, Ohio, California, Kansas, Arizona, even Hawaii. You can always count on a Showcase to bring out the best talent. College coaches from all around the country fly in to see all the rising stars compete in one place. The colleges include USC, UCLA, Pepperdine, Florida, Cal, Long Beach, Georgia State, TCU, FIU, FAU, and most importantly... LSU. Louisiana State University has been my dream school for as long as I can remember. I've dreamt of wearing purple and gold since I could walk. I wanted to be a Tiger, just like my mom and Jessie.

LSU's head coach, Coach Ron, is here. He waved at me earlier when I walked in. I had a semi good relationship with him from past tournaments and such. But this season there's more pressure than there's ever been to perform well, especially in front of him.

The sun is beating down so hard it feels like the sky is leaning on my shoulders. I've gotten pretty used to the heat, having played this sport for almost nine years of my life. But Florida heat is not for the weak. The air is thicker here than anywhere else I've ever played. Each breath feels like swallowing a spoonful of peanut butter.

The facility we're playing at is right by a swamp, which only amplifies the humidity. We've seen alligators in it and everything. The swamp is really pretty to look at, but the price you of pay of knowing that an alligator could always be right around the corner is not worth it. I live with a constant fear that an alligator will just wander onto the courts at any moment. And I know that if that happens, it will come straight for me.

There are little bugs in the air everywhere, and they get stuck in between my face and the sunglasses I'm wearing. As if the heat isn't enough of an obstacle.

I shift my weight around in the sand, my toes digging in. Sweat is already dripping down my back even though I'm just sitting here. My partner for this particular tournament is Chase Stevens. She has a freckled face like mine, but she has a few more than me. She is skinny in a does Pilates kind of way. She is fast and agile and always sees the bright side of things. She's a good partner. We've only played together once before this tournament, but we work. We have pretty good chemistry on the court. Georgia is her home state, but she is committed to Pepperdine University.

Pepperdine University is a prestigious school on the west coast. It's known as the Ivy League of the west. It's a private school located less than a mile from the ocean in Malibu, California. They have an amazing law school. That's what attracted Chase to it, although I have a feeling the beach sunsets might also have something to do with her decision to commit there. Their beach volleyball team has been phenomenal for years. The National Collegiate Athletic Association didn't consider beach volleyball a collegiate sport until 2016. But before the sport became "official", Pepperdine held the AVCA National Championships at their home beach in Malibu, Zuma Beach. They won the very first AVCA Championship and won again two years later. They were at the top of the collegiate beach volleyball game before it was even really watched.

I've never been to the school, but I hear the second you step foot on Pepperdine's campus you never want to leave. It's built into the side of the mountain and overlooks the ocean. I've never visited because I know I wouldn't fit in there. The tuition is ninety-six grand a year.

I couldn't go there, even if I wanted to. I would need a full scholarship and beach volleyball currently isn't a fully funded sport. The school is full of private school kids who can actually afford to pay the tuition.

We've battled hard through two days of matches to get to where we are today.

The semifinals.

We lost the first set. 19-21 and we won the second set 22-20.

We're in that tiny break before the third set — the tie breaker that decides who gets to go to the finals.

My heart is pounding in my chest like it knows what's coming.

Something I've never experienced while playing beach volleyball is nerves. I have played far too long to let myself get nervous. Nervousness is healthy in sports. Or at least that's what all the coaches and players around me preach. For me, nervous feels like having to give a speech in front of my classmates, or reading a poem I wrote to a friend, singing anything at all to anyone or like Easton finding my doodles the other night. Nervous is being inches from Easton's lips and not knowing what he's gonna do next.

I know nerves. Just not when it comes to sports, or beach volleyball, or third sets.

My heart pounding in my chest isn't nerves — it's the reminder of why I do this. The adrenaline coursing through my veins makes me feel alive. I'd be lying if I said

I don't love a match this close. I love 50/50 odds. I love knowing I have to earn it. I love the fight that comes with a third set. Each point is fought for with grit and passion. I live for these stakes.

Coaches have been watching from every side of the court, all sitting in shaded chairs with clipboards in their hands — making note of every good or terrible thing I do. They aren't watching anyone else. Chase is committed to Pepperdine and the girls we're playing against are both committed to USC. Coaches don't watch players who are already committed to college. That does them no good, because to them we are assets.

Today, during this match, I am the only asset they can possibly acquire. Which makes the pressure of this third set a lot heavier. It makes the outcome that much more important. I'm younger than everyone else playing, which is why I haven't committed yet. I have one more year left of high school and these girls are all about to start their freshman year of college. The only player on the court worth watching, is me. And I know that.

Our opponents look like classic USC commits. Both taller than me by a few inches, bleach blonde, and tanner than me and Chase combined. They're almost golden, and their hair is in perfect long ponytails — not a hair out of place. I don't even think they're sweating.

Must be nice.

We take the court again, ready for what could be our last set of the tournament or the reason we get to play one more match.

Once I get to the court, I glance back at the sea of people watching. I squint toward my mom and spot Easton. His hat is backwards, sunglasses on, grinning like a little kid at a carnival. If anything was my weakness, it's Easton in a backwards hat. *Damn.*

He catches me looking.

Great.

To my surprise, instead of his normal *hi* head nod he stands up, cupping his hands around his mouth and yells,

"Let's go, TK!"

Jessie whistles loudly after him, enough to make the court next to us pause. "You got this!" She adds.

My mom sits beside her, holding her phone sideways, pointing in the direction of our court. She always FaceTimes my dad so he can watch from whatever film set he's on. And if he can't watch right then she'll still film the game and post it to YouTube so he can watch it after.

Which he always does.

He's on a movie in Kentucky, and I know he was working right now, but it was nice to know he's gonna watch it later.

I smile at my personal fan club, shake out my shoulders, and turn to Chase. "Ready?" I say. She adjusts her bun and nods, calm as she always was.

"We've got this," she says to me, but I think she says it to reassure herself.

We actually did have it… for about fifteen minutes.

I dove for a ball on one of the last points, getting a mouth full of sand. My voice is hoarse from yelling for every ball. It is getting more intense by the second. Chase is laser focused. She isn't as loud as me, but she's in it.

At 12-13, Chase serves an ace, tying it up. The USC girls put up a good fight.

At 13-14, Chase goes up for a block and gets it, barely.

But barely is enough.

It's 14-14 now. Every beach volleyball game is win by two, and every third set is to fifteen points, so now… we're in overtime.

I serve the ball, putting the right-side player slightly out of system. They recover well and hit a high line shot right over Chase's block. The USC girl had dropped her elbow slightly on her swing and is facing the end line, so I take off before the shot even leaves her hand. Even though I take off early it's still a stretch to get to the shot before it hits the ground. I've never sprinted so fast. I extend my body to the extreme. My right arm reaches all the way out.

I'm reaching with every fiber of my being and I get it up. My whole body in the air and one arm stretched out. I don't know what happens after that. I hit it, I think.

Next thing I knew, I was serving again. 15-14. Match point for us. I serve confidently, but the USC girls fight a little harder for this point. They get a kill, tying the score up again.

15-15. They serve me this time. I pass and hit a shot that isn't as good as it should be. They pick it up and hit it into the deepest part of the court, just out of my reach.

16-15. And just like that, we're down. Match point them. I'm resting in serve receive when they serve Chase. Chase passes a great ball, but it's a little too tight to set it back to her. So, I do what I do best, option. I take the second ball as an opportunity to hit, using Chase's first ball pass as the set. I swing and it feels good. Strong. Powerful. But as soon as the ball leaves my hand, I know I messed up.

The USC girls let it land a half inch outside the line.

"Out!" They both scream with joy!

At 15-17, it's over. The whistle blows and the blondes high-fived like they expected to win all along. That's my least favorite part about playing girls from California — they were entitled.

I stay at the net for a second longer than I should, feeling the defeat. I don't want to look at the coaches surrounding our court. I don't want to look at the scoreboard. I don't want to look back at my mom and

Jessie... and Easton. I could feel the pity on their faces from here, without even looking.

Chase walks up behind me, patting my back. "It was a good shot, Tate. Good game."

I know she isn't mad about the last point. A set is made up of lots of points. The last point isn't the reason we lost, but it always feels that way for a while.

"Yeah," I say, taking it in. "Just... bummed."

That's part of it though. Part of the risk. Part of the thrill. You don't always win. No matter how bad you want to. We shake hands with the winners and walk off the court. A couple coaches wave politely. The Pepperdine coach walked up to Chase, patting her on the back.

They talked for a second before she introduced me. "This is Tate. Isn't she phenomenal?" she says with a big smile.

I don't feel phenomenal.

I know she means what she said but the remnants of the loss makes what she said feel like a dig.

The coach shakes my hand. He's wearing a navy dri-fit long sleeve shirt and an orange cap. The shirt reads "Waves" in a bright orange letters.

"It's so nice to meet you. Thank you for watching," I muster out.

"It was my pleasure, Tate," he says with a big grin and an accent I can't quite place.

He hands me his card and says, "Nice work out there."

I nod and say *thank you* as I tuck the card into my shorts pocket without really looking at it. It's nice of him to give me his card, but unless I got a full ride, Pepperdine isn't an option for me. I can't even put it on the table. Plus,

I don't know how I'd fit in at anything described as an

"Ivy League."

Chase and the coach continue to talk, and I leave them be.

Easton, Jessie, and my mom meet me at the edge of the sand. Easton playfully tosses me a cold towel. It smells like sunscreen and citrus. It must have been in the cooler because it's damp. I immediately put it around my neck, attempting to cool my internal temperature.

"You did good, babe," my mom says giving me a hug.

"You were insane, honey!" Jessie says, handing me a water bottle. It isn't as cold as the towel, but I like it that way. "That dive in the third set! I think people actually gasped—I mean, I know I did."

Easton smiles, his eyes soft, comforting. "You played your heart out. Always a blast to watch."

I shrug. "Didn't really matter in the end. But thanks guys."

"It still matters," Easton says quietly holding my eyes with his.

The last thing I want right now is to be comforted. It all feels like pity. Everything in my body knows they don't feel bad for me, but something in my mind just can't take even the kindest of comments after a match. I just need a few minutes to myself.

Thankfully, I'll get that time because we lost, which means we have to ref the final match.

"We gotta ref. Catch up with y'all later? Actually, where's my backpack?" I ask the group.

"I got it," Easton says, turning his back to me revealing my backpack hanging from one of his shoulders. That's sweet of him.

"I just need my phone to keep score online for the website," I state.

I open the score keeping app on my phone, but when I tap it, my phone goes completely black. Dead. "Shoot, it just died," I say annoyed.

Before I can even think of a solution, Easton holds his out. "Use mine."

"Thanks," I say, taking it from him with a soft smile.

He's being so helpful. Not that he usually isn't. I guess he isn't ignoring me, like I thought.

The screen lights up automatically. My thumb freezes. The wallpaper is... not Annie anymore. He changed it. It's a photo — grainy and sun-drenched — from years ago. I recognize it. It's from my last summer here in Florida. I had taken the photo. It's a selfie of me and Easton soaked from a water balloon fight, laughing, dripping in our clothes, standing in front of their old house. We look so happy.

I don't mention anything, but we exchange a look which says more than words can anyways.

"Well, I'll be back in a bit." I say to them.

Why did he change it? Did something happen?
I just thought I was confused before.
But now what am I? A tornado of confusion?

Halfway through final match, Chase leans toward me, shielding her eyes with one hand like she's blocking the sun. "I'm glad you're done with Ryder. I didn't realize you had a boyfriend though," she says with a huge grin. Her voice is higher than normal. She's teasing me.

"I don't," I assure her.

"Easton?" She questions in disbelief. "Are you sure?" she adds.

"Yes, I am certain I don't have a boyfriend," I say almost disgusted. I'm not grossed out by her question, but I want her to stop prying. "But you and Ryder are…" she says.

"Done," I interrupt.

She looks at me with these big, huge eyes, trying to say something without saying something. It's working "What?" I say, annoyed.

"You've seen the way Easton looks at you though, right? I mean I've never seen a guy look at a girl the way he looks at you, Tate. Like ever. He's in love with you." "It's not… it's not like that," I stutter.

Chase smiles faintly. "Okay. Just saying — if someone looked at me like that. I wouldn't let them get away."

I don't look at her. I just stare at the court, heart thumping for an entirely different reason now. This is nervous. I feel more nerves during this conversation than I have the whole tournament.

I can't help but wonder what would happen if I asked him straight up how he felt about me.

I mean we almost kissed the other night.

Didn't we?

"We're just so close as friends. I don't want to risk it," I admit.

"I thought you hadn't spoken in five years." She says firmly. "Doesn't sound like there's much at risk to me," she adds with a snap of sass, but I knew it was out of love.

I hate that she's right.

What do I have to lose? A little bit of witty banter? A smirk from him here or there? Why does talking to him about this feel so much harder than anything else I've ever had to do?

I guess now that the tournament's over, I can focus on enjoying the remainder of the two weeks I have here.

I guess figuring out what is or isn't going on between me and Easton is the new priority. It's the new risk.

I just don't know if I can take it.

Chapter 14: Izzy who?

(The summer I was 13 and he was 14)

135

16

We're nothing

EASTON

Tate slept through dinner. That last match really took it out of her today.

I've watched her play before and shamefully I've even watched some of the videos Kora filmed for Mr. Knightly, because she posts them on YouTube. She doesn't know to not make the videos public. I picked up on it a few years back when my curiosity got the best of me and I googled Tate. Her latest game popped up and I couldn't resist watching. But today, Tate was so much better. She played with this confidence she didn't have as much last time I watched her play in person. Maybe it was just the excitement of getting to watch it live but she seemed much better this time. She looked strong and fast in ways I didn't know she was. She played with so much passion. It was so very attractive.

I could tell she was upset after the loss earlier. I wanted to do something to cheer her up and get her mind off things, so I decided to make her favorite meal — homemade chicken noodle soup. It's Kora's recipe that she shared with my mom years and years ago. My mom only ever makes it when we're sick or during an odd ball cold day, which doesn't happen much here in Florida. This soup is healing. As kids, we used to joke it healed you from the inside out. On days the mom's wanted to throw something together quick they would make it for us, and they would use extra wide egg noodles. The store bought noodles are good, but Tate's favorite is when Kora makes the noodles from scratch. On special occasions Kora would claim the kitchen for herself a spend a couple hours mixing up the dough and rolling it out and cutting it into perfect long dumpling like noodles.

Since Tate took an extra long shower and went straight into my room after, I decided I'd have enough time to whip it all up from scratch the way she loves it. Homemade noodles and all. I peeked in my room a few hours ago and she was out like a light. She needs the recovery sleep. She was sprawled out, twisted up in the comforter like a pretzel, so I figured I'd have some time before she woke up to get everything ready for her.

The moms went out to watch a movie and do some grocery shopping and dad is working a late shift which leaves just me and Tate in the house. After I made the soup and ate some, I just sat here for a while — at the kitchen counter thinking. And thinking is dangerous right now.

I look around at the apartment. It's empty in that cookie-cutter apartment layout way. It's a basic little apartment but it's nice for what it is. I don't really like when the apartment gets this quiet. The grey wood floors. The eggshell walls. The granite counter tops. It's all so fresh. It's new and clean. I like it for what it is, but it doesn't really feel like home. It's at times like this, that I miss our old house. There were so many memories there. Even though we brought a lot of things with us, in the move — nothing compares to the memories walls hold. I miss the scratches on the walls and the messy wallpaper in my old room, and the game closet door that didn't close all the way. I could sit in any room of the house, and it felt comfortable.

But here it's… lonely. I've never really been alone like this in the apartment before. Mom is always here or dad. Even is he's reading silently in the corner; he's still here.

Usually, Lila would be here when the mom's leave and

Tate naps. Lila can't nap because she's got too much energy. She barely gets sleep at a night, let alone in the middle of the day.

As selfish as it sounds, I'm glad Lila's not here. Because lately wherever Lila goes, Annie follows. Annie.

I can't believe I forgot about her.

Whenever I'm around Tate, I forget everything and everyone.

All I can think about in her presence, is us.

Unfortunately for Annie, that means I forgot about her, the other night in the kitchen.

It took everything in me not to kiss Tate that night. I can't stop thinking about it. It's consuming me.

She's consuming me.

Tate's still sound asleep in my room, so I invited Walter over an hour or so ago. I had forgotten I texted him until he burst through the door with a six-pack in hand. He's wearing a cut off t-shirt. I only notice because usually he isn't wearing one at all. Walter lives his life like the world is a beach. Salt air and sand in his hair, barefoot, and usually… shirtless. Three things you can always count on him for are:

1. He'll have his drumstick in his back pocket (which he does)
2. He's probably intoxicated or holding something that's gonna get him to that state shortly (which he is)
3. He's gonna bring the fun (which he always does).

He sets the six-pack of beer down on the counter and immediately opens one.

"Where are the girls?" He says taking his hat off and throwing it on the countertop.

"Girls?" I say, confused

"Yeah, in your text you said there'd be girls."

"Here? At my parents' apartment? Are you high?"

"Well, yeah. But I can still read," He remarks back.

Walter comes from a prestigious family in the community... the Hughes family. Walter is the second born, black sheep of the family. His dad's the pastor of our church — a very stuck-up religious man who always wears a suit. And I mean always. I've never seen him wear anything else. But maybe that's because most times I see him he's in the pulpit. Walter is what me and Tate call a "PK" — pastors' kid. A pastor's kid cleans up to be a great picture-perfect Christian on Sunday but spends Monday - Saturday being a Tasmanian devil doing anything and everything they possibly can to be disobedient.

Walter is the king of the PKs. Around me and our friends, he's chill, laid back and usually high. But the second an adult enters the room he becomes an eloquent man of society — even if he's dressed like a homeless hooligan. Everyone loves him. Including me. He's been my best friend for the past five-ish years. I met him through my first girlfriend, Izzy. Walter is Izzy's younger brother. Not a whole lot of good came from that relationship, but I did get a best friend out of it. He's a good best friend.

"I said the girls, meaning my mom and Tate's mom are gone. So, I figured we could watch a movie or something," I say.

"Well, next time, please clarify that the 'girls' you're talking about are millennials. I wouldn't have cleaned up so much if I knew it was just you." I chuckle.

"What's all this?" He motions to the mess in the kitchen.

"I made soup," I say spinning the ladle around in the pot on the stove. "You want some, there's plenty…"

He interrupts me. "I didn't know you were a chef."

"I'm not. It's Tate's favorite meal and she had a rough day so, you know I figured I'd whip something up for her."

"Where is she?" he asks looking around the apartment.

I nod in the direction of my room. "She's been out for a few hours."

Walter takes a sip of his beer; his face is holding something back.

"What?" I ask.

"What about Annie?" He questions. "Does she know
Tate's here?"

I walk toward him and grab a beer. I open it and take a sip. "Not exactly. But what does it matter?" "You know I'm all for a little lady on the side but, come on. Annie isn't gonna handle that well when she gets back."

Get's back?

I don't even know when Lila and Annie get back, how does he know?

"Get back? When do they get back?" "Uh, soon. I think," he says sheepishly.

He's a terrible liar.

"Don't avoid the question," he adds.

"You didn't ask me a question," I jab. "Annie and I only went on a couple dates. It's not like we're serious or anything. We're nothing," I say a bit more defensively than I want to.

"Does Annie know that?"

His question hangs in the air. And suddenly, I feel alone again — even though Walter is here.

I hate that Walter has this maturity about him that doesn't match the way he dresses or acts. Having such responsible parents has rubbed off on him whether he'd admit it or not. He has this wisdom that sneaks out every now and then and it always reveals his true identity. His big heart is buried under layers of fake sloppiness and nonchalant vibes but deep down in his bones he's a really good person. He might say he's *all for a little lady on the side,* but Walter would never two time someone. He would never cheat. He would never treat Annie the way I am. He would never dream of it. Maybe that's because he's never much dated. Or maybe it's because I've never seen him date. I've only seen him kiss girls, and a lot of them at that — but for some reason he never really dates anyone, and he's never had a girlfriend. I'm just now realizing how it's a bit odd that he hasn't yet. I always take his advice though, for some reason. I think it's because I know that if he did date someone, he'd love them the way your supposed to love a girl. He'd do all the yearning and longing that girls love so much. He'd be like Noah from the *Notebook* or whatever it is that girls like so much about that guy — Walter would be that. So, whenever he talks, I try to listen. Sometimes it's mumble jumble weird shit and sometimes it's real, solid knowledge.

I know he's right. I should be thinking about Annie, but how can I when Tate is just in the other room. How can I think of Annie when Tate is in my house, in my eyesight, and in my head. It's impossible to think of anything with Tate lingering around in the corner of my brain I made just for her when we were kids. I can't just not want her.

I can't not want her.

So, whether it's fair to Annie or not, I'll think about Tate... because how could I not.

17

Walter's Dream Girl

TATE

It's just past eleven-thirty when I finally wander out of his room. My rumbling stomach reminds me that I missed dinner. All the lights in the apartment are off, and I don't think anyone is awake. Something about being the only one awake makes me feel like I'm getting away with something.

I tiptoe into the hallway, quietly.

A voice I don't recognize floats through the dark. "You gotta figure your shit out dude. I mean, I know what I'd do if I were you," the voice says — not quite a whisper, but close. He sounds fired up about something.

"Yeah, well, I'm not you," Easton says.

"She's your dream girl, Easton. I didn't really get it until I met her the other night. She's like — I don't know dude… like…" the voice trails off.

"Epic," Easton says, sure of himself.

"Yeah, epic, exactly," the voice I don't recognize says. "She's the legit real deal. She's athletic, she's witty, she's kind, she's beautiful in that

142

natural kind of way that just makes me sick. And her eyes... dude, her eyes are like pots of honey. I get lost in them," the voice keeps going.

"Walt, bro, you're drooling man," Easton says nervously, but I can tell he's serious underneath it. He sounds protective.

Walter. The drummer from the band I didn't know

Easton had until the other night. I knew that voice was from somewhere. *Why is he here this late?*

Forget about Annie. Hell, it seems like you already have. How could you not with Tate right there in the other room? I can't believe you haven't hit that yet," Walter says.

"Watch it," Easton says firmly. "Don't talk about her like that," he adds warning him with a protectiveness in his voice that sends shivers down my spine.

"I'm just saying. You and Annie aren't official, right?"

"Right," Easton says, but his tone switches. It sounds like he's trying to convince himself and then Walter. "The issue is, I do forget about Annie. I forget about everyone when Tate's around. It's always been that way."

Oh. What? Is he serious?

When did he start to feel this way?

"Then what are you waiting for?" Walter asks, louder now with a spark of challenge in his voice. He almost sounds jealous of Easton.

I've always wondered what guys sound like when they talk about girls. It's more honest than I expected it to be. Almost sweet. I feel bad for eavesdropping, but my curiosity is stronger than my guilt. But, if I wait any longer to eat something, I'll throw up from how empty my stomach feels.

Before Easton can answer Walter, I shut the bathroom door a little too loudly — on purpose. It's only fair to give them a chance to change the subject.

Tiptoeing into the kitchen, I go straight for the fridge. I don't even glance at the living room. They are silent now anyways, and I feel them watching me but I don't pay them any attention. It will look suspicious if I look over.

I open the fridge — nothing but orange juice, milk, and eggs.

"Hey," Walter says, breaking the silence. He gets up, walking toward me.

"Oh, hey," I reply, pretending to be surprised. My eyes meet his in the dark. They're bright blue, even with only the fridge light his eyes are still piercing.

I give him a little salute. It comes out flirtier than I mean it, but the grin that spreads across his face tells me he doesn't mind.

"You always salute guys in the kitchen, or am I just special?" he teases, stepping closer.

Easton glances between us two, clearly uncomfortable and wanting to be acknowledged as he steps a bit closer, joining us in the kitchen.

"Depends, I say, shrugging in the most nonchalant way possible. "Are you special?"

Oh, I'm very special," Walter says, leaning a hip against the counter. His smile is easy, lazy. He looks me up and down — not in a gross way, more like he's genuinely admiring me.

I can feel the color appear on my cheeks. Suddenly I wish I wasn't wearing my dad's oversized sweatshirt. It's getting warm in here and I'm suddenly aware of my sleepy zombie-like state. I wish I was wearing something a bit less slouchy. I like the way he's looking at me. I can tell he finds me attractive by the way his eyes keep glancing down to my lips and the way they search my eyes as he talks. It's nice to be looked at like this when I'm not dressed up or anything. He looks at me like I've just walked down the stairs in my homecoming dress or something.

Easton clears his throat behind him, "You hungry, TK?" Walter raises an eyebrow but doesn't break eye contact with me. "TK?"

"Yeah," Easton says. "That's TK. TK, this is Walter he's— "

I interrupt him. "We've met."

Walter's grin widens with mischief sprinkled in it.

"Easton doesn't shut up about you, and now I know why.

You're beautiful Miss TK," he says emphasizing Easton's nickname for me.

I hold back a giggle as Easton grows more anxious by the second. I can feel it.

Something on the stove catches my eye. The soup pot is out and there are ingredients spread out around the kitchen everywhere. Flour on the counter. Half used chicken stock and a few carrot tops sit by the stove. It's a mess. This can't be mom or Jessie's doing because they always clean as they go. This is a boy's work.

"You guys made a mess," I say pushing the carrot tops into my hand and walking them to the trashcan to throw them away.

"Actually, I made chicken noodle soup," Easton says. "Really? You cooked?" I ask as I peep my head into the soup pot on the stove. To my surprise there are long, thick homemade noodles. "SHUT UP!" I yell a bit too loudly.

Did you do this?" I ask Easton, who's wearing a big grin.

That's all the *yes* I need. I run right past Walter to Easton, wrapping my arms around him.

Thank you!" I say. My voice comes out high pitched and scratchy like a little kid who just got told they could have a sleepover with their bestie.

His arms don't wrap around me immediately. It takes him a second, but once he does, they wrap around my waist, and he squeezes gently.

Just above a whisper, he says, "Anything for you."

I'm waiting for him to pull away but he doesn't. We just stay like that, hugging until— "Get. A. Room," Walter chuckles.

We break apart and look at him awkwardly. Walter looks at Easton with big eyes. They have some awkward eye conversation.

After a moment or so, I decide to let their eyes talk in even more silence than they already are and make myself a bowl of soup while it's still warm. Before I'm even done filling my bowl, Walter packs up his things.

"Fine, see you later man. For the record, you invited me here," Walter says. When he gets to the edge of the kitchen he says, "Bye honey, with a wink." He then salutes me and walks out the front door like he owns the place. I shake my head, fighting back a smile. Easton watches him go, jaw tight for some reason.

"He's such a prick," Easton says, now sitting across from me at the countertop.

"I don't know. I kind of like him."

"Oh," he gasps, a bit shocked.

His response sits in the air as I grab a spoon from the drawer.

"Then you should know he's a PK," Easton adds.

"Him? No."

"Yep. The worst of them too," he tells me.

I think for a moment, "Well doesn't that make him the best of them? He's tall, has blue eyes, bleach blonde hair, and he's handsome," I say.

Easton's jaw tightens again as he starts cleaning up the counter, shielding his face from me now.

"I bet he cleans up nice on Sundays. And I he knows throws a hella good house party. Am I right?" I ask.

"The best but he is a pain in the ass," Easton mutters.

I prop myself up on the counter, right next to Easton.

"If you call you're best friend a pain in the ass then what do you call me?" I ask with eyes big and curious.

His eyes search my face, like he thinks I can give him the answer to my own question somehow. He clears his throat and looks back down at the counter he's wiping down. "I don't call you anything." *Oh. Right.*

He goes back to cleaning, moving around the kitchen as he wipes off different surfaces, cleans a dish or two, and packs up the rest of the soup. With each bite of this amazing soup, I can't help but think about the conversation I walked in on them having earlier. I wonder what Easton's response was going to be to Walter's question.

What are you waiting for?

What is he waiting for. I guess he isn't waiting for anything. How can you wait on something for someone you don't call *anything*.

I think I'm making up everything in my head.

If he really feels the way he says he feels, then what's stopping him. It's at times like this I wish I could read his brain, although it might not be the smartest decision to ever know what goes through any man's brain.

He looks up anxious, watching me eat now as he leans against the counter across from me. It hasn't occurred to me til right now that he's probably worried I heard that conversation with Walter. I guess his anxiousness isn't misplaced considering I did hear every word. Even though I had heard all the things he didn't want me to hear, nothing feels different. I think it's because part of me has always known Easton feels something deeper for me than he's ever let on. The presence of wonder is always in the air with us. It's what makes all the moment's we have together special. There's something about us that was different.

Magical. Maybe even, chemical. But just when I think I have him figured out he says something that changes everything I thought I knew.

Nothing he could say would make me feel differently for him. I was kidding myself five summers ago, when I thought I could forget him. No matter how much I try, he's always there. In my heart. In my mind. And right now, he's right in front of me. I should just break the ice and tell him why I left. But I can't. I won't.

We sit in the low light, the clock on the microwave flips to 1:02 A.M. The air between us feels warm, like the scent of vanilla clinging to my skin from my shower earlier. The shower I took was long and healing. An everything shower makes everything feel better. It washed away the feelings of a tough loss, but it didn't wash away what I feel for Easton. I wish it was that easy. I double shampooed my hair and shaved my legs. I used a sugar scrub that was already in the shower too — vanilla sugar scented. I use the same one at home, but it wouldn't fit in my bag for the flight here. The scrub is definitely Lila's. Growing up, we always loved the same scents. Lila wouldn't mind that I took a little scoop of her vanilla sugar scrub. So, I did.

I've always been a vanilla girl. For as long as I can remember, I've loved the smell of vanilla — warm, sweet, comforting. My mom always wore this perfume from *Bath and Body Works*. She worked there when I was a really little. It was in a clear bottle with little gold sparkles all over it, like fairy dust. The label said *Warm Vanilla Sugar*. It sat on the top shelf of her bathroom closet, right next to a small container full of hotel shampoo and conditioner bottles she collected, "just in case."

My mom isn't one of those moms who wore a ton of makeup. the most I ever saw her wear was mascara, a hint of blush, and chapstick. It would be strange to see her in any more than that — she didn't need it. She was too beautiful to hide behind anything. But she did wear perfume. *Warm Vanilla Sugar* was her signature scent. She smelled like the house after we bake cookies — warm, sweet, safe.

By default, I too became a vanilla girl. I always wanted to be just like her, so as soon as I was old enough to wear perfume it's the only scent I wanted to wear. So guess what my sweet mama got me? Yep, my very own bottle of *Warm Vanilla Sugar* perfume. I was over the moon. That was one of my favorite birthdays.

Lila Mills is one year younger than me. Almost to the day — her birthday is three days before mine, so every year, for three days, we're the same age. We loved that when we were little. We shared everything back then.

Even Easton.

As we got older, our interests solidified. I loved sports and Marvel, Easton loved Marvel, music, and theater, and Lila loved theater, singing, and some sports. Some of those things overlapped but not all of them. Easton was older so we always just did what he did. He always kept it fair… most of the time.

When I first got here I was sad she wasn't here but right now, sitting in front of Easton, I'm not too upset that it's just us.

I like not having to share him this summer.

I wonder if Easton can smell the vanilla scrub on my skin.

"Hey, Easton? I say, as I finish my last bite of soup.

"Yeah?" He says with his big hopeful eyes. The anxiousness on his face is gone for a moment.

"Wanna go to the pool?" I ask, bluntly.

He looks at me blankly, then glances at the stove clock to check the time. "The pool?"

"The pool," I confirm, setting my bowl down on the counter.

A slow smile tugs at the corner of his mouth — the same one I've always loved. The one that means he'll do anything I ask.

"Okay," he says. "Let me grab some towels."

"I'll put on my suit." I say, scampering off into my room like a little kid.

Chapter 17: Think You' ll Remember This?

18

Meet Me at the Beach

TATE

I wake up to the smell of pancakes.

I don't know how long Easton stayed out last night, or if he ever came back. I don't want to see him, which is why I've been lying in his bed with the covers over my head for the past thirty minutes. That's when the aroma starts drifting under the door. I find it easiest to pretend that there aren't warm fluffy pancakes being made fresh right outside my door, but my nose tells me otherwise.

Part of me wants to think that it's Easton out there making the pancakes, dropping little chocolate chips in them. I want to think that he's made me a plate and a cup of coffee. It would be a peace offering after last night. An apology for kissing me without warning. For holding me like he did. For making me know what it's like to be his. It's rude for him to do such a thing, when I know it doesn't mean anything. To him it's just a kiss. In my mind I believe that I deserve an apology from him for not knowing that he's the reason I stopped coming back to

Florida. I deserve an apology.

I deserve an apology. I deserve an apology.

I keep repeating that phrase in my mind, trying to convince the rest of my body that it's true.

If it's true that I deserve an apology, why can't I just walk out of this room right now with my head held high? If Easton is the one in the wrong, then why does it pain me to see him again? The words he said last night combat my way of thinking - *we were just kids.* I hate it, but I know he's right. I'm holding something he said to me five years ago over his head. I can't walk out of my room with my head held high, because I don't deserve to walk out there at all. I'm ashamed.

I've held this thing over Easton's head for years and he didn't even know why.

Deep down in my heart I know he deserves an apology from *me.* Maybe even more than I deserve one from him.

I finally work up the courage to make my way into the kitchen. To my surprise, Easton isn't in there. Or anywhere. The couch is untouched. His blanket is folded, hanging over the back of the couch. His pillow is puffed up like a marshmallow, like it wasn't slept on.

Mr. Mills is standing in the kitchen, pouring my mom a cup of coffee. Jessie is on the phone down the hallway. I wonder who she's talking to?

"Hi honey," mom says as she sips her freshly poured coffee.

I pull the sleeves of Easton's oversized sweatshirt into my hands. I grabbed it out of his closet last night. It's dark forest green with little patches over where the fabric has grown thin. The words *Colorado State* are patched on the front in a college jersey font. It's Mr. Mills' from college.

"Hi mama," I say, sitting down next to her at the bar. I steal a sip of her coffee, but it's not as sweet as I like mine.

"I haven't seen that one in a while," she says, grabbing the hem of the sweatshirt. "it's seen better days." "It's been loved is all," Mr. Mills chimes in.

As kids we used to try on Jessie and Mr. Mills clothes to dress up like "grown-ups" when we played house. For some reason we always loved this green hoodie. To this day, I'm not really sure why.

Mr. Mills places a plate stacked three pancakes high in front of me with a reassuring nod. "Syrup?" He asks.

"Easton said I should warm it."

"He did?" I ask. The only thing I like more than chocolate chip pancakes is chocolate chip pancakes with warm syrup straight off the stove.

"Yep," Mr. Mills says as he drizzles the warm maple syrup over my pancakes.

I can't help myself from looking around the room for him, even though I've already looked.

"He's not here babe," my mom says, knowing exactly who I'm looking for.

"Oh."

I take a bite of the pancakes. They're delicious, but I can't help but taste the guilt. It doesn't feel right to be enjoying such a thing when there is so much left unsaid between me and Easton.

"He left this for you though," Mr. Mills says, sliding my

Captain America mug across the counter. There is a pink sticky note stuck to the front of the mug, covering the Captain America shield.

It reads:
MEET ME AT THE BEACH. – E

A smile starts to creep onto my face.

"What's that about?" My mom questions.

"I'm not sure." I shove two more bites of pancakes in my mouth in a hurry, then grab my mug, and head for the door.

"Slow down, you'll choke!" Jessie says worried. "I'll be back."

"Be quick, they'll be here so…" my mom's voice is cut off because I'm already out the door, practically running down the apartment stairs.

I don't have time to think about who *they* are before I'm consumed by the thought of why Easton wants to see me and why we couldn't just talk in the kitchen. Maybe because he wants to be alone? Maybe because he regrets last night? Maybe because being in the kitchen isn't the most productive place to talk after last night?

* * *

When I get to the beach, I don't join him immediately.

I see him out there all alone, just sitting on a beach blanket, with the mug that matches mine in his hands. He's so peaceful like this. Just sipping his coffee and watching the waves. I lean against the old wooden fence that leads down to the ocean and for a moment, I just watch him. This is the Easton Mills I remember. Before he said what he said back then. Before I stopped coming back.

He's calm, reserved, quiet in a way that isn't shy.

Somehow, he's more confident and cool now. This version of him. This him is what made forgetting him so impossible.

I want to draw what's in front of me right now. I want to capture him exactly like this, in this moment. I wish I could paint. I would paint this moment in deep blues and light grays and the dark brown of his hair. I'd learn to paint just to keep this moment. I'd frame it in an antique frame and hang it in our house one day.

I walk up to him, sitting down beside him. My feet rest in the soft sand, but he doesn't look at me. It's like he doesn't even notice me.

"I got your note," I say looking out at the water, like he is.

"Did you like the pancakes?" He asks, still not giving me even a glance. He takes a sip of his coffee.

"I took a bite but then I rushed here."

"Rushed? You must have really slept in. I hope they weren't cold."

"They weren't. The syrup was warm," I say to reassure him that his dad took his advice.

With that, he tilts his head toward me. I feel it, but I don't look back. I just let him look at me. I'm starting to wonder why he asked me out here. The whole walk over I was sure it was to talk about last night, but now I'm not so sure. I don't know how much more small talk I can take.

My coffee is going lukewarm in my hands, but my skin feels hot all over, like the sun has decided to spotlight me.

Easton breaks the silence. "I didn't sleep last night," he says, eyes still focused on the waves.

My stomach dips. *Neither did I.* But I don't say that.

"I kept thinking about what happened," he pauses, setting his mug down in the sand. "...in the kitchen."

Every muscle in my body tenses. He said it — the kiss.

My mind flashes to his hands firmly against the small of my back. I remember how it felt like I'd stepped into something dangerous and safe at the same time. I grip the mug tighter like it's my anchor.

"What about it?" I ask, trying to sound casual, like the memory isn't tattooed behind my eyelids.

He finally looks at me, and the force of it almost knocks me backward. His gaze is steady, unblinking. "You're acting like it didn't matter. Like it was just... some mistake I made," he says, voice solid as a rock, like maybe he had practiced saying that exact line multiple times. Like he had rehearsed it for this exact moment.

"Wasn't it?" My voice comes out sharper than I intended, a weak shield.

Easton shakes his head slowly. "No. Not to me." He drags a hand through his hair, like he's searching for the right words. "Tate, I've thought about kissing you for years. You're the most epic person I've ever known. Do you realize that? Everyone else comes and goes, but you've always been this…" he gestures toward me helplessly, "this hurricane that I can't get away from. And

I don't want to."

My throat tightens. He says it like it's the most obvious truth in the world. Like I should've known he's felt this way the whole time.

"I mean…" he exhales hard, his voice rough now, "you're brilliant. You walk into a room, and everyone can't help but notice. I can't help but notice. Always. Even when you're pretending you don't see me. You laugh and I feel it in my chest. And last night—last night was the first time I stopped pretending I didn't want you, Tate."

The words wash over me in waves, pulling me under before I can find the surface. My chest feels heavy, too full of everything I don't know how to say.

Epic. He called me epic.

But all I can think is…*he doesn't know the whole me.* He doesn't know the parts of me that have grown bitter. He doesn't know the way I've felt for the past five summers. He doesn't know how broken I've been, or how much of me shutting Florida out was about him. And the thought of Annie haunts me too. What would she say if she saw what we did last night or what he's saying to me right now?

I take a shaky breath, trying to build a wall inside myself before I drown in his sincerity and his dark brown eyes again. "You're just saying that because you're caught up in all this… nostalgia. We were kids, remember?" I throw his words from last night back at him like a weapon.

His jaw tightens. "Yeah, we were kids. But I'm not a kid anymore.

And I know what I feel now."

I look out at the horizon because it's safer than looking into his eyes. The ocean doesn't ask me to choose. The ocean doesn't demand I know how I feel.

Inside, though, I'm chaos.

What if he's serious? What if he means every word? What if I let myself believe him and then I'm the one left bleeding again?

And still, underneath all the doubt, there's a part of me that aches to believe him. That aches to let him hold me like last night wasn't a mistake, but a beginning.

There was a version of me that would have killed to hear him say these words. To hear him confess his desire for me.

I finally whisper, "Easton…" but my voice cracks, betraying me.

His hand brushes against mine in the sand, tentative, almost asking.

"Tell me you don't feel it too," he says, quiet but certain. "And I'll never bring it up again."

The air between us hums, electric, waiting for me to decide.

And the truth is — I don't know if I can.

The only truth I know right now is that the Easton I know wouldn't kiss me if he was with Annie, but my head is spinning too much to be sure. I stare at him, his words still hanging heavy in the salty air. His hand is so close I could close the gap in an instant, but instead I pull mine back into my lap.

The silence stretches until I finally find the courage to ask what's been gnawing at me since last night.

"What about Annie?"

Easton blinks, caught off guard. "What?"

I force myself to look at him this time, my heart pounding so hard it makes me nauseous. "You keep saying all these things, and you…" I swallow, the words scraping my throat. "You kissed me, Easton. Like it meant everything. But Annie…" I say as her name burns in my mouth. "Is that even real? Because if it is, then why would you do that to her? Why would you do that to me?"

He drops his gaze, jaw tight, like he's wrestling with an answer. For a moment, he doesn't look like the boy I knew or the man in front of me — he looks like someone caught between two worlds.

"Tate…" his voice is low, careful. "Annie and I… it's not what you think."

"Then what is it?" My chest feels raw, like the waves are crashing against me, breaking me down grain by grain. "Because from where I stand, it looks a lot like you get to play the good boyfriend and still kiss me in the kitchen when no one's watching."

He exhales sharply, dragging is hand through his hair again. "I thought I could make it real with her, I really did.

I tried. But the truth is, I've never been all in. Not with

Annie. Not with anyone. Because its always been you."

My breath catches, traitorous, like my body wants to believe him even if my brain doesn't.

Always been me?

But the other half of me screams: *If that's true then why*

Annie at all? Why not stay this loner? Why let me carry five year's worth

of silence alone?

I cross my arms tight against my chest, trying to keep my insides from spilling out. "That doesn't make it better,

Easton. It makes it worse."

Easton's eyes change, and suddenly he's not holding anything back. "You're right," he says, his voice sharper now. "It does make it worse. Because Annie's never been you, and I knew that from the start."

My stomach flips. I want to look away, but I can't.

"She's easy," he continues, his words tumbling out fast, like he's afraid if he stops, he won't get them out at all.

"She doesn't expect much from me. Doesn't push. With her, I could… pretend. Pretend that I was fine, that I didn't care about what happened with us. That I hadn't spent years replaying the last thing I said to you. Annie was safe."

Safe. The word stings more than I expect. Like a knife twisted in both our backs.

He shakes his head, his voice breaking just slightly. "But safe isn't love. Not the kind that rips you apart. Not the kind that makes you sit on the beach at dawn, just hoping she shows up, because you can't stand the idea of her not knowing how you feel."

I blink hard against the tears threatening to fall. He says it like it's the most natural thing in the world, but to me it feels like an earthquake splitting me open.

"Tate…" He leans in a fraction, his eyes begging me to hear him. "Every time I was with Annie. Or Izzy, or Ryan or any girl, I thought of you. Every time. And last night when I kissed you, it wasn't some accident or weakness. It was me finally doing what I've wanted to do for five years."

My chest feels like it's caving in, fighting between fury and longing.

He's using Annie as a shield. He kissed me knowing she was still in the picture.

He's saying everything I've ever wanted to hear, but it's tangled in something ugly. Something I don't know if I can handle.

I press my hands against my knees, grounding myself.

"Do you even hear yourself?" My voice trembles. "You just admitted she was a placeholder. That's not fair to her. And it's not fair to me either."

Easton flinches, but he doesn't look away. "I know it's messed up. But I can't take it back. All I can do is tell you the truth now." He steadies himself with a calming deep breath. "Me and Annie went on like three dates. We kissed in her car after the movies one time, but that's it. It was just a couple dates. I didn't even realize she thought it was more until you looked at me last night like I was the biggest hypocrite on earth."

The truth. Its lands heavy between us.

My heart stutters. "So, you're saying…" I trail off.

"I'm saying, I never promised her anything, and maybe I should've been clearer, but that's the truth. She's not my girlfriend. She never was. She's a girl I liked hanging out with when I didn't want to think too hard about what I really wanted." His eyes lock on mine, steady and unflinching. "But what I really wanted…was always you."

The words hit me like a wave, knocking the wind from my chest. All the anger I'd been clutching onto starts to slip through my fingers, leaving me exposed and shaky.

Always me.

I try to cling to my doubts — to the years of silence, to the things left unsaid. But he's right here. Closer than he's ever been, his voice raw and certain in a way I've never heard before.

"You drive me insane," he whispers, leaning in just enough that I can feel his breath against my cheek. "You make me feel like I'm alive and drowning at the same time.

No one else has ever come close to that. Not even for a second."

My chest burns, but this time it's not anger — it's the ache of wanting him, of finally letting myself admit how much I've missed this, missed *him*. Because he makes me feel the same way.

"I hate you for saying that," I whisper.

He gives a half-smile, soft and a little sad. "No, you don't."

Before I can stop myself, I turn toward him. My shoulders brush his, and it feels like setting down a weight I didn't know I was still carrying. His hand finds mine in the sand, warm and steady, and this time I don't pull away.

The truth is, I don't know what tomorrow looks like, or if I can forgive everything overnight. But right here, on this beach, with his confession echoing in my chest — I want to believe him. So, I let myself.

His hand tightens gently around mine, like he's asking permission without words. And for once, I don't resist.

Easton leans in slowly, almost cautiously, like he's afraid I'll change my mind or that I'll vanish if he moves too quickly. His lips brush mine, light and careful, nothing like last night's more desperate kitchen kiss. This one is softer, sweeter — the kind of kiss that feels less like a fire and more like a promise.

For a few seconds, the world goes quiet. Just the waves rolling in, the salt air, and the warmth of him.

When we pull apart, our foreheads linger together. It feels like we're sharing the same air. My chest aches, but it's a good kind of ache.

Then my phone buzzes in the pocket of Easton's sweatshirt that I'm wearing. The sound slices through the moment, making us both flinch.

I fumble pulling it out, my pulse still racing, and see my mom's contact flashing across the screen.

MOM: Hey, where are you guys?

"They want us back," I tell him.

As we stand to leave, his fingers graze mine, just enough to remind me of what happened here.

19

The Bubble

TATE

Easton held my hand the whole walk back from the beach but I dropped it before we walked inside. We haven't as much as labeled what we are yet, so we don't need our family members asking what we are if we don't even know ourselves yet. He gave me an understanding look as we joined everyone in the kitchen. I don't have to tell him why I dropped his hand because he already knows.

The kitchen is full when we walk in. Jessie's at the stove flipping more pancakes. Mr. Mills is sitting in his chair in the living room now, reading the newspaper like it's 1998. Walter is rummaging in the fridge for something, probably orange juice. He seems like the kind of guy who like orange juice. That must have been who my mom was referring to earlier.

"Walt? What a surprise," I say playfully standing at attention with my hand saluted like we did the other night. He does it back without any hesitation. His bleach blonde curls fall lazily around his eyes, and for once his eyes don't have a redness too them. I think, right now, he is completely sober. It's nice to know he's just as playful when he isn't

162

high.

"The pleasure is always mine, honey," he says, with the orange juice carton in one hand.

I smirk at the nickname he's given me. It's cute in a sarcastic kind of way. I think that's why I like it so much. When I glance over at Easton, his jaw is tight like it was the other night in the kitchen. He clearly doesn't like the nickname as much as I do.

"TATE KNIGHTLY!!!" A voice screeches from down the hall. A voice I haven't heard in years, but I'd know it anywhere.

I turn just in time. Lila tackles me like a football player, almost bringing me to the floor with the force of her hug. If she wasn't so tiny, she would have knocked me flat on my back. When she pulls away, she is bright-eyed and happy. She's barefoot and wearing one of Mr. Mill's old band tees. She looks different, skinnier, and her hair is cut right above her shoulders in a cute blonde bob. Growing up she had long wavy beach hair, but somehow this haircut fits her. Her body is petite and cute and her eyes are light blue, like the sky. The kind of blue you can't believe is real. She is beautiful in all forms of the word, just like she's always been. She squeals my name again out of excitement, arms wrapping around my shoulders so tight I swear she might squeeze my heart right out of my chest. She's so close, that for a moment I wonder if she can smell the vanilla sugar scrub of hers that I've been using.

"How are you? You look amazing!" I tell her.

"Thank you," she says posing for me with her classic duck lip/peace sign combo that was popular in 2012. It's a joke, because as kids we wanted big lips, so we made this stupid duck lip face all the time and added a peace sign for some reason. We thought we were so cool, until Easton started making fun of us for it. It became a signature joke between us three, because eventually his teasing us for it ended with him just joining in on the joke. We'd use it as a selfie face, or we'd do it as a signature sign off at the end of our weekly FaceTime calls.

Easton laughs at her and makes the same face, holding up a peace sign adding to the laughter from us all. And for a moment, it feels like all the summers before. All the summers when everything was normal. Everyone in the kitchen, us three laughing and smiling. It's just missing Nate and my dad.

Even though, somehow, it feels perfect.

Well, perfect isn't real. Perfect is sold to us by TV shows, movies, social media, cereal commercials, and makeup adds.

Just as Lila starts to tell me how she is, out of the corner of my eye, I notice an unfamiliar silhouette in the living room. Jet-black hair, parted just off-center, that falls in soft sheets down her back. Skin so light it glows against the couch.

Annie.

She turns her head just enough that I catch her side profile. The bridge of her nose points upward as she laughs at something Mr. Mills says. Her nose doesn't slope evenly; there's a little raised hitch in it. She smiles careful and calm as she listens to whatever Mr. Mills is talking to her about. She's wearing a big black *Guns and Roses* t-shirt that must be thrifted or a hand-me-down, because it has thinly worn holes everywhere. The white long sleeve she wears under her shirt almost blends in with her skin. She is translucent. Her jeans are baggy and have holes in them right above her knee. She's not looking at me yet. She doesn't even know I'm here.

I enjoy the last moments of calm we probably all have. I look at Easton to see if he see's her too. This moment feels like the calm before the storm. That big grin that was on his face just moments ago at the beach isn't there anymore. It's fallen onto the floor, wiped clean off his face.

He sees her.

He looks back at me, eyes wide. He smiles a shy smile. The one that still lives in my bones. But there's something flickering behind it… a question that I don't know the answer too yet.

What do we do? We didn't talk about this scenario. Or any scenario really. There wasn't enough time.

Lila catches our glance at each other and her eyebrows furrow together. "What's wrong?" She asks us both.

Easton and I exchange the same look at each other again. We didn't talk about what we'd tell our family either.

We should have been talking instead of kissing.

"Nothing, just so happy for all of us to be back together again," I say, because it's not a lie. It's not what I'm thinking. I'm thinking, *I kissed your brother.* But she doesn't need to know what I'm thinking right now. I don't see a world where that's productive. Especially since I know her feelings about that whole idea.

Lila always loved when we played the parents in house and she got to be the kid, but in real life, she was never super for the idea of us liking each other. When she was really little, she'd tease us about it because she thought it was funny. As she got older, she became less and less a fan of the idea. I can't imagine how she feels about it now.

I hug her again to alleviate the awkwardness in the air and it works. "God, I missed you, Lil," I say.

My face hurts now from how big my smile is. A pinch of the smile is nervousness, and the rest is pure joy of getting to see Lila in front of me again. I didn't realize how much I'd missed her until now. She smells like strawberries and vanilla and sparkles… if sparkles had a smell.

Her face is the same and different all at once. A little older. A little braver. Her face is slimmer, more mature, but her eyes still shine like they always have.

She walks toward the stove. "I saved you the last pancake," she grins. "Walter tried to steal it, but I threatened to break his drumsticks."

Walter shouts from the fridge, "She's not kidding!"

They share a glance that I can't quite put a feeling to. It makes my stomach twinge. Their look unsettles me for some reason. I make a mental note to ask Lila about it later, when we're alone.

I watch her as she moves. We have so much to catch up on. I don't know any of the things I should know about her. I don't know is she has a boyfriend. I don't know if she's had her first kiss. I don't know if she's thinking about where to go to college yet. I don't know why she cut her hair. I don't know anything.

I swallow my guilt.

Everything in me wants to tell her about Easton and what happened last night and what just happened at the beach. But something in me tells me to wait. To keep it to myself, so that's exactly what I do. Now is not the time.

Suddenly the air in the living room shifts — a soft throat clear, a polite little step close. The attention goes to Annie.

She crosses the space between us, moving like she's on a mission. Her hair is perfect — pin straight and shiny. It's unsettling, really. She seems more fragile standing in front of me than she did on the couch. Not fragile like sweet and precious, but fragile like frail and weak. She smiles at me with this small, practiced smile, attempting to look kind. But I see right through it. I'm not easily fooled. Something being an athlete teaches you is that people aren't always honest. Whether its coaches, partners, club directors, or other kid's parents… someone is always lying. I've gotten pretty good at telling the difference. Her smile is plastered. It's the smile she gives the cashier or the waitress or the little kids at Sunday school. It's painted on like the deep red lipstick she's wearing.

Ring ring… 2012 Taylor Swift called, she wants her lipstick back.

"Hi," she says, voice just an octave too soft. "I'm Annie.

I've heard so much about you. Tatum, right?"

I blink at Annie while my heart hammers a confused beat. *What do I say? I've heard about you to. I actually let who you thought was your boyfriend kiss me last night. Or hi, yes, I heard you were Easton's place holder. OR OR, Hi Annie I'm the girl you've heard about but clearly already hate.*

None of those feel fitting.

Before I can respond, Easton chimes in. "It's Tate. Tate, this is Annie. Lila's friend from church." *Ouch.*

I can feel Annie's pain as soon as those words leave Easton's lips.

"Oh, well, hello *Tate,*" she says my name like a curse word she's not allowed to say or something.

This whole thing was better when I thought I'd never have to actually meet Annie. Oh, what a nice time that was. More peaceful back then. I took those twelve hours for granted.

"Oh—hi," I say, not too excited, not too unenthusiastic, but trying to cover my annoyed state. I'm a lot of things but

I'm not fake. I won't plaster a smile on just to please her or anyone else around me. What you see is what you get.

"How was church camp?" I ask, trying to keep the conversation going, to be polite.

Annie nods like it was lovely. She tilts her head just a bit. "It was really good. Walter picked us up this morning. Easton was supposed to come to, but I guess he got… busy?" She questions, now looking at Easton like she's reminding everyone in the room that *she* came here for him or that *she* has some claim on him.

"Yeah, what's up with you bailing dude? What happened?" Walter asks.

"Didn't really sleep well last night."

Walter raises his eyebrows, knowingly and then scrunches his nose up with a slow nod. "Right, okay." Then he winks at us.

Great.

Annie looks Easton right in eyes, shooting daggers at him, and a bit angrier now than she was a moment ago, "Is that so?" She says through gritted teeth.

I look over at Easton, taking in his appearance. His eyes are tired. I feel a bit of pride in my chest that I'm the reason he yawns every couple of minutes and that his eyes droop a bit. But I know with the tired, disheveled state we are both in, even a simple man's mind could assume we were doing the worst of things all night.

Which we weren't, but we sure look the part right now.

Something shifts in the air. Jessie goes stiff at the stove. Lila scrunches her face up like she feels it too. Even Walter looks away, burying his grin with the carton of OJ he's drinking straight from. No cup. He really knows how to make himself comfortable. I kind of like that about him.

"You know, I'm super happy to meet you Tate. Easton wasn't sure you'd come back." Annie looks straight into his eyes, threatening something but I don't know what. "With the way he talks about you, I'm glad to even be in the same room as such a rock star." The way she says rock star makes it sound like a dig. But I give her the benefit of the doubt. She's got a lot going on right now. It does look like I'm stealing her man right now, so…

"No, I'm not a rock star. Easton's the one with the band."

"Rock on!!" Walter says with a punk rock tongue out face, making us all giggle a little.

"You know, I feel really stupid right now." She looks at

Easton with a glare, tears starting to well in here eyes. "I should have seen this coming."

Everyone in the room goes quiet. Annie has made it awkward, but no one moves.

"Can we take this outside?" Easton asks her quietly.

"Has he played you his newest song? What was it called again,

Easton?" She's starting to cry.

Everyone looks at him, awaiting an answer. Mr. Mills takes this as his opportunity to leave. He grabs his coffee mug and heads off to his study. Lucky duck, escaping all the drama just like that.

"He won't play it for me, but I saw it all written out. What was it called again?" She says, starting to get a bit hysterical.

"Annie, it's not what it looks like," Easton says, taking a step toward her but she takes a step back, keeping the distance between them. "Yikes," Walter says.

"Isn't it?" Annie says with a pound of hurt in her voice. You could hear a pen drop.

Lila looks at me and then at Easton. "Wait, what's going on?" she questions.

"I'm sure whatever's going on can be resolved. Let's all just take a breath," my mom says.

Jessie takes a step toward Annie, resting her hand on Annie's shoulder. "It's okay Annie, why don't you go talk to Easton in private? You guys can settle things, yeah?" she says looking over to Easton.

Annie moves away from Jessie's grasp. "The name of the song is *I love you like the Knight.* K-N-I-G-H-T," Annie says looking at Lila.

Lila's eyes go wide and so do mine.

I love you like the knight? He loves me?

And everybody else's in the room, except Easton's because he isn't surprised.

The song is about me. He does he loves me. So many thoughts run around in my head. I can't get them straight.

Walter breaks the awkward silence with the sound of his breath leaving his lips. The tension is high, and everyone can feel it.

"Let's go outside," Easton says without raising his voice.

He remains cool, calm, and collected, even in the heat of this moment. He puts his hand on the small of her back and leads her outside away from everyone.

Lila looks at me and the joy that was once behind her eyes, is gone. It's replaced with a look of betrayal. She shakes her head in disapproval.

"Guess everything's back to normal," she says with a hint of disgust.

She sprints toward her bedroom and I follow. When she gets to her room she turns, grabs the door and looks me dead in the eyes. "Welcome back I guess," she says as she slams the door.

I'm not sure how, but I end up in Easton's room.

I sink onto the edge of his unmade bed and stare at the wall where his old Marvel poster still hangs. It looks exactly the same as it did when we were kids, just hung on a different wall. Everything feels the same and everything feels different. The second I think I have something figured out, something decides to come back from church camp.

I mean, I just found out Easton likes me like an hour ago and now I find out he's written a song about me… confessing his love?

I blow out a heavy breath and tuck my hair behind my ears. I want to hear it more than anything, but with everything that just happened, I doubt that will happen anytime soon.

The floor creaks. I don't have to look to know it's him.

Easton closes the door behind him, slow like he's trying not to scare me off. Having the door closed feels like a sin. Growing up we weren't aloud to have the door closed, for obvious reasons. I guess now, we're old enough to be trusted.

He stays there by the door. His back against the wall and his hands shoved in the pockets of his old jeans. His eyes find me right away.

"Hey," he says softly, testing the waters.

"Hey," I say back, but my voice is thinner than I want it to be.

He crosses the room in a few careful steps and sits next to me, close but not touching. I can feel the heat of him, like a sun I can't decide if

I want to stand under or not.

"I talked to her. She wasn't happy obviously, but she understands," he says, rubbing a hand across the back of his neck. "I'm really sorry for the way she treated you back there and about what she said— about the a…"

I wait for him to finish the sentence but he doesn't, at least not the way I thought he was going to.

He sighs, "It's not… it's not what you probably think it is."

I swallow, my fingers curling into the hem of his comforter. "It sounds like you wrote me a love song." He hesitates and then looks at me. "Maybe." "When?" I ask.

"Uh-huh" he admits. His voice is quiet and a little unsure. "Like eight months ago. Right before Ryan broke up with me…" he stops himself, shaking his head.

"Why did y'all break up?" I ask him.

"I played her the song, hoping she would think it was good, but I guess she saw through it. She knew it wasn't about her," he admits

"Oh," I say shocked. Who knew, even though I was absent from his life I was still causing ripples?

"She said, *whoever she is, you should be with her. But she's not me.* And we never spoke again."

"I'm sorry."

I can't believe it.

"It's not your fault. None of this is. I'm the one that's sorry. I'm sorry for putting you through this and for putting everyone I date through the ringer just because they aren't you."

I laugh at him. He sounds like someone from a silly romcom.

He can't be serious.

"Don't laugh," he says.

"It's funny," I say with a half laugh. "You act like I'm this *Victoria Secret* supermodel or like Gracie Abram's or something."

"You're better."

"UGH, you being cute is gonna take me some getting used to."

"Well get used to it." He puts his hand on my cheek, pulling me into him.

He kisses me gently. I can feel his smile against my lips. He's happy. I can feel the happiness radiating off of him. I can feel his lips curl into a smile against mine. It makes me believe all the sweet things he said. It seals the deal.

I pull away, pushing his chest. "What made you suddenly want to confess how you feel to me? Why now?" I ask curiously. *I have to know.*

"Because…" he trails off as he kisses me, deeply, passionately and then just pulls away, his eyes still closed as I look at him. He opens them. He wears the sweetest look I've ever seen and somehow looks straight into my soul as he says, "That is exactly what I always thought it would feel like to kiss you. I spent so much of my life just wondering what it would be like, and it's better than I ever imagined. I thought I could just kiss you and that be it, but I can't Tate. I can't just kiss you and not want everything else too. Not when it's you."

"When it's me?"

He looks at me like I'm the only girl he's ever seen.

"Tate Knightly, it's always been you."

I look at him. I take in his hopeful eyes. They're dark, deep, and that soft brown that always looks a little sad when he's trying to be honest.

I can feel a smile forming on my face. I believe him. For the first time since being here, I fully believe that he's always been secretly in love with me the way I have been with him.

"Prove it," I say with a grin.

It's a dare. Not just the words I said, but the way I said it and the way I looked at him when I said it.

His head tilts a little to the side, like a puppy dog… unsure of how he could do such a thing. The darkening of his eyes tells me he knows exactly how to prove it to me. His bottom lip rest in between his teeth. He's thinking, questioning me.

I nod my head slightly, to tell him yes.

I want him to show me just how much he loves me. I can look in his eyes and know that he does, but right now I want to feel it.

His eyebrows furrow, still unsure of exactly how this works.

So, I lean in and kiss his cheek, as light as a feather. I start the kissing, even though I don't really know what I'm doing yet. I'm still so new to this. I just do whatever feels right. I kiss right above his cheek bone, and then right by his eye, and then his chin, and then the tip of his nose, and then his cheek (the spot right by his mouth). His breathing has sped up, forming a rhythm I want to join. I pull away just a little bit, still close to his face. He wraps a hand around the back of my neck, his face close to mine, our breath mixing. He smells like coffee and sugar and I love it. I want to taste it, but I don't lean in. The ball is in his court right now.

"I don't want you to think this is what I meant when I said I don't just want to kiss you. I meant like singing to you and making you coffee and driving to see you and…"

I cut him off, "I know what you meant Easton. I want all of that too."

He smiles, nodding slightly. "Okay, I wasn't sure if you did and…"

I cut him off again, "Stop thinking so much and kiss me."

And he does. His thumb brushes against my jaw, tilting my face up to meet his. For a second, I think he might pull away like he's changed his mind or something. But instead, he leans in, slow and certain this time, lips finding mine with a deep kind of hunger. It's not rushed or stolen. This one lingers. Easton's breath is weary against me, his hand sliding from my jaw to the back of my neck, holding me like he can't let go.

He doesn't just kiss me. He claims me.

His mouth presses into mine like he's been holding back for years, and I realize I've been holding back too. It's not careful like it was before. It's not safe. It's desperate.

My fingers find the hem of his shirt, curing into it like it's the only thing keeping me alive. I feel his laugh vibrate against my lips when I tug him closer. He pulls back for half a second, his eyes are dark, searching mine.

"Tate," he's whispers, like saying my name out loud makes this real. "Tell me to stop and I will."

I shake my head before I can even form words.

"Don't."

The moment the word leaves me, he exhales sharply, and then his mouth is back on mine — harder, slower, like he's pouring every ounce of restraint he's ever had straight into this kiss, His hands grip my waist, and I swear I can feel the tremor in them.

Everywhere he touches feels alive. His thumb tracing lazy circles against my hip. His lips brushing along my jaw before finding my mouth again. My hands are in his hair now, pulling, grounding, begging him to get closer.

It's messy. Breathless. My heart is racing so fast it feels like it's trying to break free of my chest. But in this moment, pressed against him, I know one thing for certain. This time, this isn't just a kiss. It's the beginning of something neither of us can undo.

Easton's mouth moves to my neck, then lower and back up until he's kissing the sensitive spot just beneath my ear. I grip his shirt tighter, my breath catching like he's stolen it straight from me.

"Easton," I whisper, and it comes out more like a plea than his name.

He groans quietly, the sound buried against my skin, and his hands tighten on my waist. One hand slides higher, rushing against my rib cage, like he wants more but he's still holding himself back. The restraint in his touch only makes me ache more.

When his lips find mine, again, it's hungrier. Sloppier. He kisses me like he's afraid we'll never get this chance again and I kiss him back the same way, because I don't trust tomorrow either

I pull at the hem of his shirt, lifting it up just enough to feel the warmth of his skin beneath my fingertips. His muscles shift under my touch. He exhales sharply, like I've undone something in him. He pulls back only far enough to look at me, his chest heaving.

"Tell me this is real," he says, voice raw.

"It's real," I breathe. "It's always been real."

That's all it takes. He lays me not so gently on top of his bed. He crawls on top of me and starts kissing me like its all he's ever wanted to do. He moves to my neck and back to my lips. He stops for a moment, resting his forehead against mine as if to steady himself. His hands are anything but steady. They roam my sides and my hips. He runs them up my stomach til he reaches my rib cage and pauses, as if to ask for permission. I smile and his lips crash into mine again, there's no hesitation left. It's just us unraveling in the only way we know how.

Together.

20

Let's Talk

EASTON

I can hear my own heartbeat in my ears as I walk down the hallway. It thumps like a threat: *Don't screw this up. Don't screw this up.* I can't believe I just said everything I've been wanting to say to Tate since she left so long ago. I can't believe I've kissed her, and it feels exactly how I've always dreamed it would. I can't believe she feels the same.

I'm upset at myself for how everything went down though.

The way Annie was here and the way she spoke about Tate when I took her outside to talk. I keep replaying it. Mostly because I feel bad for how it all went down.

Right outside the apartment door, Annie perched herself on the stair railing. Her legs crossed neatly, hands folded in front of her like she's waiting for an appointment. We just stood there in the silence. I realized I should say something since I'm the one who said we should come out here, but I was at a loss for how to explain exactly what's going on. I'm not even really sure I fully understand it myself. And every second I stand here makes my stomach twist tighter.

She seems softer than she was inside.

"Hey," Annie said, tucking a piece of her black hair behind her ear. She looks up at me with those big brown eyes. They were soft, careful, and a bit too open. She knew what was coming. I always liked Annie's eyes. They reminded me of

Tate's.

I'm terrible for even thinking that. My stomach flipped at the thought. I'm a terrible person.

I hate how careful she is with me. It makes whatever I was gearing up to say meaner somehow.

"Hey," I said back. My voice cracks a little. I clear my throat.

I leaned against the wall across from her. It felt stupid to stand so far away but I couldn't stand next to her right now. I needed the space. If I was any closer, she'd try to hug me or maybe even worse. I had Tate inside and I didn't want this to get messier than it already has. I fold my arms across my chest to help me stay still and look a little less nervous.

"Annie," I started, and immediately my chest knotted up because I didn't want to do this to her. I really didn't. She's a very sweet girl and she's Lila's best friend. She didn't do anything wrong except care more than I could.

"I wanted to talk to you about... about us."

She didn't flinch, like she knew this was coming. She just blinked. "Okay," she said.

I watched her face for any signs that she knew where this whole thing was going, but she looked good. She's always good at keeping her expression neutral and soft. Super unreadable. It's one of the things that made her so easy at first. She didn't expect much from me. I thought that would make things simple. It didn't. Still, I knew she could feel what was coming. How could she not?

"Annie," I said again, slower this time. "You know I care about you.

You're sweet. You're… you're good. But this… whatever we were doing… I don't think I should've let it happen."

Her eyes flicked away from mine, then back to me so fast I almost missed the flash of something sharp underneath. "Is this because she's here? Be honest with me Easton, I deserve that much," She asked me. "Because it feels like it's always been about *her*."

She didn't say Tate's name. Just *she*. It landed like a punch to my jaw. But she's right. She did deserve to know the truth.

I exhaled through my nose. "Yeah. Well, no, but… yeah… it is," I admitted.

Her mouth twisted, just a fraction. "So, what was I, Easton? Just a placeholder?" *Yes*.

"No—" I started, but she cut me off with this quiet laugh that didn't sound like a laugh at all.

"God, I should've known," she said, voice low but it shook a little with each word that left her mouth. "I knew it.

I knew the second Lila told me she was coming that this was gonna happen. I was sick the whole week thinking about how you would respond to her being here."

"Annie—"

She leaned forward, her hands folded together so tight her knuckles went white. "You know what's pathetic? I knew you were never really here when you were with me. I could see it. Your eyes were always somewhere else. on your phone, or out the window, or God-forbid writing a song about *her*. I'm such an idiot," she scoffed.

She spit the words like it burned her tongue. *Her. Tate.*

I closed my eyes, feeling ashamed for how careless I was with Annie and her heart. It wasn't intentional, but somehow that doesn't make it much better. "I'm sorry. I really am," I admitted truthfully although I don't think she believed me.

"Oh, you're sorry?" She huffed out a bitter laugh that sliced right through my rib cage. "That makes it better, huh?

You're sorry you strung me along so you wouldn't feel like you were alone for five seconds. Thanks for that."

"That's not fair," I said, sharper than I meant to. "I didn't do this to hurt you."

She sat back against the stair railing, arms still crossed over her chest, just like I was. "No, you did it because you're a coward, Easton."

I swallowed that comment because she wasn't wrong. I am a coward for leading Annie on and I'm a coward for not having told Tate how I felt so much sooner. "I should've told you sooner. You deserve better, I know," I tell her.

She tilted her head, letting her soft dark hair slide over her shoulders like a curtain. "No, what's not fair is that the whole time, you knew that I wasn't her. That's what this is right? You're picking her. After five years you're gonna run back to your little childhood crush?"

My jaw clenched. "I'm not running back. I never stopped—" I caught myself before all the words could leave my mouth. But the words that I didn't catch in time were out there now, hanging in the air like something alive. She put it together, none-the-less.

Annie's smile was small and meaner after that. I didn't know she could look that way. "God. She must love that. Sweet

Tate Knightly, stealing the boy she's had wrapped around her finger since she was born. It's perfect, isn't it?"

I hate that she was right. "Don't talk about her like that," I told her.

Her eyebrows shot up, slow and mocking. "Why? It's true, isn't it? She shows up and snaps her fingers, and you drop me just like that. You must be blind if you can't see that."

I uncrossed my arms and stood up. I couldn't take this. I wouldn't take this. My palms were sweating, my head was pounding. "Annie, this isn't about her stealing anything. You and I… we weren't gonna work. You know that."

She stood up too, eyes blazing, her voice low enough that the rest of the house wouldn't hear. "You know what pisses me off most, Easton? I liked you, like really liked you. And you used me to pretend you didn't still want her. And now you're gonna go back to her and she's gonna pretend to be sweet and innocent like she didn't just—"

I cut her off. "Stop. You don't know her. Don't talk about her like you do."

She laughed again. Harsh and sharp this time. "I know enough. I know she left five years ago and now she's back and you're crawling around at her feet like a lost puppy."

I looked at the floor because if I looked at her, I'd say something I'd regret later. I ran a hand through my hair, tugging until it hurt. "I'm sorry, Annie. I didn't mean to hurt you. But I can't pretend with you anymore. I won't."

She stepped back, crossing her arms even tighter somehow, hugging herself like she's the only one who can keep her warm. "Whatever. I'll go. Go play summer house with her. Just don't come running back to me when she's far away again."

Her words stung. They really did, but not enough to make me want anything to be different. And she's wrong about Tate. Tate's not leaving again. She's here now and I'm not screwing anything up this time. I'm not letting what happened five years ago ever happen between me and Tate ever again.

She took one last look at me. She's so hurt and angry. Mascara is now running down her face. I barely recognize the girl I kissed in my car for the first time a few months ago.

"I'm really sorry," I say again, but it sounded empty even to me.

Annie turned her face away so I couldn't see her eyes, then she left.

When I came back inside, I was scared for a moment that when I walked into my room Tate was gonna tell me that everything I had just said on the beach was misplaced and wrong, but she didn't. She let me explain it all. And I did.

I talked to her, I kissed her, I touched her, I loved her.

I've always loved her, and now she knows it.

Love is a silly thing though, isn't it?

I've known Tate since she was born. Me and mom were at the hospital when she was born. There isn't a version of

Tate that I haven't loved. She's stubborn and strong. She'll argue with a brick wall, but she also loves so deeply and fiercely that she'll break herself to show that she loves you. I've always known that it was supposed to be Tate and me.

Not because our mom's said so, or hoped so, or prayed so, but because for me, no one compares to Tate.

We're like this book that you keep up on the shelf and you read it every now and then. You've read it cover to cover and no matter how many times you read it, you love it even more each time you read it. I've had our story up on the shelf for as long as she's been around. No matter how far away she's been, or how how little we've talked, I've kept the book up on the shelf just in case. And now, I finally get the chance to start a new chapter with Tate. That book can finally have the ending I've always hoped it would.

For as long as I can remember, Tate Knightly has been mine. I don't really believe in soulmates or true love or the idea that there is only one person out there in the universe made for me. I think that's why I tried so hard with Izzy, Ryan, and Annie. I wanted to believe that if I tried hard enough, I could fall for them to the depths of what I had fallen for Tate. But no one was ever as sweet as Tate, in that genuine way that doesn't think twice before helping my mother in the kitchen, or helping Lila braid her hair. No one was ever as honest as Tate; she never spares me my feelings. She tells me the hard things, the things I don't want to hear but need to hear. No one was ever as blunt as she was about anything. Tate has this thing about her. It's this look that just captivates me. Her big hazel eyes look at me, and I can't help but fall into her. Her little button nose that scrunches up when she laughs, no one ever had that. I always used to tease her that she looked like a rabbit, but it was a positive thing when I said it, though I don't think she ever took it that way. No one was ever as humble as Tate. She'd give all she had at whatever she did and never expect anything in return. She never speaks highly enough of herself, even now. She spends her days pursuing her dreams and her nights dreaming about them, but she won't ever boast about the amazing things she's accomplished. Kora always has to mention them in a group of people. Tate's cheeks get all pink when Kora talks about the awards and wins, because she feels like it's bragging but really, it's just her. No one was ever as silly as Tate. No one makes me laugh the way she does. Maybe it's because we grew up together, but our humor is one in the same. When she's not around and I make a joke only she would laugh at, it's then I'd miss her most. No one has ever been Tate or anything like her, and maybe that's the issue. I've never wanted anyone to take Tate Knightly's place in my life.

I've spent five years trying to find someone to fit the void she left. No one fits but her.

* * *

I woke up with Tate asleep on my chest. It was the best sleep I've had in a long time, but especially since she's been here. I've always imagined this as something we'd experience some day.

For a while, I just stay here, letting our breaths fall into rhythm. I can't help myself from playing with her hair. It's so much longer than the last time I saw her. I love the golden hues that streak through her hair like the sun kissed her head. She smells like vanilla and sunshine, and I can't get enough of it.

I want this moment to last forever. I want to bottle it up and keep it on me at all times. But even the best moments have to end.

My mom cracks the door open quietly creaking it open one inch at a time. "Tatey?" She says just above a whisper.

I don't know what to do or where to go, but I don't want to wake Tate, so I don't move a muscle.

Mom freezes when she see's us. Her eyes get so big I think they'll pop out of her head. Slowly she brings a hand up to her mouth, covering it in shock. But to my surprise, she doesn't look mad. Not even a little bit.

"Oh," she says when he hands finally leaves her mouth. "Is this finally happening?"

"Shhh," I say as quietly as possible. I try my best not to move as I look up toward the door.

My mother's eyes question me again. She won't leave until she has answers.

"I hope so," I tell her.

She nods her head in understanding. "That explains earlier with Annie then," she sighs. She looks at us, studying the way we fit so perfectly together. She looks happy until her brows furrow together like she might be holding something back.

"What?" I ask, because I always love having my mom's opinion. She's one of the wisest women I know.

"You only get one shot with a girl like Tate, Easton." She says looking at her sleeping on my chest and then me again. "Do you think right now is the right time?" She questions.

I know what she's asking. *Are you ready to commit to this?*

Are you ready to commit to her?

I am, but I can tell by the look in her eyes, she doesn't think I'm ready yet. I ignore her eyes and say, "I know, mom.

I won't screw it up, I promise."

She nods as a smile creeps up her face. "You guys fit. I've always known that," she says.

"Me too," I say looking down at Tate's long eyelashes and freckled cheeks. *Oh how I love her freckles.*

"I support whatever's going on okay, but just please keep the door cracked," She threatens playfully.

I giggle a little, causing Tate to move around on my chest a bit. I think about what we could've done with the door closed, if we had wanted to, just a couple hours ago. I'm not really sure how Tate feels about all the physical stuff, but I want to take it slow. It's not about any of that with her. Just being looked at by her and talking to her is enough. But physical intimacy is a big part of relationships, and I know that. I personally haven't gone all the way with anyone yet. Not because I didn't want to, I just have this pit in my stomach at the thought of not waiting for my wife to go that far. I've run all the bases, a lot. But I've never crossed home plate.

I know Tate had a boyfriend back home. My mom showed me pictures of them when they first went public on Insta. He's a football player with blonde hair. I didn't really think that was her type, but I guess I haven't really been around her much as of late, so I wouldn't really know what she was into. I couldn't really imagine her kissing him. Sometimes when mom would mention this dude she was with, I'd get angry. Not like throw a punch angry, but I'd have a headache and want to be left alone angry. It bothered me to think somewhere out there was a football dude kissing my girl, or worse. I hope not worse.

My mom is religious. Not in the beat you with the Bible kind of way, but in a pray every morning and night, sings worship while she folds laundry kind of way. One thing she believes strongly in, is waiting til marriage to have sex. I try to honor that, as her kid, but if I was planning on breaking that rule, I don't think I could break it under her roof.

"Mom, stop, you know that's not what's going on," I tell her, because she knows we're both pretty innocent. Or at least she thinks we are.

"Hormones honey, they make you do crazy things at your age," she warns.

I guess she has a point, but it's different with Tate. I'd wait forever if it meant my first time got to be with her. I've always secretly hoped when I do go all the way, it would be with Tate. I think it's because I've always seen all the other parts of life with Tate too. I don't just see dating and kissing and superficial things. I see late night drives, grocery shopping, cooking dinner, waking up next to each other, traveling to see her, marrying her, having kids with her, having a home together. I see it all with Tate. She's the only person who I can see past today with.

Mom starts to close the door, but I stop her. "Mom?" "Do you think this is dumb? Me and her?"

She opens the door all the way and stares at me with the same look she gives me when I used to ask to drive the car to Walter's house on a school night.

"Do you love her?" She asks bluntly.

I take a deep breath and look at the beautiful, weird, stubborn girl in my arms. "More than anything," I say with more confidence than I've ever had about anything.

"Then no, baby, it's not stupid," she says, pulling the door almost closed behind her as she leaves.

I do.

I love Tate Knightly.

21

Is He Your Sweater?

TATE

The ocean air hits me before I even open the truck door. It's salty and warm, thick with the sound of waves folding over themselves just ahead of us. Walter kills the engine, but neither of us moves right away. For a second, we just sit there, our elbows almost touching on the middle console.

Walter DM'd me on Instagram after lunch and asked me if he could pick me up to hang. Easton is at one of his jobs, but I'm not sure which one. Lila still isn't talking to me, and the mom's have been running around shopping and trying new coffee places. So, it's been a bit lonely in the house. I've tried to talk to Lila, multiple times, but she won't have it. She just looks at her phone and walks away or pretends to get a phone call. My guess is that Easton asked Walter to keep me busy today while he's at work.

We haven't really said much since he picked me up.

The windows were down, and the music was loud the whole drive down to the beach, but now we just sit here in silence.

"Ready?" He asks, flashing that perfect cool-guy grin that makes him look half boy, half trouble. Easton makes him sound like a man child. Like he can't do anything for himself or like he doesn't know what he's doing. But he doesn't seem so clueless to me.

"Not even a little bit," I admit. "Especially since I don't know what we're doing," I add.

He laughs, tips his head back against the seat. The last rays of sun catch in his hair, making his messy strands glow golden. He's so different from Easton. He's lighter somehow. He doesn't seem to care for things as deeply as everyone else. Walter is like a breath of fresh air in a stale world. It must be nice not having to care so deeply. Sometimes I wish I knew what that was like.

"We're at the beach," he says, "Nothing bad can happen at the beach."

"You must have never seen Jaws," I laugh.

He doesn't laugh though. Easton would have laughed at that. Most things I say relate back to a movie reference or quote. It's that way with Easton too. That was one of the many things we had in common.

"You'll be fine. You just gotta have a little bit of trust," he says confidently.

I don't respond because I'm not sure how to. I think I might actually trust him, but I'm not sure why.

"You do trust me, right?" He asks me with his eyebrows furrowed.

I shrug, fighting a smile. "I guess."

"Rude," he says, mock offended. He opens his door, hops out and jogs around to my side before I can even grab the handle. He swings my door wide open, offers me his hand like we're about to step onto a red carpet instead of a messy beach. I appreciate him being a gentleman. I guess chivalry isn't dead.

It isn't until now that I realize we're alone. It isn't a big deal, I hang out with guys like this all the time back home, but this feels different. If Easton hadn't asked him to hang out with me, I might be worried Walter was trying to move in on me or something. I'm sure it's just his way of helping his buddy out though.

I roll my eyes but take his hand anyways. I can't let him know I think what he's doing is sweet. His palm is warm, rough from the drumsticks I guess or maybe it's from working out. His wash board abs and softball sized biceps make me believe he spends a good amount of time in the gym, or maybe it's from all the surfing. He does seem like the kind of guy who could casually rep out fifty pull-ups, just because.

Outside the wind lifts my hair, tangling it around my cheeks. I squint at the ocean. It's wide, blue and endless. I love it. It's really bright out. I reach back into the truck and grab my sunglasses.

I see a surf board sitting in the truck bed.

It looks longer than me.

"No. No no no. I don't surf," I say walking away from the truck, slightly annoyed.

Before I can get too far, Walter grabs my hand and pulls me back toward him and the truck. "Well, you're going to today."

My chest is heavy all of a sudden. If you think alligators scare me, think again, because sharks are a whole new level of scary. My favorite movie as a kid was *Soul Surfer*. Which is odd for someone who hates sharks, I know, but it definitely kept me out of the ocean. I've never been able to get past not knowing what's swimming under me.

"You're not gonna make me stand on that thing, are you?" I say.

He's still holding my hand, and I haven't let go. His hand is so much bigger than mine, it almost swallows my hand whole. We both become aware of it at the same time and Walter releases my hand, then playfully shoves my shoulder. "No, I brought it so we could use it as a dinner table. Of course you're gonna stand on it, TK"

Oh. Why did he call me that?

It's weird hearing Easton's nickname for me roll so casually off his tongue, but I find myself wishing he had called me *honey* like he did the other day.

He pulls the board out like it's weightless, tucks it under his arm, and starts walking backward toward the beach. The sun is right above the water, just about to disappear behind the horizon. The sight looks like something from a movie poster.

"Come one. Surf's decent. You know you want to," he teases.

I don't, but I follow him anyway. The sand is soft under my feet. I like the sound of my footsteps in the sand. It makes a squeaky noise with every step. When we reach the water's edge, he drops the board and turns to face me. The wind snaps at his shirt, tugging it away from his chest.

"Okay, lesson one," he says. "Panic later. Balance now." *How corny.*

"I'm not gonna be good at this," I say. "I have terrible balance."

I've tried to ride Nate's skateboard back home on multiple occasions. I'm never any good at it. He makes fun of me for it because no matter what I do or what he teaches me, I always fall. I doubt Walter will be any better of a teacher than Nate. Although, he might be more patient.

Walter tilts his head, "You're an athlete, no? Like going D1 kind of athlete. Aren't freak athletes supposed to have good balance?"

He lays the board down in the sand and kneels down beside it.

"I'm not a freak athlete," I admit.

"Easton begs to differ. Have you ever even tried to surf?"

He asks

I shake my head *no*.

"Then you don't know yet," he says as he pats the board.

"Hop on," he instructs me.

I look at him, then at the board, then back at him. "On the sand?" I ask confused.

"Did you think I was just gonna throw you into the water? We gotta make the sharks work a little harder than that yeah?" He says, accompanied by a soft laugh.

"I don't know, I kinda thought you'd feed me to the sharks to be honest." I say.

"Nah, not yet," he says, rolling his eyes. "With the way you're looking at me right now, I doubt we'll ever make it out there."

"I didn't realize you were looking at the way I look at you," I say turning the question back on him.

"Well—" he stutters, and I can feel the awkwardness creeping into the air. I said it as a joke, but he seems to be scrambling for words. But before he can say anything, I pull off my jean shorts and t-shirt and toss them on the ground, leaving me in my bathing suit.

"Teach me how to surf, Walt. I'm ready," attempting to push the awkwardness out of the air.

I sigh, toes on his board now, and as I plant my feet where I would imagine my feet should go. Walter steadies the board with one foot.

"Yes ma'am," he says, stepping close enough that I smell the sunscreen he applied the first time he came to the beach today and whatever cheap cologne he's wearing.

It's a mix of salty and sweet. "Bend your knees. Arms out.

Look ahead, not at your feet. Never look down."

I obey, mostly to what he teaches me. I'm a great surfer, if the objective is to surf sand. Which honestly sounds fun and safer. I guess in some ways, as a beach volleyball player, this is kind of my territory.

I haven't forgotten about the sharks though. I keep messing up on purpose in the hopes that it will get dark and we won't be able to go out into the ocean.

He stands right behind me, helping me with my hip placement. "Sideways. Not forwards," he says.

His hands hover near my hips like he's ready to correct me if I decide that "my way" is more sufficient than his. The second I try to shift my weight, his hands gently grip my hips and move them back into the correct position.

"Watch it," he says with a teasing laugh right in my ear. "Just do this and you're ready for the water." *Ugh.*

NO. No water.

He lets go of me, like he realizes just how he's holding me.

"Easy for you to say," I murmur.

His smile softens. For a second, he looks at me like he wants to say something else, something real, but then he just pats my wrist, pulling me toward him and out of the way.

"So, where's Easton today?" he asks me.

"He's at work. That's why you're hanging out with me, right? Because he asked you to?"

"Uh, no. I didn't know what he was up to. I just wanted to hang out." *Crap.*

"Really? Why?" I ask nervously.

You're telling me that this super cute bleach blonde surfer boy who happens to be my kinda boyfriends' best friend just randomly wanted to hangout with me?

"Because I wanted your company... is that not ok?" He asks like we're old friends who hang out all the time but, we aren't.

"No, it's just... can I ask you something?" I say.

I want to switch the subject. There's no way a good-looking guy like Walter doesn't have a girlfriend. Since Lila isn't talking to me, I haven't gotten to ask her about Walter, so I'll ask him instead.

"What's going on with Lila?" I ask him.

He looks down at me, eyebrows furrowed and confused.

"Lila Mills?"

I shake my head *yes.*

"Nothing. Why?"

"I don't know, the other day in the kitchen I just thought

I caught a vibe or something between you two. And you picked the girls up, so I thought maybe..." I trail off, not really knowing how to explain what I thought.

"No, Lila's like my little sister."

"You don't think she's beautiful?" I say, shocked. Lila is definitely beautiful.

He thinks for a moment. "She's attractive, she's just not my type."

Hmmm, I guess I was wrong.

"What is your type?" I ask him.

His eyes stare deep into my eyes, searching for something. He looks at me like what I asked him is a trick or something. He breaks eye contact and looks past me at the ocean, the skyline, the sunset.

"Actually, we'll get in the water another day. The sun's getting real low." He picks up the board and starts walking back to the car, avoiding my question.

I laugh at his unintentional Black Widow/Hulk reference.

I love a *Marvel* reference.

The sun is getting lower, but we still have time to get in the water. Even though I previously didn't like the idea.

"What? We're not gonna surf?" I ask him, standing right where he left me, pointing back at the ocean.

The sun kisses the horizon, spilling gold all over us. The sun is giving him this golden hue. It's angelic.

He turns back to face me, but he doesn't say anything.

He's staring through me and suddenly, I'm confused.

What is going on? His silence makes me anxious he's gonna say something he shouldn't.

"Okay, we'll go," I say. I grab my clothes and walk past him to the truck.

Something just shifted and for the life of me, I can't place what. I'm starting to wonder about Lila. Maybe something did happen between them, and I just struck a nerve. But even if that was the case, I don't know why I struck a nerve. He's the one who wanted to come out here in the first place.

In the car, we sit next to each other quietly, again. I keep my arm in my lap this time. It feels dangerous to put my elbow up on the middle console again. Walter's playing a mix of 2000s bands. That's the only sound that fills the air for a while. I look over at him while he drives. His blonde locks fly around in the wind. His skin is tan, like a Greek god, except for a little patch of skin on his nose that's slightly burnt. If he was a Greek god, he'd be the son a Poseidon. His eyes are a deep blue just like the ocean, but they've turned a deep grey now as he focuses on the road in front of us. I think about how Easton had described him to me — a preacher's kid, with a rebellious side or something like that. But other than the redness in his eyes from smoking weed, he didn't seem like such a bad guy.

"Why do you smoke weed?" I ask him, to break the silence.

He doesn't look at me, but he responds. "I like it." "That's it? You just like it?" I persist.

"Yeah."

"But don't people who smoke weed to like try and escape something? You know, like they don't like their reality or something?"

"Are you diagnosing me with depression?" He asks with a sarcastic scoff.

"No no no, I'm just curious what you're trying to escape," I admit honestly.

He thinks for a moment, "My dad's a preacher and my mom's on the board at the country club. So, most of my life is church services and family service hours at the homeless shelters or country club dances or shit like that. I like that stuff, but I don't love it like my parents do."

"What do you love?"

"When did we start playing twenty questions?"

I wait for him to answer me, hoping the silence draws out an answer.

"I just want to drum and catch waves, you know. I want to soak it all in before I'm an adult and I have bills and a wife and kids. If I had my dream, me and Easton would make it big as a band out in Nashville. We've talked about going there. Even if he doesn't go, I think I will," he says with a smile creeping on his face for the first time since leaving the beach. He glances over at me, nudging my arm. "What do you love?" he asks.

"No no, you're playing twenty questions. Not me."

"Come on, I already asked. Please?" He leans over and bats his eyes, barely looking at the road.

"Fine! Just keep your eyes on the road. I don't want to die,"

I say harshly.

He turns back to face the road with a laugh.

"I love my family, good coffee, movies, you know stuff like that," I tell him.

"Don't hold back on me now. I know you love more things than that. You're like dripping in drive and passion. Tell me about it."

"I don't know," I tell him. I don't ever really talk about my dreams out loud anymore. That was Easton and I's thing and when I left, I kept it like that. I just don't talk about it.

"You know," he says. "I have some weed if you think that will loosen you up."

"I'm an athlete. I don't do that stuff," I defend.

"OK then. I'll just keep driving around the block until you decide to tell me," he teases throwing me a smirk.

Someone's in a better mood.

I believed him. He would hold me hostage until I answer honestly. I take a breath and think about my response. I release a long breath because I know nothing, but the truth will satisfy him." I love beach volleyball and honestly, it's the only thing I've been really focused on for years now because I love it. But it consumes all my time, and I don't know... I feel like I'm missing something. Everyone tells me they love the way I play volleyball you know, it's like out of the box and creative, and recently I've just been thinking a lot about that. Because I come home from practice and tournaments and I'm always like…angry or frustrated. It used to make me so happy and bring me so much joy, but, it just doesn't anymore."

I take a big breath because I just said all of that like I couldn't get it out fast enough. Walter doesn't react the way I think he's going to. He just sits there and looks at me.

Like what I said isn't the most bizarre thing he's ever heard.

"Okay. So, you don't love beach volleyball. I asked you what *do* you love… but I love the passion."

He's right, so I tell him. "I love to write. Poetry mostly, but also, I love movies. I think I want to follow in my dad's footsteps with like movies and stuff. So, I've been thinking about writing a screenplay. And I want to act and model. I know it all sounds outlandish and like a lot of different things but that's exactly what I want it to be. I want to be all those things because I don't want to just be one thing and right now, I'm just a volleyball player. In my head and in my bones, I know I'm so much more than that."

Walter doesn't say anything at first, he just keeps driving and then he does the last thing I think he'd do. He laughs.

"That's like super insensitive Walter, I just poured my heart out to you, okay? I haven't told anyone that… like ever,"

I say looking out the window and even though I don't want to admit it, his laugh is making me feel stupid. Maybe having dreams like that is stupid. I just confessed all this to him, and he doesn't even care.

"What, honey, no no." *Honey.*

That does something to me. I don't know why. It's like an old couple pet name, but it makes my stomach do somersaults every time he says it.

He continues, "I'm laughing because when we get out of the car, I'm gonna have you sign my board. Do you know how much that's gonna be worth when you make it big?" He says with a little laugh.

I can't tell if he's serious.

"Will you pretty please write me into one of your screenplays. I am willing to dye my hair, but I draw the line at cutting it."

Now I'm the one laughing. He's being serious.

He rambles on, "Do you think I could act, like seriously. You could write like the next *Mr. And Mrs. Smith* for us. Think about it. You give me like bad ass Angelina Jolie vibes, but the real question is… do you think I can pull off Brad Pitt?"

He looks at himself in the rearview mirror fixing, his hair and making a ridiculous smolder face, checking himself out. I actually do think he cold pull off roles like Brad Pitt., but he definitely strikes me as more of a Matthew McConaughey. Walter has this stature, like he knows exactly who he is. He has a nice face and a pretty Hollywood smile. And he has that mop of blonde curls on his head. He's a casting agents dream. At least I think that's what my dad would say if he saw him.

"Yeah, you have that look about you. I'll keep you in mind,"
I tell him.

He pulls into the apartment complex, parks the truck and leans back against his headrest. "You didn't mention Easton at all," he says softly.

"What?"

"When I asked you what you loved. You didn't say
Easton. I guess I just kind of thought you would." *What's the point he's trying to make?*

"Okay, so I didn't. Does that matter?" I say.

"I don't know. Do you love him?" He asked me bluntly without making eye contact.

I overheard Jessie talking to Easton the other night. He admitted to loving me to her while I was lying on his chest, but he hasn't directly said it to me yet.

But do I love him? How does one answer that? I don't know what romantic love feels like. Whatever I had with Ryder definitely wasn't love, so does that make what I feel for Easton love?

I sit with Walter's question for a beat too long. He looks at me, and I realize I haven't answered him yet. I wonder how long we've been sitting in silence.

"Between you and me, Walt. I don't know. I just spent five years thinking Easton hated me. And now… well now I know he doesn't hate me. I'm still coming to grips with that, I think."

"But you know he loves you. Either you love someone or you don't Tate. It's not science," he says plainly.

I've always loved Easton. I know that. Our parents know that. Lila knows that. Even my bones know that. But I haven't told him I love him.

Something in my stomach knots up. If I tell Easton I love him, it means forever. It means I'm his and he's mine. Even though we've always been each other's in some way, if I admit to loving him romantically to the the depths that I do, then there's no turning back. Our friendship will be ruined, because we'll be two people in love. Right now, we're two friends who have always loved each other — that's it.

"What is love anyways?" I ask him. "How do you know something is truly love?" I say looking out the window in front of me. I'm not sure if I'm asking him or myself.

He's silent for a moment, then he says, "For me, when I feel love… I feel it here," he says pointing at his chest. "My heart starts to pump different around the person I love. I become aware of every rise and fall of my own chest. It tightens when they look away from me, and it warms when their eyes meet mine. I feel all the abundance of love and all the lack of it, right here." His right hand hasn't left his chest. "Love is easier to feel when it's with someone you just met. Until they walked into your life, you only know their absence. You don't realize you want or need them until they show up right in front of you. You live your whole life wanting this person who you don't even know yet. You don't know what they look like or how they sound or where they're from, and then one day they just show up in your life and you just… know." He looks deeply into my eyes. "And you can't get them out of your head, and your chest is tight all the time because, because you just… want them." He pauses.

What is he saying?

He looks away for a second and then finds my face a again and continues, "But when that person is someone who's been in your life forever, it can feel like… like…" he searches for the words like their loose in the air waiting for him to grab them. "Like when you find your favorite sweater at the bottom of your closet after a long time of not knowing where it was. You know you didn't get throw it away or donate it to Goodwill, because how could you do that to something you love so much. You know you didn't sell it and you know you didn't let your best friend borrow it, because you love the sweater entirely too much to share it. But when you find it, you realize it was in your closet the whole time. It had just fallen off the hanger and gotten covered by some other stuff. You put it on immediately, it's familiar and fits just right. You want to wear it everyday, because nothing in the world feels as good as that sweater does to you. You won't take it off, because how could you?"

What on earth is he trying to say? I can't believe I let him drive me this high.

He looks at my lips and then back up to my eyes. He says, "To me, it's one or the other you know?" He's rambling and I'm not sure why.

"I don't get it," I tell him.

He lets out a sigh. "When you've loved something for so long you can't really picture your life without it, but really you've already been living without it. You know?" He says, but it just leaves me more confused.

"It's your favorite sweater but you only love it because you loved it so long ago. And truthfully, are you gonna wear it everyday or just... when you want to feel comfortable?" *Oh.*

He faces me, leaning over the center console a bit. "Is Easton your sweater?" He asks looking deep into my eyes. He's trying to tell me something with his face, but I can't read it. I don't know his eyes as well as I know Easton's.

I can't read Walter's eyes.

"Because he's a good guy Tate, but I don't know if he's ready for you. And he deserves to be worn more than when you just want something familiar. And you deserve something you want to wear everyday," he says with his face is too close to mine.

My breathing picks up it's pace, but I slow it by backing away from him.

How the hell would he know what's good for Easton or me?

"So you think I'm too good for Easton?" I ask, my anger visible.

"Yes," he says bluntly.

My eyes search his face for some sign of regret for his brutal honesty, but there isn't a drop to be found. He means every word.

"You're a bad best friend," I say, intending to hurt him.

He doesn't react how I hoped. He looks down at my lips again. "We both are, just for different reasons."

"Best friends don't hit on their best friends girlfriends," I accuse him.

"Best friends don't waste each others time either," he says.

That hurts, but part of me knows he's right. If I told Easton I loved him, I'd be wasting his time. I'm not gonna up and move to Florida just because I want to date him and be with him. I'm about to go to college and compete at the D1 level and Easton wants to go to Nashville to sing and perform. It doesn't make any sense.

I won't let Walter get to me like this. Me and Easton have always been in the cards. We'll figure it out somehow, because we have to.

"He'll leave everything for you," he says softly. "But you won't leave everything for him." It's like he's reading my brain as I think.

"You're wrong," I tell him.

"I hope I am," he says with a broken smile.

He looks at me with his heavy puppy dog eyes, that say *yes, I like you.* Because only a person who likes you can look at you like he's looking at me. This look in his eyes, is unsettling. It's hungry and sad and curious.

I'm sweating and my hands are fidgeting. As I look at him, I realize that he's not dumb or unaware. He knows exactly what he's doing by inviting me to go do something. He knows what he's doing by getting me alone and he knew what he was doing by not telling Easton about it? He knew what he was doing by accepting my dreams and making me laugh and holding my hand for too long and grabbing my waist. He knows exactly what he's doing when he looks at me with those big, blue, ocean eyes and blonde Greek god curls. *Walter likes me.*

My stomach drops. For a moment I feel something I've never felt for Walter.

A singular butterfly takes flight.

I scrunch my face up, mad. I swallow hard, trying to push the butterfly down in my stomach.

Not now.

I just got Easton.

I won't let Walter mess this up.

"Thanks for the surf lesson," I say getting out of his truck and slamming the door shut.

* * *

Five years. It took Easton five years and who knows how many girls to confess his feelings for me. *Why did it take that long?* In a way I feel like I've been waiting for him. That moment we had on the beach felt like it was always supposed to happen. Even though I tried to ignore it, I knew me and Easton were bound to happen at some point. I think when I boarded the plane to come here, I knew something was going to happen.

There was so much left unsaid between Easton and I.

The moonlight shines on my journal, as I scribble little doodles. I can't get Walter's question out of my head.

Is he your sweater?

Do I love him?

How dare he ask me such questions. How dare he look at me with those eyes and look at me like he feels things for me. I can't believe him.

Before going to the beach with Walter, I thought I knew exactly what I wanted. I wanted Easton. But what Walter said rings in my ears… I don't think he's ready for YOU. He said you like I was a hurricane or a forest fire or something that comes in and destroys a town, or a house, or a family. I can't help but feel like Walter might be right.

What if Easton is my sweater?

I think he is. The question is… is that a good or bad thing?

What if everything we have feels so perfect because I've always known him? What if we hold each other back? What if everything we have is bound to break because we aren't made to be more than what we are right now? What if Walter's right?

The only problem is that he didn't get lost or magically disappear, I took him off the hanger and threw him on the ground five years ago.

And now that I "found" him again, do I even have the right to put him back on? UGH, I hate this analogy because it's so confusing but it also makes perfect sense.

What if by keeping him in my closet, I'm keeping him from being something else like… a blazer or something. Or someone's everyday shirt, you know, like Walter said. He deserves to be loved like that. Can I do that?

Maybe he is my sweater.

But to Easton, I am the girl who lost him on purpose. I am the girl who tried to forget him.

I look down at my journal and realize what I've drawn. A curly headed boy with bright eyes. The kind of eyes you can drown in. The boy's shoulders are strong, like a surfer who carries his board while he runs to the water every morning. His lips are full, and he's laughing.

I know him, his name is Walter Hughes.

22

Your Dad's Bedside Table

TATE

I avoided Easton like the plaque when he got home. I was worried he'd smell the guilt and uncertainty on me. I was on the back porch when he got home, so he didn't see me. He texted me he was getting cleaned up, so when he took a shower I snuck into his room and got under the covers. I don't know what to think or feel, so I pull the covers up to my chin and close my eyes. Maybe if my eyes are closed, tears won't fall as easily.

Why am I like this? Why when I feel things do they feel like the only thing I can feel? When I was with Easton on the beach, all I felt was the longing I've felt for him for years. It's the spark I always knew we had and we'd finally gotten to ignite it. Why then if I felt that way on the beach, did I feel guilty when I heard him tell Jessie he loves me? *Why? Why? Why?*

These must be the hormones Jessie was talking about. I can't seem to control them. They have a mind of their own. I can't trust my feelings anymore. They change too much. I must listen to the facts. That's what my dad would say. He would tell me to make a list of all the factual things. So, that is exactly what I do.

FACTS:

1. Easton loves me.
2. Walter… I think likes me… Wait no, that s not a fact because he hasn't actually said but…
3. Walter has feelings that I don't understand.
4. Easton is the first boy I've ever liked.
5. Easton gets me. Like the real me. The me I've always been.
6. Walter is Easton's best friend.
7. Easton doesn't know I went to the beach with Walter.
8. I subconsciously drew a picture of Walter in my journal.
9. Easton loves me.
10. And I lo…

My mental list gets interrupted by Easton quietly walking through the door.

"Oh, hi," he says, surprised to see me, but also happy too. He flashes his perfect smile in my direction.

A smile forms on my face as I look at his shape in the darkness of the room. The bathroom light shines through the doorway behind him, giving Easton and his muscle's a backlit spotlight. His hair is wet, leaving drips all on his face and chest. My eyes make my way from his eyes to his towel that sits low on his hips. His abs are defined, sharp, and strong.

"You like what you see?" He adds, but he doesn't chuckle in his usually playful manner. He's really asking me.

I do enjoy the sight in front of me, but I think I'd like it better if I could touch him.

Suddenly, everything I was thinking has washed away. All I can think about it Easton.

"I don't know, I think I need a closer look," I tell him.

He walks up to me, shoulders back, eyes locked on mine. He is my ultimate temptation. When he gets to me, he grabs my chin, gently making me look at him. I guess the angle of my face is now making my eyes more visible to him than they were before, because the second he see's them his face changes from sexy to worried. Although his concerned face is still pretty sexy.

"What's wrong?" He asks me.

I shake my head. "Nothing," I assure him, hoping he doesn't press me. "Just kiss me." I add as I try to lean up toward his lips, but he stops me. He sits down beside me, gently.

"What's going on TK?" He asks, face full of worry.

I shake my head again, silently begging him not to make me talk to him. I don't know what'd I say. "Whatever it is we'll get through it. You're the strongest girl I've ever known," he continues as he pulls me in for a hug. He smells like his manly body wash, like pine and cinnamon. His wet hair now dripping on my shoulder, but I don't mind. He pulls away and looks at me with the same amount of concern as before, "You don't have to tell me, but look at me. If it's too much to carry, I will take it and carry it for you. OK?"

He loves me. That's what he just confessed.

The truth is, he's confessed he's loved me before. Hearing him tell Jessie the other night was just the first time I heard a verbal confession. It's phrases like that, where he tells me he'll carry my burdens for me, that make me realize he's loved me for longer than I've known. I was always just too blind to see it. So caught up in my own feelings that I didn't realize just how much he cares for me.

Because isn't that what love it? Isn't love sacrificial? Isn't love laying your self bare in someone's arms and trusting that they won't hurt you? Isn't love handing someone a loaded gun and trusting that they won't pull the trigger? Isn't love, just that?

But how can I tell him that today at the beach with Walter, for a moment my heart fluttered for him? How, after this week, could I tell him that? I don't want to tell him that. I don't even think he needs to hear that. It doesn't matter anyway.

Sitting here, looking into his big, beautiful, brown eyes, I know what I want.

The ocean is scary and cold and vast. It's dark, mysterious, and ever changing. The ocean is wild and free and doesn't know where to stop. The tide, it pulls you in, but it never lets you up for air.

I much prefer the forest. It's dependable and kind. It's homey and forgiving. It's warm and strong, like the coffee that I drink each morning. It's dependable and loyal. It's bark is rough, but the wood underneath is soft and smooth. And when I look in Easton's eyes, that's what I see — the forest.

I want to tell him what Walter said, but really what did he say? He questioned my feelings for the boy I've loved for my entire life. What difference will it make if I tell Easton about the beach and the surf lesson? It doesn't change anything.

I want Easton. Just like I always have. And I want him now.

"I love you too," I say it like I've said it a thousand times before.

Easton's eyes go wide. That's not the response he was expecting, nor was it what I intended to say. But I feel it when I looked in his eyes. I feel every single butterfly that's ever lived within the cage of my ribs take flight

when he looks at me. Only he can do that. Only my Easton Mills.

"You do?" he says, still in shock.

I nod my head, pulling his face to mine. "I think I always have," I admit.

Right now, in this moment I don't know why I was even making a mental list in my head before he walked in. This is all there is. Him and me.

"No one's home," I say, even though I know he knows that too. I bite my lip before I say anything else stupid. But right now, I want him. All of him.

"I know," he says, paired with his boyish laugh this time. He wipes a tear from my face. My whole face fits in his hand. I like feeling this little. As an athlete, it's not often I don't feel like the biggest person in the room. But next to him I feel small, but not in a meek way. He makes me feel feminine. He makes me aware of who I am.

He's looking through me. If he could read my mind, he wouldn't still just be looking. He'd be all over me, like I want him to be. He doesn't seem to get what I'm implying by mentioning how we have the whole apartment to ourselves. I can think of a couple ways we could productively fill our time. We're just not on the same page... yet. I take his hand off my face, and he's full of concern again.

"You can tell me stop," I tell him slowly.

He laughs his little boyish laugh, quieter this time. "You're not doing anything," he says. He's never been more clueless in his life than he is in this moment.

How can he not feel that I want him closer?

I put my finger on his lips. Not shushing him, just pressing my finger into his bottom lip, gently.

"What are you—?" He starts.

I drag my finger down his face, down his neck — slowly, taking my time with it. His confusion is dissipating by the second. When my finger drags over the little dip by his throat, he lets out a breath I don't think either of us knew he was holding. His chest is rising and falling faster now, and his face softens. I think he's getting the hint. I drag my hand down his chest, feeling every dip and crevices of his muscles on the way down. I'm not looking at his eyes anymore. My eyes follow my hand, taking him all in. My hand gets as low as it can, until my hand rests on his towel.

"Wait," he says. He's looking straight into me. He's not upset. He's flush, and his face is full of curiosity. "We can't," he adds, fighting everything in him.

"Why not?"

His eyes go wide, shaking his head. "Because…we…"

"Can't? Won't? Don't want to?" I ask him with.

I lean into him, hand still on his towel. "I don't want to rush it Easton. But I know I want it to be with you," I admit. I get as close to his lips as I can without kissing him. "What do you want?" I ask him.

He doesn't answer me. I can feel him wanting to give in. If he told me right now that we should wait to make such a big leap I would respect that, because honestly, he'd probably be right. But right now, all I know is that I love him and I want to know what it's like to be his. Fully and complete his.

He stays quiet, closing his eyes attempting to focus. I guess he can't focus and look at me at the same time. He shakes his head in disapproval and I play out the next thirty seconds in my head. He's gonna say we should wait, and I'll say he's right and we won't take this step for who knows how long. But he doesn't do that. He crashes onto my lips pulling me into him. He kisses me like he's finally giving in to everything we've been denying. It isn't rushed. It's desperate in the most controlled way. Like he's thought about this moment before. His hands find my face, holding me there, like if he lets go I'll disappear.

He looks at me like I'm not real.

I tug him closer by his towel, not because I'm bold, but because I'm terrified he'll change his mind. His breath mixes with mine when he finally pulls back just enough to whisper, "Tate… have you ever done this before?"

I shake my head, "No," I say. My voice is shaky, but honest. I've never wanted anyone else enough to even imagine this, I don't ask him if he's ever done this before, because honestly, I don't really want to know.

His eyes soften instantly, like the weight of what I just admitted matters more than anything. "Me neither."

Something about him admitting that makes me fall for him all over again. He could have lied. He could have played it off. But he's here, as vulnerable as I am.

"Okay," I whisper. "Then we'll figure it out… together."

The way he kisses me after that feels different. Softer.

Slower. Like he wants to memorize every inch of me. His

towel slips, but he doesn't even notice, because his hands are everywhere else. They're running through my hair, tracing down my spine, pulling me against him until there isn't any space left between us.

I sink back into the mattress, pulling him with me, my heart pounding so loud I'm sure he can hear it. He stops, hovering just above me, searching my face like he's looking for any sign of hesitation.

"Are you sure?" He asks me.

I nod, smiling at him.

He kisses me with a smile I can feel against my lips. He pulls his sweatshirt off my body, and I push my shorts off. Leaving me in nothing but my little blue bra and black lace thong.

He stops everything to look at me. It's not more skin than he's seen when I'm in a swimsuit, but somehow right now, it feels different. "Whoa." He says and I kiss him, pulling him down on top of me.

"It's just me," I say attempting to calm whatever nerves he has.

He smiles until he realizes something. "Shoot, I don't have a…a…" He trails off. *Shoot is right.*

I love that he doesn't have a condom. I love that he doesn't have some, just in case. I love that he doesn't have one buried in his wallet. He really is more innocent than I give him credit for.

I rack my brain as to where we could find one? "Your dad's beside table," I blurt out. His face scrunches up, "Gross."

"It's not like it's used," I giggle softly.

"Won't he know I took one?"

"You think he counts his condoms?" I ask with a smirk.

"I don't know how much my parents do it… maybe?"

But then he says, "Fine." He wraps his towel back around his waist and runs off. He comes back, but it takes him, longer than I originally anticipated. He comes back, dropping his towel and joins me on the bed. "You already put it on?" I ask, surprised.

"Yeah, I didn't want you to see me not know how to use it, so…"

I laugh, not at him but with him. This kind of stuff isn't awkward when you're doing it with your best friend. You can laugh and giggle and kiss and it doesn't matter. It all feels right.

He crawls back on top of me and kisses my forehead. I run my hands over his back and pull him closer. I can feel him as he rests in between my legs. We kiss deeply, passionately. He slowly moves to kissing down my neck as his hands explore my body. The room is silent except for our breathing and our whispered confessions. He can't decide where he needs me most. We can't get enough of each other. I love being the person he loves. I could be this forever. He looks deep into my eyes, "Ready?" He asks.

I nod in agreement and with that, he pushes into me. I suck in a breath so sharp it almost hurts. My nails dig into his shoulders without meaning to. My body adjusting to a kind of closeness I didn't know was possible between us.

Easton stills completely, his eyes squeezed shut like he's holding himself back from everything he wants. His chest heaves against mine, warm and solid. "Tate," he whispers, voice strained. "Talk to me? You okay?"

I nod quickly, even though my voice catches when I say, "Yes." I swallow, my lips brushing his gently. "It feels… different. But good. Just go slow."

He exhales shakily, his lips ghosting across my cheeks like he's praying. Then he moves. Just barely at first, a careful pull back and press forward, like he's terrified of breaking me. The feeling steals the air from my lungs.

Every shift inside me is new. It's strange, but not in a bad way. It's just new. Underneath the ache, there's this… fullness. Like something I didn't even know was missing is suddenly here. My body learns his rhythm before I even realize it, matching him, clinging to him.

"God, Tate," he groans softly, biting back a sound like it's dangerous to let it slip out. His eyes meet mine and he says, "You're everything."

I believe him. He's the only boy in the world who has ever made me feel this special. I believe that to him, I am everything. I know that he would flip his world upside down for me. Or that he would turn himself inside out if it was what I wanted. He loves me. I know that if I let him, he'd make me the center of his world.

I love him for it. For his passion for me. *For us.*

I don't even realize I'm crying until his thumb brushes away a tear that slips out.

"Should I stop?" He asks.

I shake my head, whispering, "No, just don't stop looking at me."

So, he doesn't. His eyes stay locked on mine with every slow, steady movement, and it makes me feel like he's not just inside my body but like he's inside my soul. If soulmates did exist, I found mine.

When he finally lets himself move a little deeper, a little faster, I grip his back harder. I've never seen him so hungry for something. For me. He freezes again, panic flashing across his face. "Too much?"

It's a rare thing to see Easton flustered, but the thought of hurting me makes him that way.

I shake my head furiously, clutching to him. "No, don't stop. Please."

His body tenses under my hands. "I can't hold it much longer, I'm trying."

Something in him breaks. He kisses me hard, messy, like he's drowning and I'm his air. His pace quickens, still careful but less hesitant, and I wrap my legs around his waist, pulling him closer, needing him closer, wanting him closer.

The ache shifts into something warm, pulsing, overwhelming. I'm lost in it, in him, in the sound of his breath catching every time I move with him. My name falls from his lips like a prayer, like he's begging over and over, until I feel myself unraveling beneath him.

When it happens, it's not loud or wild. It's quiet, like the ocean receding after a storm. My whole body shudders against his, my lips pressed to his neck, whispering his name like it's the only word I've ever known. The feeling is indescribable. It's like reaching a mountain top and taking a breath of that cold fresh air that knocks the wind out of you, but you love it. It's like an explosion of every feeling you've ever felt all at once. It feels like everything. I've never felt anything like it. Seconds later he follows me, eyes wide looking into mine until he can't take it anymore.

His eyes close and he comes completely undone.

I relax against my pillow, bringing my hand to my lips.

It's only now I realize what we've done. We just had sex. I, Tate Knightly, just had sex with Easton Mills. We took each other's virginity. And we can't give it back.

Something about that thought makes me giggle.

He follows, collapsing against me with a low, broken sound that I know I'll be hearing in my dreams for the rest of my life. "What?" He asks.

"That was… fun." I say with a giggle.

He's flat beside me on his own pillow now. His eyes looking over at me with a sparkle in them. I can't help but think I put that sparkle there. I'm proud of that. He looks more adorable in this moment than he ever has somehow. I love him.

For the first time, in my whole life of knowing Easton, I look at him in a different way.

He's not just Easton anymore.

He's my Easton and I'm his Tate.

Some moments you just know you'll remember forever.

This is one of those moments.

We stay there for while, both breathless. Our hearts beating so fast I can't tell which one is mine and which one is his. His hand grabs my hand, his thumb brushing over my skin like he can't stop touching me.

"I love you too. Always have. Always will." He says low and confident.

23

With You Two

TATE

Summer is wasted if you don't spend it at the beach. That's what my mom always says. As a kid, I always knew her favorite place was the beach. Like out of any person in the world, no one loves the beach more than my mom does. As I got older, I realized my mom does love the beach, but not in the die-hard way I always thought she did as a kid. My mom loves coming to Florida, not for the beaches and the ocean and the sun. She loves the beach because the beach has Jessie.

It wasn't until I stopped coming to Florida that I realized I agreed with my mom. The summer was indeed wasted if I didn't spend it at the beach... or spend it with the Mills. Summers back home were never the same. Sure, I went to the pool with my friends, had ice cream late at night in the kitchen, listened to Carly Rae Jepsen, and still got a good tan, but I didn't ever have as much fun as I did when I was here. Something about your best friends just makes everything better. I was lucky enough to have two.

Lila and Easton.

Currently, I am not on talking terms with Lila. Which is unfortunate, considering the close-knit quarters of the apartment. Easton keeps trying to talk to her and so do I, but Lila is a D1 avoider. She'd been gone most the day, I think to hang out with Annie.

The mom's left today for their girls' trip at the resort. Jessie's friends with the owner so she gets a discount. Every summer they go for a two-night stay. The days sound like a dream, full of massages, and mud masks, and they get their hair done. They might not like makeup, but they sure do love some self-care. Since they've been gone it's super quiet in the house, with none of us speaking to each other at all. So, Easton had the bright idea to go to the beach tonight.

As kids, on Sunday nights, we three would go out the beach and make s'mores. Easton would carry the wood and matches, I'd carry the graham crackers and chocolate, and Lila would carry the bag of marshmallows. She'd eat the marshmallows the whole walk to the beach. The marshmallow would be all over her face when we finally got to our beach spot. She'd sit there and tell us she didn't eat them, despite the evidence being all over her lips.

We've been sitting around the fire for half an hour and no one has said much of anything. The only sound filling the air is the ocean behind us and Easton's guitar. He's been slowly strumming the start of a song, with an occasional hum leaving his lips every now and then.

The first note rings out like it's been waiting for me all along. My chest tightens, and suddenly the air around me feels heavy. Like the fire, the ocean, and even the sand beneath me were listening too. Easton follows low, unsteady at first, but sure enough to pull me in. He didn't sing like someone showing off. He sang like someone confessing. I watch him as he pieces together the parts of a song that he's making up as he goes. His eyes don't leave my face. Every word seems to weave itself between us, the silence none of us are threatening to break, until Lila does.

"So, like, what is this exactly? What's happening?" She says, looking straight at me. Her eyes shoot daggers into me.

"We just wanted to do something fun, like we used to when we were kids you know," Easton says, clearly oblivious to the intent of her question.

Lila isn't stupid. She wants to know about us. "Easton, don't be coy. I mean you two," she says pointing as she draws an invisible line between us.

Lila has always wanted to be sophisticated. She's been using words like coy since she was four.

"What do you wanna know Lil?" I ask her before Easton can say anything else..

"Everything," she says it deliberately. Like she deserves to have been told the truth the second any of this started between us. I guess in a way we blindsided her. But to be fair, I don't think either of us were thinking straight. We were all blindsided in a way.

"Why are you even back Tate? We barely even talk anymore," she says. Each word digs into my skin like individual daggers.

"You aren't happy I'm here?" I ask her.

"I didn't say that. I'm just so confused. I don't see you for years and then all of a sudden I come home from camp and you're here, and Easton's breaking up with my best friend, and he's looking at you like, like, like he's always looked at you," she says, her voice getting louder with each word like she'd been holding this in for a while.

I guess I really was oblivious to the way things used to be between me and Easton. Jessie and mom saw it and so did Lila. The only one who couldn't see it was me.

"I'm sorry Lila… for not coming back."

She interrupts, "You know. I thought it was me."

Her eyes are heavy, dark, sad. She's fighting back tears like her life depends on it.

"No, no, no. It wasn't you. Please don't think that," I plead. I don't want her to think that she had anything to do with why I left or why I stayed away.

Easton suddenly stops strumming his guitar and sits forward, leaning into the moment. "It was me, Lila. That last night she was here, I said something really shitty," Easton confesses.

I didn't need him to do that, but it's nice to hear him say it and nice of him to take ownership, even though it was both our faults really.

"What'd you say?" She asks directing her anger at Easton now.

Does he remember exactly what he said to me. Does he really remember the soul crushing moment I spent five years wishing hadn't happened? I'm now waiting on his response as eagerly as Lila is. He has the floor.

"You remember the fireworks at the end of the summer? Well, me and Tate used to go together ever year down to the beach and watch them. You weren't old enough yet to come with us. But that summer was the summer I met Izzy, and I got all confused and I basically blew Tate off to…" "To go with Izzy. What a jerk," Lila says as she puts the pieces together.

"I was a jerk. And the worst part is…" He hesitates like he can't get the end of the sentence out. "I called her a kid. I told her to leave me alone and to grow up because I knew it would make her leave me alone and it worked. For five years she stayed away. I've never regretted saying anything more than what I said to her that night. So don't blame yourself, Lil. You had nothing to do with it. I'm the only one to blame." He's looking at me now. Eyes full of something. Love, I think. Maybe a bit of remorse too.

"It was both of our faults," I add.

"No, it was all me." His eyes are soft. Hearing him take ownership of this is making me feel so many things at once. I want to hug him for releasing the guilt I've been carrying on my back but mostly I want to drop my s'more in the sand and run over to him. I want to straddle him and kiss him and tell him I love him. But the moment at hand isn't over.

"That doesn't explain everything," Lila says, still upset but a bit less hectic now than she was earlier.

What does she mean?

"What's going on right now. With you two?" She asks us.

Easton and I eye each other, both silently begging the other to answer the question. I want to tell her that I love him, but I think she already knows that. She's not asking what our feelings are for each other. She's asking what we are. And, honestly, I haven't thought about it. I like the idea of there not being a name for it. We're just Tate and Easton.

There doesn't need to be a label like *boyfriend & girlfriend*. It would sound weird coming out of my mouth to call Easton my boyfriend. Maybe he thinks the same about me, because neither of us say anything.

"Are y'all like dating or together or talking or is this just a summer fling?" She adds to her pile of questions.

We've never even been on a date, so I don't really think we can say that we're dating. Although, I very much would like to go on an official date with Easton, even that would feel a little odd. I've always hated the, *we're talking* thing, because what does that even really mean? I talk to twenty people a day, doesn't mean I want them to touch me and kiss me and sleep next to them. It's a stupid phrase. Even if that was the stage we were in, I would call it something else like… *enjoying each other's company*. Although that does make it sound like we just sleep together. Maybe *talking* is a term for that reason. It's casual. I don't really know what me and Easton are, but I don't think it's just a summer fling. I'm too nervous to be wrong. Too nervous he'll correct me if I say we are together. But being together or dating would imply that we've talked about the future and what life looks like after the summer if we do choose to stay together. Which we haven't.

"Tate's my girlfriend," Easton says super confidently. He says it like we've talked about it. He makes me believe him. I nod my head in agreement like we've had that conversation before or that I knew for sure that's what we are. But I didn't until just now. I'm not mad about it.

"Gross," Lila says with a face that could only be described as disgusted. "You broke up with Annie like two minutes ago. Seriously Easton you disgust me."

"Annie and I never dated," he defends. His eyes stare into

Lila, begging her to stop making everything so awkward and tense.

"If you and Tate are a couple already, then I would call what you and Annie did dating. Which is probably why she's taking it so hard. You're so selfish bro, you are always only thinking about yourself," she says angrier now than ever. She looks at me. "And you. You don't as much as call for five years and then you show up and think you can just wreck everything? We had a good thing going here and then you roll into town and hurt my best friend and start messing with Easton again. All while playing the innocent card, like all of this isn't your fault." "Lila," Easton threatens.

She throws her hands up in defeat. "What? Am I wrong?"

My chest is starting to feel tight. I'm trying to count my breaths. I'm trying to drown out her voice. Her voice that is telling me all the things I deserve to hear. All of this is my fault. I know that deep down, but I don't want to believe it. I wanted to believe that I could come back to this place, and it would be like before. But before we were kids and things were easier. Back then it was princess movies and pop tarts.

Out of everything she's said tonight. The words that ring in my head over and over are *she's my best friend*. Annie probably deserves that title because she's been around. I'm suddenly jealous of Annie again.

She's gotten to curl Lila's hair for their school dances, and I haven't. She's gotten to pick her up and take her to the mall and help her pick out new clothes in the fitting room and I haven't. She's gotten to lay around in her room with her while listening to Taylor Swift and talk about boys, and I haven't.

Suddenly, Lila isn't the only angry one. I'm angry too. I'm maybe madder at myself than anyone. For leaving. For coming back? For not calling? For not thinking about how me and Easton's relationship would affect her?

I'm mad at me for forgetting that I was once Lila Mills best friend.

And now, to her, I'm nothing.

"I'm sorry," I mutter out. It breaks in the air.

I almost think it doesn't reach her ears because she says,

"Leave it to Tate Knightly to wreck the summer."

"That's enough Lila. You're not being fair," Easton says voice raised a bit.

Half of me wants to run into the ocean and never come back and the other wants to lay curled up in Easton's arms and listen to him tell me that it's not my fault. But everything

Lila says is true.

Sometimes the truth hurts. Sometimes it slaps you in the face. Sometimes it yells at you and calls you exactly what you are.

And tonight, Lila is telling me the truth.

And then the truth hurts: I'm a bad friend.

Lila stands there furious. She looks at the ocean for what feels like an eternity. Easton reaches for my hand. He lays his palm on the back of my hand, trying to comfort me. But I don't want his touch right now. I want to make things right with Lila. She turns around and lets out an annoyed sigh. She looks at our hands and rolls her eyes.

"Unbelievable. You know what would have been fair Easton?" She says.

"Don't," he warns her.

But she doesn't listen. "She should have never come back, and you know it." She storms off back toward the house.

The words ring in my ears. *She*, like I wasn't even in the room anymore. I've never seen Lila so upset. I've never been the cause of her frustration like this.

"She'll cool off. She's just gotten a lot more opinionated since the last summer you were here. Really, she'll come around," he says squeezing my hand.

I look at his face. Even after all of that he still looks at me like there is no one else he wants. And for the first time, I feel guilty because of it.

"Maybe not this time." I stand up, leaving him in his chair, mouth open like he doesn't know what to say. His lips are parted and inviting but kissing won't fix what just happened. Especially not with my heart pounding the way that it is right now. I can feel every pulse of my heart pounding in my head. The air is feeling thick as I try to suck in a breath. My hands are shaking, but the worst part is my skin feels like it's crawling.

I can't be here. I keep walking, faster now. My legs feel heavy in the sand, each step is harder.

What is happening to me?

He follows behind me as I trail off toward somewhere, anywhere that isn't here. I just need to be alone for a minute.

I need to walk on the beach and hear the waves crashing and clear my head. But before I get to far, Easton grabs my hand, turning me toward him.

His eyes are full of hurt. It makes me want to reassure him that everything's gonna be okay. He's not the one I want to get away from."Where are you going?" He asks, trying to mask the hurt in his voice."

"Somewhere that's not here," I tell him trying to catch my breath.

"Why? Did I do something?" he pleads.

"No, no. It's not you. I just need to breathe," I say, each word coming out in between a breath. I'm scared now that

I'm not okay. He can't see me like this though. I push away from him, taking a step back. But he grabs my shoulders, stopping me.

I feel like the world is sitting on my chest. It's hard to take in a breath. Am I dying?

Easton turns me to face him. My hand is on my chest now. I'm clawing at my chest, begging it to let me breath. My lungs are failing me, the air is failing me, my body is failing me. I can't even function.

"Tate, look at me. What do you need from me?"

I shake my head back and forth fast, my fear of dying growing bigger by the second. I don't know what I need.

I don't even know what's happening to me.

"Tate?" He asks me. His voice sounds desperate.

I need to breath.

But no words make it out of my mouth. They sit in my throat, begging to be let loose but they don't move. They're as stuck as the air is trying to get into my lungs.

I'm facing him now. Concern is painted on his face. He grabs my face in his hands.

I need air.

But still the words don't come out so I pat my chest over and over again hoping he understands that I need to slow down. I feel like my body ran a marathon and forgot to tell me.

"You're scaring me Tate. Talk to me," he begs.

I shake my head in between his huge hands. I can't talk.

I can't breathe. I can't do anything.

I am frozen in front of him.

I look at him, just in case I am dying. I'd want him to be the last thing I see.

24

Panic

EASTON

What do you do when someone is having panic attack? I'm eighty-five percent sure that's what's happening to Tate right now. Everything Lila said was harsh. She was fuming. I know she is hurt by us dating and honestly, I predicted her not taking it super well, but her reaction was super uncalled for. It's at times like this that I remember what a difference two years can make in person's maturity. We could have had a meaningful and intentional conversation if she was more mature than she is acting right now. I've been trying to talk to her since she got home from camp, but she just wouldn't have it. All of this could have been dealt with maturely if Lila would just not let her feelings determine every word that leaves her mouth.

It isn't until now that I realize she's grown to be this hyper-independent, opinionated young woman. She used to be more like Tate, who is also both those things… but Tate thinks before she says things. She knows who she is, what she wants, and what she believes in, but unlike Lila, she picks her battles.

Lila is acting a lot more like Annie. A bit selfish. A bit like her life is the only life there is. It doesn't take away from the fact that Lila is the sweetest girl I've ever known. She's just being influenced and I know that. Now more than ever, I wish I had never said all that shit to Tate five years ago. If I had just treated her the way she deserved back then, then tonight would have been a normal night at the beach, sitting by the fire, eating s'mores, sharing stories and playing my guitar.

This is all my fault.

And here Tate is not able to breathe because of me. I've never dealt with someone who's had a panic attack. I've never had one myself. All I know is what I've seen on TV. *Great.* The extent of my knowledge on panic attacks is boiled down to a scene I watched in *Teen Wolf* like eight years ago. If I hadn't seen that episode of Stiles losing it in a locker room, I don't think I would even know what Tate was going through right now.

My hands are on her face as she taps her chest with her hand. She's grasping for air.

What do I do? Mouth to mouth? No.

Make her count sheep? No, that's for sleeping, I think.

I pull Tate down into the sand with me. Tears have formed in her eyes. Her face holds an expression I haven't seen on her before. She's scared. I love her, but I can't keep looking at her if she's this sad and hurting and full of fear. She looks at me like I should know what to do. But I don't. I'll be damned if I let her know that though. I wipe her tears and say, "You're having a panic attack. Have you had one of these before?"

She shakes her head *no*.

"It's gonna go away, OK. It feels like it's not gonna end but it will," I promise her.

She nods softly as a tear rolls down her beautiful, freckled face. I wipe it away. "Come here," I tell her as I pull her toward me.

I sit back in the sand, pulling her really close me. I sit up just a bit higher than her so that her head can lay on my chest. Her ear is right over my heart. I wonder if she can hear how sped up it is and how nervous I am. If I could take her pain I would. If I could switch places with her, I would. In a heartbeat.

I have the overwhelming feeling to tell her to breathe, but I know that's all she wants. If she was capable of breathing, she would be. I want to comfort her, and slow her breathing, but how?

As I hear the waves crashing in the distance, an idea washes over me.

I focus on my own breathing. I calm myself down. I even out my breaths so that her head begins to rise and fall at a steady, calm, rhythm. I feel anything but calm, but I'll fake it for her. "Try and take a breath with me?" I say.

"Can you do that?"

She remains quiet but she nods her head *yes*.

I dial in even more now than I was before. Making my breaths deep and long.

I run my hand through her hair as she tries to match my tempo. I run my thumb along her earlobe, and rub her shoulders and neck with my one free hand. I want to distract her from whatever is happening in her body and mind right now. I want to force her to slow down. It feels like it's working. Her breaths are getting choppy, but slower.

Her hand grips my sweatshirt, tight. Her tiny little hands cling to me like I'm air itself. Slowly her hand loosens on my shirt as her breaths become more normal. More matched to mine.

I stare up at the stars as she continues to come down from the high of her panic attack. The stars are clear tonight. The clearest I've seen in a while. I wonder why I ever stopped looking at the stars. I used to look at them every night on the front porch with Lila and Tate. I guess when she stopped coming, a part of my childhood ended. I stopped doing childish things like looking at the constellations and eating ice cream out of coffee mugs. I quit picking up seashells and making forts in the living room out of my *Star Wars* bedding. I stopped making cookies with my mom and riding my bike… it all just felt childish after Tate didn't come back. Why would I look at the stars if I didn't have the person I wanted next to me pointing out all the constellations and trying their hardest to find a shooting star. Everything about being a kid felt pointless when she left.

But now that she's here on my chest on the beach and I'm looking up at the stars, I realize I can only be this version of me when I'm with Tate. My dreams are bigger, my words are heavier, my time is more valuable when I'm around her. Everything just matters more when Tate is with me. Everything is better and brighter.

Even the stars are brighter when she's around.

Tate sits up, pushing herself off my chest. When she looks at me, her cheeks are tear stained, and she has little red spots under her eyes from all the crying. Her freckles pop more in this moonlight. Maybe it's the tears left on her face that make her glow, but right now she looks the most beautiful I've ever seen her. Never in my life have I met someone who looks beautiful after crying…she might be the only one.

"I'm sorry," she says. Her bottom lips quivers. She must notice because she pulls her lip in between her teeth, attempting to calm herself down.

I don't want her to think having a panic attack is something she should be ashamed of. "Do not apologize. You can't control that kind of thing. And even if you could, I would have sat here with you through it all the same."

A few more tears fall from her eyes, and this time I'm not sure why.

"I don't deserve that," she says with her eyes closed. I can tell she's having a lot of inner dialogue right now. Her head seems like it's still spinning, so I grab her face and kiss her. Her lips are soft and salty from the tears. It's a gentle kiss at first. I want her to know she's safe with me. But one kiss is never enough with her. I part her lips and let my tongue slip into her mouth. She lets out the sweetest sound against my lips, and it sends shivers down my spine. I can't help but kiss her again and again and again, until I'm the one that's breathless.

I pull away from her mouth just enough to say, "It's not about deserving. If it was, I'd never get a chance with you." I kiss her again, softer this time.

Now she's the one to pull away. She puts a hand on my chest. Through tears she says, "But you don't wreck my life the way I wreck yours."

Her words hang in the air. I want to tell her she's wrong, but we both know she's right. Lila was mean about it, but she had a point. Us dating affects me a lot more than it affects Tate.

The difference is that Tate is most likely going to wreck it. My life that is. With anyone else, I would leave. The thought of a girl coming into my life and making parts of it hard sounds miserable. The smart thing would be to just let this be a summer thing. To just kiss and hold hands and cuddle under the stars and watch the sunrise together. But I don't just want summer with her. I want winter, spring, and fall too. I want every season. I've never wanted all the good and all the bad of someone before.

I want Tate during a panic attack. I want her when she wins a huge tournament. I want her when she loses. I want her when she's sick. I want her when she's sad, and mad, and happy. I want her when she's pale and when she's tan. I want her when she's sleeping and when she's awake dancing in the kitchen.

Unlike Tate, I don't know exactly what I want.

The thing is, the odds aren't in our favor. Lila knows that. Even my mom knows it. I saw it in her eyes the other night when she asked me if I loved Tate. The question felt silly at the time, because of course

I love Tate. *How could I not?* My mom has always known how I feel about Tate. She wasn't asking that, really. She was asking… *are you willing to do long-distance with her? Are you willing to travel to see her? Are you willing to support her? Are your ready for that kind of commitment? Are you ready for that kind of love?*

I want to think I am ready. But something flickered in my mom's eyes that night. Like maybe she didn't think it was the right time. Maybe she agrees with Lila. Maybe she thinks Tate will wreck my life or break my heart or I'll do either or both of those to Tate.

But I'm more than willing to run the risk. "No one's wrecking anybody," I assure her.

Her fingers draw shapes on my leg, or maybe she's drawing letters in her pretty penmanship. I wonder what she's saying. She stops to look at me. "You can't promise that, and neither can I." She's right.

"Come on." I grab her fidgeting hand and pull her up out of the sand. Her eyes are still down on the sand, avoiding my eyes. I lift her chin with my finger, making her look at me. "I want to show you something."

* * *

The song isn't much, but it's about her. The chords aren't complicated, it's just a steady strum and a soft melody. It's the realist thing I've ever written. Even the ocean can tell I'm nervous.

She bats her eyes at me, full of curiosity. "Is this the one about me?"

I nod. If only she knew how much of my music is about her. She's always my muse, even when I think she's not… somehow she works her way in. "Yeah, but all of them really are."

She moves closer to me, crawling up toward me. She leans over my guitar and kisses my lips. Just a quick peck. "Thank you. I'm flattered to be Easton Mill's muse," she says as she kisses me again. Against my mouth she says, "but…"

Buts are never good.

She scrunches her nose up, keeping her eyes closed. "Do you think we're making a mistake with all this? Lila seems to think so."

I could care less what anyone thinks because I truly believe this will work. So, if she thinks this will work, then that's all I need. "I don't think this was ever a mistake. This was meant to happen. We both know that. To be frank, I don't really care what anyone thinks about us, but us. Okay?" She nods her head, but I don't think she's fully convinced so I keep going. "Let me tell you something. Wrecks are accidents. Car wrecks. Shipwrecks. You know? It implies that it's unexpected, not supposed to happen, right? Nothing about this is an accident. You and me? You can't wreck something if you always knew that it was gonna happen. I always knew we were gonna happen."

She sits back, "You did?"

I nod, strumming my guitar again. "I always hoped." She looks out at the ocean, hiding her face from me. I wish I could see her eyes. I know they're glowing in the moonlight. She sits silently, the only sound circling the air is my strumming.

After a few minutes she says, "I just I don't think I believe that you've always wished for me. It seems too much like a fairytale."

Maybe she's right. Maybe that is what we are. Fairytales are magical. That's what being with her feels like. Magic. "What if it is a fairytale?" I ask.

She tilts her head to the side, contemplating my words. I can't see her face, but I can feel her thinking. "Fairytales aren't real, Easton," she says bluntly. "If they were then everything would be perfect, and Lila would love that we're together and we wouldn't live states away and I would have just come back five years ago."

"Fairytales have all different kinds of endings. Why can't we be each others?" I ask.

She turns around, putting her hands on my knees. Her eyes are heavy and shiny from the tears threatening to fall. "You're going to Nashville and I'm going to college *not* in Nashville," she says looking deep into my eyes. She's inferring that we'd be long distance.

"You don't think I know that? Long distance is not that hard. Not when we've waiting our whole lives for this," I say, my voice raising unintentionally.

"I can't do long distance," she says, like it's not even an option. "It's never fair to either party and I just won't do that to you or to me."

Sure, long distance isn't ideal, but it's doable. I'll follow her wherever, as long I get to have her. Even though I know she won't want to hear it, I say, "Then I'll go wherever you commit to college, and we'll make it work. I'll work and you can go to school and then—"

She cuts me off. "And what about you? What will you have out there?"

I want to say *you.* But I know that's not what she means.

"You'll follow me to wherever and then I'll be all you have in a new place where I'm trying to create community and find friends, and do well on my team, and be in classes, and probably working and you'll just what? Wait around for me? I can't keep asking you to do that," she says rambling.

"You didn't ask me to do it the first time. I chose to."

"I know. I know."

"I love you, Tate. That's not something I take lightly," I reassure her.

She smiles a little half broken smirk and bites her lip. She nods, accepting she's lost this round. But something behind her eyes is still fighting. I want to silence the voice in her head telling her to doubt us. But I don't know how, so I just look at her. She's looking at me, eyes tracing over my whole face like she's trying to memorize me.

I do the same to her.

She's so beautiful without even trying. It pains me to look at her and not kiss her. I want her in every way. I thought after the other night, that I'd regret sleeping with her. Not because I didn't want to, but because I thought I'd feel guilty for not waiting like I thought I was going to. But it felt so right for Tate to have that part of me. It felt right to be that intimate with her.

I can't stop replaying that night in my head. The way she felt, warm and soft. The way she smelled like vanilla. They way her hands made my skin come alive. The way she gripped me and held onto me like I was her lifeline. The way she kissed me like I was her air. Her noises are the things I keep trying to replay in my head most. They way she gasped like she couldn't breathe, and the moans. God, the moans. Hearing my name leave her lips with that low desperation — I could never get tired of it.

She gets this look in her eyes when she wants something. There's something special that sits behind her eyes when the something that she wants is me. Looking in her eyes right now, I can tell that's exactly what she wants. She wants me.

Luckily for her, I always want her.

She grabs my guitar and leans it against the other chair. She crawls onto my lap, straddling me. Her face is just slightly above mine. I don't know if it's the darkness or the tears that still well up in her eyes, but I can't really read her. She brings one finger to my chin, lifting my face up to meet hers. Her legs are warm, closing the space between our hips. I know she can feel me against her. I don't know what her plan is, but I know we can't have sex on this beach.

I can see us now. I'll carry her back to the house, kissing her with every step. I'll lay her on my bed, and we'll relive the other night. But better this time and hopefully longer. "Tate," I say, but she kisses me before I can give her my plan.

She rolls her hips into mine and runs her hands through my hair. What a deadly combo.

My hands are on her hips, guiding her toward me. My hand ventures up her back, finding the skin there. She's cold from the wind. My hands must be colder because she flinches at the contact, but then she melts into it.

Her lips haven't left my lips in minutes. At this point, I would do whatever she wanted me to do, wherever she wanted to do it. I'll face the consequences later.

Something about this moment feels different. I don't understand until my lips taste like salt and her hips slow down. She kisses me gentler and gentler with each kiss until she pulls away and shakes her head.

In the most broken voice I've ever heard leave her lips she says, "I love you, Easton Mills." And then she kisses me again.

I love her too, I always have. But why is she crying? I don't understand.

She pulls away again and something in her face has changed. I wipe the tears off her face, but she pushes my hand down.

"I won't be the reason you don't go to Nashville. That song, it was beautiful, Easton. You won't waste your talent on me." She kisses my head and stands up, backing away from me like she doesn't want to. She turns her back and doesn't turn back around once.

I want to grab her and pull her back down to me, but I can't.

I'm frozen. Time keeps moving but I am paralyzed.

"Wait," I finally say, but she is almost back to the house before the words come out. She can't hear me. And even if she could, she wouldn't have turned around. She's made up her mind.

I just lost her.

25

The Whole Bottle

TATE

When I walk inside my head is pounding again. But this time I can't tell if it's coming from me or the house. Music is blaring over multiple speakers. The apartment doesn't look like the apartment anymore.

It's breathing, pulsing with color… everywhere. LED lights flash around bleeding blue and purple and green into every shadow of the apartment. Music rattles the walls in tune with the beat in my chest. The floor's slick with the sheen of spilled beer and sticky soda. There's Chinese takeout everywhere. There are towers of white cartons with greasy fingerprints smudging the flaps. It's a graveyard of chopsticks and half-empty soy sauce packets. And the wigs. So many wigs.

I've never been to a house party, but I've pictured myself at one before. I can't tell if this is better or worse than I imagined. We weren't at the beach that long, were we? The amount of people and the organized wig theme gives away a predetermined plan for a party, that Easton and I weren't invited to, or made aware of. This is definitely Lila's doing.

Lila passes behind me. Her long purple curls bounce like a cartoon villain. She's wearing a full face of makeup. Glitter all over her face, and a bold red lip. She's always making a statement.

I wonder if there is someone here she's trying to impress. I would tell her she doesn't need a drop of makeup to look pretty, but she wouldn't listen to me if I said such a thing, so I keep my mouth closed.

I'm still shocked at the state of the apartment. We were only at the beach for an hour or two maybe. *How did all of this happen? Why is all of this happening?*

I just left the love of my life on the beach. I wanted to come back to a warm bed to have a good cry. My eyes are dry now. I'm just angry.

I march straight to the kitchen. My eyes are scanning the room for Lila, who has somehow disappeared. There are wildly too many people in this apartment. People are dancing and jumping around in the living room, girls are taking shots in the corner, and there's a group of guys sitting around the table playing some sort of poker game. How could you focus on betting your money in this kind of climate? I can't even put two thoughts together.

All I know is I need to find Lila.

I'm searching the apartment for her petite figure and current mop of purple curls, but all I see are wigs. Bobs, Afros, pixie cuts, and even a Dolly Parton wig. I'll never find her like this. The smell of Chinese food is making me nauseous. I love the taste, but I can't stand the smell.

I'm leaving the kitchen when I see him. The only person in the house not wearing a wig, other than me. Walter.

He smiles when he first spots me, but his smile fades once he searches my face.

Shit.

I must look awful.

I don't need this right now. In fact, I shouldn't even be in the same house as him. Especially right now. I don't want to see him.

My head is pounding, my eyes are stinging, and I feel more alone than I've felt since I got to Florida. I want my bed, not Walter. I want Easton, not him. I want to be home, not here. I don't want Walter. He is the last person that I should be turning to right now, but unfortunately he's walking up to me.

He's here and he's tall and sweet and he looks at me like I'm a mess, because I am a mess. He doesn't see me as this perfect, dream girl. He see's me for the unraveling, snotty, crying mess I am right now. And he's standing in front of me and he's touching me and holding my shoulders and asking what's wrong and wiping my tears and nothing I could do could wreck his life.

He tries to hug me… and I let him. I want to be comforted more than I care about who's comforting me right now. I feel sleazy for letting him hold my face in his hands, but it feels so nice. It feels nice to look at him and know he didn't know me before this summer.

He doesn't know my scraped knees or sun-kissed cheeks. He doesn't know my princess jammies and pigtail braids. He doesn't know all the phases and moments that make me. He just knows the girl standing in front of him.

And right now, I'm sad. Broken. Hurt. Destroyed. And the only one to blame is myself.

"What's wrong? Where's Easton? What did he say? Did he do something? I'm gonna kill him," He asks so many questions, but I can't find the answers to any of them. I feel lost in a maze of memories and the future I thought I could have with Easton. I'm standing in the middle of the maze, blindfolded, alone, and scared.

He can't think the state of my well-being has anything to do with Easton. I can't let him believe that. It does, but it's nothing Easton did that makes me feel this way. It's everything I am that makes me feel this way. "It's not him. I—I—I…" I mutter out through tears that start to come out faster than they were before.

"Hey, it's OK. It's OK. Come on," he says putting his hand in mine. He tries to pull me toward the hallway, but I resist, shaking my head.

I can't go anywhere with him. Not without a drink first.

My throat is dry, and my heart is empty. I'm craving that vodka from the back of the fridge. I never thought I'd crave such a thing.

I open the fridge and search for the tall clear bottle from that night in the kitchen with Easton. It was mostly full then, and it's half full now. Plenty left in the bottle to numb whatever I'm feeling right now.

The concern on Walter's face has doubled. "Shots?

Right now?" He asks, voice dripping in concern.

"No, the bottle. Right now," I say as I twist off the top of the bottle, bringing it to my lips. How long do you sip in order to measure out a shot? *Two seconds? Three? Five?* By the eighth second, someone pulls the bottle from my hand.

I was expecting to see Walter holding the bottle, but it's Easton.

He isn't sad. Or angry. Or anything. His face is frozen, completely emotionless. "We need to talk," He says to me, expressionless.

"We just talked," I answer back, snagging the bottle from him, taking another swig. This one a little shorter of a sip this time.

It burns down my throat. I can't hear anything, and I can hear everything all at once, but the only thing I hear clearly is, "Haven't you done enough?" I think Walter says.

I think he says it to Easton but I can't really tell. I didn't know alcohol works this fast. Because Easton responds calmly. "You're just gonna let her drink like this?"

I'm looking at them both. They're mad at each other?

At me? I can't tell.

Great, I wrecked that too.

"I wasn't planning on it, no," Walter says sharply, eyes digging into Easton. He seems angrier that Easton now.

"What *were* you planning on?" Easton asks, this time there's some emotion. He's accusing Walter of something that hasn't happened. That isn't happening. That wasn't going to happen

"Don't," Walter says, his voice like a threat. A moment passes between them — a look that says a thousand words. There is something behind both their eyes that I can't explain. It's not meant for me.

I take another sip from the bottle. My goal is to forget. Forget the conversation on the beach. Forget choosing the right thing. Forget ever coming back here. Forget ever knowing what it was like for Easton to be mine. I need to forget all of it.

I want to forget all of it.

Walter grabs the bottle this time. He takes it straight from my lips, spilling the liquid from the bottle on my shirt.

I don't react how I think I should.

"Sorry," he says, but I don't really care that he spilled it on me. At this rate I probably won't remember anything… hopefully.

"TK, I need to talk to you," Easton pleads again. He grabs my shoulders to focus my attention on his face.

"She doesn't want to talk to you," Walter says before I can get out what it is I want. Walter's right though, I don't want to talk to Easton. I don't want to give Easton any more chances to convince me that I'm wrong.

Easton will destroy his whole life and his whole future as long as it has me in it. I can't believe it took me this long to realize that. I won't let that happen. I want to believe that we would work in the long run. I want to believe that we have the bones to make it, but reality is a bitch. Neither of us are in a position to commit fully to one another. I can see that now.

Easton is smart, really smart. No equation, graph, or problem stands a chance against him, but that's the issue.

Love isn't any of those things. It's not something you solve with numbers or a sarcastic comment. I'm not even really sure I know exactly what it is, but I know it's not that.

Love is knowing that Lila isn't gonna be mad at me for using her vanilla sugar scrub. Love is Mr. Mills wanting Jessie and my mom to have a girly sleepover in their bedroom and him sleeping in his office chair all night so they can do that. Love is my mom raising Nate and I almost completely on her own so my dad can chase his dream of making movies.

Love is doing the thing you don't want to do for the person you love most.

Not because they asked you. Because you know it's what's best for them.

Love is sacrifice.

Easton is going to choose me, even if everyone and everything tells him not to.

We both can't be that way. One of us has to choose what's best for him. And it's not gonna be him. So it has to be me.

So, Walter's right, I don't want to talk to Easton. I can't.

I won't.

"Don't speak for her," Easton says, shoving Walter's chest.

"Am I wrong?" Walter says looking at me.

I want to tell him — *yes, I'll talk to you right now, today, tomorrow, forever* — but that's exactly why I can't. If I talk to him right now, I won't be able to stop. I already walked away from him once — no twice. I can't do it a third time.

"Easton, I need you to leave," I plead with him, tears still streaming down my face.

"My house?" He says, like what I suggested is crazy. I guess it is his house.

"You're right, I'll go, I tell him.

Without another thought I push past him, bottle in my hand and on my lips again. I have to pack, and book a ticket, and find a cab. I'm not drunk but by the time I'm leaving I'll be too drunk to drive, and I can't tell my mom or

Jessie I'm leaving. They'll convince me to stay.

Right when I get to Easton's door, I hear Easton say *shit* under his breath and the next thing I know he's grabbing my hand. I'm facing him now. His eyes are heavier than they've ever been. "You know that's not what I meant," he squeaks out.

I know he wasn't asking me to leave, but I'll take it as an invitation. I don't want to be here. Well, I do want to be here, but I can't be here. It's better for everyone if I leave.

"Tate, please, just talk to me. What are you gonna do?

Drive to the airport and book a ticket and hop on a flight.

You don't have that kind of money."

I hate that he's right. Booking within the hour is gonna be wildly over my price range. I guess I haven't really thought past packing my suitcase.

"I'll figure it out," I tell him.

He stands at the door as he watches me throw all my things into a suitcase. I feel like I'm in a TV show with a live studio audience. I feel his eyes watching me as I move across the room spinning in circles trying to find what I need to get out of this house.

"Why the sudden change of feeling? Huh? Why let me know what it's like to have you and then change your mind? Why Tate? Because Lila doesn't support us? Really? I don't believe that, so tell me why? What is it?" His voice cracks as he begs me for an answer.

When I gain the strength to look up at him, a tear falls down his face. Every fiber of my being wants to wipe it away for him. But then I remind myself I'm the one who put the tears there. I can't have my cake and eat it too.

"It's not about Lila. It's about me and you," I tell him.

"Then what is it, Tate? Tell me and I'll fix it," he says coming into the room fully. He joins me on the floor, a few feet between us.

"That's just it. I can't just tell you what to do Easton." I take another drink from the bottle. It's empty. *That was quick.* "You will put your whole life on hold for me. Do you hear how crazy that is?"

"How is that crazy? I love you, Tate," he says each word with heavy emphasis.

"There is so much I want to do and accomplish. I want to go to college and make friends and become an actress and model and writer and all the things I've always secretly wanted to be. I want to become her. And you're so talented. You'd be wasting your life if you followed me around. I won't let it happen. I won't," I say, rambling and slurring my words. The alcohol has hit me in the face. *I guess half a bottle of vodka does the trick.* "I won't let us break each other," I tell him forcefully. He's not gonna change my mind.

"You're breaking us right now," he says as tears well up in his eyes.

"I'm saving us right now," I correct him.

"I love you. I love you more than I thought I could love a person. I see my entire life with you," he goes on but I start to tune him out. I can't keep hearing about what he feels. I can see his heart break in front of me with each second longer he stands here. I've made my mind up.

I grab his face, making him look at me. I need him to hear my next words. So, I choose them carefully. I want them to be truthful, but I need them to hurt. With my voice raw, on fire from the alcohol I say, "I love you too, but I won't change my plans for you. That's the difference."

Another tear falls down his face. His face scrunches. I just crushed the little bit of hope he had left in his tank from the beach. His tank is empty and so is my bottle.

"I'll go," he says.

I shake my head. I'm the one making the mess, I should go.

"Stay the night. Enjoy the party. You should fix things with Lila tomorrow before you go. But please wait to talk til your both sober," he says, getting up and looking at me one last time before walking out the door.

When he finally leaves, the tears I've been trying to hold in finally flow out like a river.

Before I know it, I'm in someone's arms. Their arms are strong, sculpted, muscular. He smells like sunscreen and the beach. "He's gone," the voice says. His voice is hoarse, a bit scratchy. Walter. "He's staying at my place"

I shove away from him, getting a full look at his face. He doesn't seem to be upset at my shoving. So, I shove him again. Harder this time. He just takes it. Again, I shove him, tears falling down my face. I'm angry. I want what I cannot have. So, I shove Walter again, and again, and again. Harder and harder each time. He just lets me push him. He lets me take my anger out on his muscled body. I push and push until my hands hurt and my arms grow heavy. He hasn't even moved from his original spot on the floor. I can barely move him.

He's strong and immovable.

He grabs my hands and looks up at me. "Do you want me to go?" He asks calmly. *Do I?*

"I don't want to be alone," I confess honestly.

He nods his head, understanding and silently agreeing. Even if I had said I wanted him to go, I know he would have lingered in the other room. He wasn't gonna leave me. Whether that was for me or for Easton or for himself, I'm not sure. But either way, I'm thankful.

"Do you want me to get Lila?" He asks, like I don't want him in the room with me. Like I would want a replacement. Like maybe he doesn't think being alone in this room with me is a good idea.

Shaking my head no, I say, "I'm not sober enough to talk to her. And she probably wouldn't want to see me anyway. You can go though. You seem uncomfortable."

One of his eyebrows raise and a smirk creeps on his face,

"You were just hitting me, so."

I pat his chest, softly. "Sorry about that. I don't usually drink."

"You don't say," he says, as cool as a cucumber. Like everything that just happened was normal. Moments ago, I was hitting him and now he's looking at me like it's completely fine.

"I don't want to leave you, but I don't think staying is smart," he says, looking down at his hand which is holding his other hand, or wait — is holding my hand.

I'm holding his hand.

When his eyes trail back up to my face, there is a sparkle in his eye. His shoulders sink, releasing the tension in his shoulders. He moves his thumb over my hand, back and forth. Shivers travel down my spine that don't need to be there.

"I'm not drunk," I tell him and I'm not sure why I do.

I don't know what comes over me, but the second I looked up at him — really looked at him — I feel it.

Walter's eyes flicked away, jaw tight, the corner of his mouth twitching like he's fighting with himself.

"Please don't," he mutters, low like a warning. His hand rakes through his messy hair, and I know he isn't talking to me. He's talking to himself. He's begging himself to not act on what he wants.

"Don't what?" I whisper, scooting closer, my pulse thudding. His curls are falling around his face, framing it perfectly. He's the perfect mix of boy and man that makes me want to lean in. Everything feels fuzzy and blurry, but with his face this close, I'm forgetting why I even feel this way or why I was mad in the first place, or how I ended up on the floor.

His laugh is tight, sarcastic. "Don't make me do something stupid."

And that's it. I press my mouth to his before I can think any longer about what I'm doing.

He freezes for a half second, lips still, body tight. Then, his hand comes up to my jaw, rough and gentle all at once, pulling me in deeper like he's been holding this back since the moment we met. And for the first time, I think maybe he has been. The kiss breaks something open in both of us, messy and intense.

Walter kisses like he talks. Witty. Sweet. But underneath it all, there is so much heart and passion. His hand slides down my side, fingers splaying at the small of my back, pulling me into him. I grab his shirt, knuckles white against the fabric, tugging him closer until there isn't any space left between us.

He tears his mouth from mine for a second, forehead now leaning against mine, breathing hard. "Tate," he whispers, voice shaky, "I can't. He's my…"

I cut him off with another kiss, harder this time, and he gives in, groaning against my mouth like a surrender. I don't want to talk about Easton. I don't want to think about him. I want to forget him. After tonight, I'll be gone so none of this will matter. It won't matter that I broke his heart, or that I abandoned him, or that I kissed his best friend. It won't matter.

That's what I tell myself as Walter's hands travel up and down my body. They slide over my hips, his thumb grazing the edge of my bare skin just above my jeans. My body isn't on fire, it's melting. I'm like an ice cube in the summer heat, losing my form in the presence of this man. Every nerve begs for more of him.

I know this is dangerous. I know it's dumb. I know this is Easton's best friend. But in this moment, I don't care.

And judging by the way Walter pulls me in tighter, neither does he.

26

Dead

EASTON

Dead. I feel dead.

If it wasn't for my heart pounding in my chest I would think I had already gone under. It wasn't until I make it to Walter's place that I can process everything tonight has thrown at me. Tonight was my last chance, my last moment with TK and I blew it.

Walter's ceiling fan swirls above me, but the hum doesn't drown out the noise in my head. Four hours ago, Tate was in my arms, smelling like vanilla and coconut and something that's just her. I thought if I held her tight enough, she'd stay. If I just got to talk to her one more time, the outcome would change. That somehow, I could change our fate.

But it was my idea…*Let's go to the beach, let's fix things with Lila, let's talk it out.* What an idiot. What a self sabotaging, blind idiot.

And those eyes, geez, her eyes looking at me are burned into my brain. Hazel, shining with tears that she tried with all her might to blink away. They haunt me every time I close my own eyes. I wanted to cup her face and promise her it would be okay. But I didn't know if it would be. I wanted to kiss away the cracks and her doubts. But I don't know if I can. She was slipping right before my eyes, and no matter how far I reached, she just kept drifting further.

So, instead of being there for her like I want to be, I asked Walter to stay with her. To take care of her. Because for as wild as he is, he always comes through. Because he's always there for me, and now he's there for her. He's a best friend, a brother, a constant. The one person I don't have to worry about. I thank God for him.

And now, lying here in Walter's bed, I can't stop picturing it. Tate, drunk and falling apart, Walter steady beside her. His hand in her hair, his voice telling her to breathe. Him being the one she leans on while I'm stuck in this bed like a coward. The thought burns so deep it makes my stomach twist. *That should be me.*

But she doesn't want me. I have to respect that.

How did it come to this? Why did it come to this?

I want to say I saw her visit ending differently than this, but I think the version of her being here that I imagined never included the festivities that occurred. In the version I pictured, we caught up on life and maybe hugged goodnight. But we've done so much more than that. I never imagined even having the opportunity to tell her how I felt back then, or how I feel now. Part of me wanted to believe I didn't still feel so in love with her… but then I saw her and it all just came rushing back. I should have known better. I should have known myself better. I'm always so… present. I love being where I am and being fully there in each moment. When Tate stood in front of me in the kitchen the other night, I couldn't help but kiss her because that's what I wanted and it's what felt right. Mom's always told me my greatest gift and my greatest curse is how intentional I can be. When I'm doing something, I only do that thing. Maybe it's because I don't multi-task as well as I'd like or maybe it's because I love living each moment to the fullest, but either way it usually gets me in trouble. The reason I liked Izzy all those years ago was because I knew she was here, in Florida, with me. I didn't have to worry about calling her and waiting for the summer to see her again, she was already here. And that's the thing, Tate's never *just* here, unless it's the summer. And she hasn't been here in years, so when she finally was, I took every risk I wish I'd taken before. At first I thought it was out of fear of not having the chance again, but really I think it's because I knew we wouldn't ever make it pass the summer.

That's all we're allowed to have. Just the summer.

Because if I'm really honest with myself, Tate and I don't work in the real world. Us being together means flights, planned occasions, and late night FaceTimes. It means constant texts and dedicated trips to see each other — all because our worlds, outside of summer, never mix. They never have and they never will.

Even so, losing her feels as bad as I thought it would. I don't think I'll ever get used to this. I feel like I'm actively bleeding out. *Why is heartbreak such a pain?*

I turn my phone over and over in my hands. Face down, face up, face down, face up… just praying her name will light up on the screen. That she'll change her mind. That she'll say she still wants me. But Tate doesn't backtrack and I know that. She never has. Once she's decided, that's it. She doesn't flinch. She doesn't bend. It's one of the things I love most about her. And tonight, it's the thing killing me.

I keep replaying the beach. Every word, every silence, like some cruel highlight reel. Rewind. Play. Rewind. Play. Rewind. Play. No matter how many ways I twist it, no matter what I say differently in my head, she still walks away. She still leaves me in the sand with nothing but the sound of the waves and my chest hollowing out, almost like she's supposed to.

A week. That's all I got. A week with her. A week where the world felt right again.

And now it's gone.

And I don't know if I'll survive losing her twice.

Tate's not perfect. She's quirky and a bit dorky. Often stuck in her ways and a bit too stubborn. She giggles at my stupid jokes because she gets them and she loves my mom the way I do. She's beautiful but not in a model sort of way. She looks kind and friendly and full of laughter. Her eyes are bright with wonder and joy and she knows me for exactly who I am. She knows me better than I know me, and I know that's why she left. Because she's right, I would wreck my life to love her. I would change everything if I could, if it meant I got to have her. But she also knows my fatal flaw…my need to be present.

I chose someone else over her all those years ago because it was easier and more convenient. Who's to say I wouldn't do that again once she leaves. I like to believe I wouldn't, but it doesn't really matter what I believe, it matters what she does. I'd never do that to her again, but how does she know that?

I left her one last thing. One last try. One last effort. I can't be left with any what-ifs this time. It will either save me or solidify my fate as the nail in the coffin.

Just when I'm finally starting to drift off to sleep, my phone buzzes.

It's Walter.

27

We all make mistakes

TATE

The morning hits me like a punishment. My eyes crack open only to slam shut again, the light burns through my skull. My head throbs in a steady rhythm, each beat sharp and merciless, like someone pounding on a door from the inside. The room spins when I try to move, like a slow, nauseating carousel ride I didn't ask for. I'm in Easton's bed, but Easton isn't here. There's an arm over me. It's tanner and more toned than Easton's. I turn my head and see the curly blond head of hair that belongs to none other than Easton's best friend. I'm getting flashbacks from last night. I remember he tasted like beer and fortune cookies and his huge hands around my hips. My hand in his hair and my legs around his waist. I am officially the worst human to ever walk to earth.

My mouth is as dry as the desert, tongue heavy with the sour taste of whatever I drank last night. I swallow, but it does nothing. The faintest sound of my phone buzzing across the room feels like cymbals crashing in my ears.

My stomach twists with every breath, a coiled threat waiting for the wrong movement to snap. I press the heel of my palm against my eyes, but it doesn't stop the pounding or the sickly waves of nausea coursing through my stomach. My skin is cold and clammy. I feel like I haven't slept a wink. But I look over at the clock and I've slept over nine hours.

This is the aftermath of bad decisions. The price of forgetting for a night. There is a reason I've never done this before and likely won't ever again.

Walter's arm rises and falls with my deep breaths. I slip out from under his arm. When I stand up, I'm left in nothing but Walter's shirt and my pink underwear. *God, I hope we didn't sleep together.*

I tiptoe out of the room. It's almost noon when I finally make my way out.

The house feels like it's holding its breath.

There are sticky rings on the coffee table from all the beer and confetti is sprinkled around like dead stars across the wood floor. A half-eaten box of lo mein sits in Mr. Mills chair in the living room, but I can smell it from here. I almost hurl at the smell. I'm getting flash backs to being over the toilet a few hours ago that I forgot happened until now.

I'm the first one up. I put my hair up into a messy bun and walk barefoot into the kitchen, bracing myself for the mountain of half-empty cups and sauce-streaked paper plates. I crack the back door open to let out all the smells from last night. I hear the creak of Lila's door down the hall, like something hit it, but it doesn't open.

I walk toward it, opening her door.

Lila's there, sitting cross-legged on the floor, barefoot. Her hair is wild and free now of the purple wig. She's picking bottle caps and fortune cookie wrappers off the floor, humming something low to herself.

She looks up when she hears me, and for a second, we both just stare. Her eyes are rimmed with sleep, but there's no fight in them this morning — just a tired truce.

"Hey," she says.

"Hey."

I grab a trash bag from her bed and drop down next to her. We work like that for a few minutes. Me picking up cups and her picking up the smaller things. It's silent, but not in a cruel way.

I look up at her every once in a while. For the first time, to me, she looks grown. She's seventeen now. I can see it the set of her jaw, and the prominence of her cheek bones. But she's still her. My Lila.

I hate that I've missed so much.

There is a mountain of unspoken words between us. We haven't so much as looked at each other since the beach last night.

Finally, she blows out a breath, looks down at her hands.

"I was a bitch last night."

I glance at her... my best friend who used to be more like a sister to me than a friend. I feel like a stranger to her now.

"Yeah," I say, a ghost of a smile tugging at my lips.

"You kinda were."

She laughs, and for a moment, everything feels like it used to. "Gosh. I know. I didn't even mean it like that."

I lean back against the wall. "It's okay," I say reassuring her.

She shakes her head, blonde hair falling into her eyes. "No. It's not OK. You're back and I should be... I don't know... better? Happier? But it's just... I don't know, Tate.

You left," she says bluntly.

This was never about me and Easton. The whole argument, her whole fight was about me and her. I abandoned her.

The words sting, but they're not poison. She's just being honest. I pull my knees up, resting my chin there as I watch her play with the edge of the garbage bag like it's a fidget toy.

"I did," I admit. "I left. And after a while I stopped calling or texting, or… anything really. You had friends, new people. I saw the photos, you know? You and Annie. You and all those girls. You didn't need me anymore."

Her eyes snap up, wet and sharp. "That's not true. You were always my best friend, Tate. Even when you were gone."

I wipe my palm on Walter's long sleeve shirt. "Then why did it feel like you replaced me?"

Lila swallows, looks away. "Maybe… maybe I tried to. Maybe it was easier. You were my favorite person. And then you were just gone. You didn't come back. Every summer you'd show up, blow through like a a hurricane. Make everything bright and messy and fun and then you'd leave. And I'd be here. We'd both be here. Me and

Easton left picking up the pieces."

His name pierces my ears. I close my eyes. The floor is cold under my bare feet, grounding me. "I'm sorry, Lil. I should've reached out or come back or something."

She shrugs her shoulders "I should've too. I should have never said all those things about you and Easton, that was wrong."

We sit there like that, surrounded by cold Chinese food and crumbled napkins, and for a second, it's like we're kids again, building blanket forts in the living room. I nudge her knee with mine. "You were right, though."

She lifts a brow. "I know. But about what?" "Last night. What you said about me and Easton.

About me… wrecking things."

She sighs so deep I feel it in my own ribs. "I don't want to see either of you hurt. I love the idea of you two. You know that right? You're the story in my head of the perfect fairytale. My brother and my best friend being meant for each other is kind of a dream scenario. But Tate—" she catches my eyes, and her honesty stings more than her anger ever could. "He's not ready for you. To be completely honest, I don't know if you're ready for him either. He loves you so much it scares him. You have this whole life ahead of you, and we all see it. He's just starting to figure out what he wants. You'll get in each other's way, and you'll hate each other for it."

I feel my throat tighten, not with anger but with the worst thing of all… understanding. "I ended things with him last night. It was awful." I whisper, "not that there was much to end but…"

Lila moves the hair out of her face, tossing another bottle cap into the bag. "Because of me?" She asks.

"No," I confirm. "Because no matter how much we love each other, our lives don't mix. And no matter how much I want them to, it doesn't change the fact that they just don't. Not right now at least."

She plays the bottle cap in her hand, silently agreeing with me.

"I feel like I've been waiting a lifetime for him, Lil," I say

"Well then, what's a few more years?"

Her words hang in the air. Not because she's wrong, but because she's right. If we can happen now, then we can happen later.

"What if later never comes?" I ask her.

She grabs my hand, takes a deep breath and says, "Did you ever think this summer was gonna come?" I shake my head *no*.

"The greatest things aren't ever things we expect. They're things we hope for, but that's what makes them special. There's no guarantee that we'll get it in the end. You just have to hope," she says it like it's a quote from a romcom or a book she's read, but I know that that truth bomb was a hundred percent Lila Mills.

"Then I have to go," I tell her.

"Then you have to go," she says with eyes heavy.

This is either going to be the stupidest decision of my life, or the greatest. The hardest thing about making these kinds of decisions is that you don't know if you've made the right choice until later.

Lila studies my face for a long beat. Her room is so quiet we can hear the birds waking up outside her window.

Finally, she rests her hand on my knee. "What's the plan?"

Before I can say anything, she adds, "That's not Easton's shirt." Her eyes go wide as she does the mental math, figuring out who's shirt I could possibly be wearing.

A smirk works its way onto her face.

My mouth hangs open, trying to find an excuse that makes me sound not like a terrible human, but I can't find one. *I just fell asleep next to your brother's best friend. I got drunk and made out with the first guy I saw. I don't know what happened, I just woke up in Walter's clothes.* Every scenario I come up with makes me sound just as awful as I am.

The part that makes me the sickest, is that part of me feels a slight longing for the bed I woke up in, and the boy lying in it. I shake my head and the thought away.

"Please don't tell me y'all slept in Easton's bed?" She questions, still a bit in shock.

When I don't answer Lila, she laughs the first true laugh I've heard from her in years. "Oh, he's gonna burn that bed. And maybe Walter. No, Walter will probably be dead," she rambles.

"We didn't sleep together," I defend. *I hope that's true.*

"Then what did you do?" she asks me.

"I was sad, and he comforted me."

Her eyes dig into my soul like knives. "And gave you his shirt?" She puts her hands in the air.

"Lila," I say pleadingly. But I don't have to beg her the way I thought I would.

"I won't tell Easton. But for the record, running to Walter isn't gonna make anything better for anyone." "You're not mad at me?" I ask.

"All of this wouldn't have happened if I would have just told you how I felt. We're both to blame."

My face softens. Maybe she's more mature than I give her credit for. "If I had the opportunity to kiss Walter, I would take it to. So, I don't blame you."

I laugh out loud and then realize how loud I'm being. "Shut up. Have *you guys* ever?" I ask, just checking to see if Walter was truthful to me about them back at the beach.

She shakes her head *no.* "He see's me as a little sister, which is extremely unfortunate because I would do anything to touch those bleach blonde curls."

I'm filled with relief when she answers. I didn't realize how badly I hoped they weren't a thing until now.

Last night my hands were running through those bleach blonde curls, but now isn't the time to bring that up. I need to back to my room and pack, and somehow tell Walter I'm leaving.

"I should pack," I say. I walk toward the door dragging my feet a bit.

"I'll come see *you* this time." Lila says with a smile.

I turn back around with a smile plastered on my face. I run toward her and fall on the ground, collapsing on top of her. "I love you, Lila." I say in a sing-song way.

She laughs hard and pushes me off her. "I love you too."

* * *

When I walk into Easton's room I see the last thing I thought I'd ever see. Walter is sitting in the middle of the floor, slightly bent over my suitcase. His biceps contract as he folds my clothes and puts them into the body of my suitcase. He's shirtless, probably because

I unintentionally stole his shirt this morning. Now that I'm sober, I take all of him in. His back is tan and toned, each muscle defined. His sweatpants sit low on his waist. His back is to me, and something in my stomach clinches when I see the little marks on his back. They aren't deep or anything. He looks like he got a back massage. I know in my heart that I put those marks there, but I can't for the life of me remember. He must feel me starring, because he turns around spotting me. His face immediately smiles. "What are you doing?" I ask.

"Packing you up," he says like it's obvious.

"Wanna get rid of me that fast huh?"

"I booked you at flight at 4."

My face falls, "Oh, you really do want to get rid of me."

"You said you wanted to go home, so I pulled some stings with my uncle. He's a pilot for Delta. Got you on the next flight," he says sweetly.

"What? Why did you do that?" I ask walking toward him, joining him on the floor.

"You said it was what you wanted. Still is, right?" His eyes have this glimmer of hope in them. Like after whatever happened last night I might want to stay.

I don't know what comes over me, but I wrap my arms around his neck and squeeze him as hard as I can.

"Thank you, Walter."

"Anything for you *honey*. But you gotta promise me something." His words tickle my neck. I pull away to look at him and his face is close to mine. Our lips too close. "You gotta write me into one of your movies. Okay?"

I laugh and shake my head in agreement. "I think I can do that."

My eyes are looking straight into his, holding his eye contact until his eyes drop to my lips. I follow suit and look at his lips. Full, soft, and pink. I want them on mine again.

As slowly as possible I lean into him, giving him all the time in the world to stop me, but he doesn't. I kiss him so lightly I almost think I'm not kissing him at all. He reaches for my face, pulling me closer to him, and kisses me deep and long, like it's the last kiss he'll get. The second I start to let my body mold into his, he pulls away. My face still in his hands. "I know I'm not Easton. I know I don't have this long history of knowing you, even though I would give anything to have known every version of you. But I really like *this* version of you. The dream chaser, the writer, the artist, the realist. He knows you better than I can right now, and I know you love him. I know he's your sweater, but he's not the only one who's going to miss you when you leave today. I know he knew you, but if you gave me the chance, I would give my left kidney to get to know you today and all the days that follow after. You make me wanna do more than just play drums and surf and smoke weed. You make me feel, alive."

"Wait, if this is about last night. I don't know what happened but—" I say, stopping him from his confession.

"Last night?" He chuckles. "We kissed, a lot, and then you threw up all over your clothes."

"Oh," I look at his big blue eyes. So big and vast and full of things I've never explored. "So nothing happened?" He shakes his head *no*. "You told me all about the movie you wanna write and fell sleep on my chest. That's it." Oh. That's really sweet.

"What about your back? It's all... scratched?" I say slightly embarrassed.

He chuckles the cutest little laugh. "You scratched my back for hours. You just started running your fingers all over my back while you talked. I was fighting my demons trying to stay awake. It was so relaxing." "Oh," I don't know what to say.

"So, it's not the sex that made you feel alive?" I question.

He shakes his head. "Your mind. The way it works, thinks, creates and the way you look at me and the way your hand feels against my skin… it's all so electric. You're electric. You just being you is what makes me feel alive," he says, honestly searching my eyes.

How does someone respond to something like that?

"If you're asking to date me, you know that can't happen."

"I'm asking for you to let me text you, and let me call you, and maybe even FaceTime you. I would never ask you to put your life on hold for me. But I'll settle for a friend, because I think that's all either of us can be for each other right now."

He's right and he's so sweet. He sounds so mature. He's got his head on straight. He doesn't want to join himself to me, he just wants to watch and hear about all the things I do.

"I could use a friend," I say with a smile.

"Good. Let's get you packed then. You're future awaits." He says folding the last of my clothes.

"Do you think I'm making a mistake?" I ask him honestly.

"I think you're doing what's right. Even if it sucks right now. But that's the hardest part about making the right decision. It feels wrong for a while until you can see that it was right. It just takes time. And time takes patience. And patience takes discipline. Which for you right now, is focusing on getting committed. So that you can focus on all those dreams you have for after college. I'll let you in on a secret. Boys are stupid. Me included. I've watched my sister get her heart broken time and time again and every time she's stuck picking up the pieces on her own because some douchebag guy decided he could find someone better. She's always so lost, all because of a guy. The best thing to do, is do what you have to do for you. The right guy will come along."

He's so much different than I thought. I feel bad for having run away from his truck after the beach.

For ignoring him.

For not getting to know him better while I've been here.

But he's right. I don't have time for boys right now.

"You're right." I tell him as I zip up my suitcase. "Are you always this good at giving advice?"

"Having sisters makes you a wise man. What can I say?" he jokes.

I giggle until I fall back down to reality. "What are you gonna tell Easton?"

His face hardens as he ponders my question. "That he'll be okay. That he should go to Nashville. That he should write every feeling he feels about you down on paper and do what every heart broken musician does. Use the pain."

I'm glad Easton has friend like Walter. I asked because I wondered if he was going to tell Easton that we kissed but by the look in his eyes right now, I think last night and today were our little secret. And honestly, I can live with that.

Walter checks his watch. "He's gonna be okay, but you won't be if you miss your flight! Let's go."

I rush to get ready and finish grabbing my last-minute things.

I leave my mom and Jessie a note explaining things vaguely. Lila will know how to handle them when they get home, so I don't worry too much.

The whole drive to the airport, I look out the window of Walter's truck. Walter has rolled down the window, so the wind's in my hair. I resist the urge to look over at Walter. It will be easier to leave him if I stop thinking about how I'll miss him once I'm gone. How can someone become so important to you so quickly?

It's weird how his lack of need to keep me here makes me want to know him more. It's nice to be seen for the person I want to become. Walter is the first person to truly believe that I can do all the things I want to do. He has a faith in me, a confidence that makes me actually believe in myself. I have a feeling he's gonna be a good friend. Someone who reads my scripts, shares my successes on his Instagram story, texts me *happy birthday* and random pictures of the ocean, just because he feels like it.

He's right. He doesn't know me like Easton does. Part of me loves that. There's no expectation. No need to explain why I feel differently than I used to. No history or past. It's a blank slate, and empty canvas. It excites me.

He kisses my cheek after he gets my luggage out from the bed of his truck. I watch him drive off and when I turn around to walk toward the entrance, I'm met with the last person I expect to see.

Easton Mills.

28

Only you

EASTON

I don't say anything when I see them. A kiss on the cheek is nothing, especially between them. The love of my life and my best friend. I let any harsh thought that comes to my mind when his lips hit her cheek wash away, like water off a ducks back. I know them, and I know they wouldn't do that to me. Especially not that quick. What am I saying? Especially not at all. It's inconceivable. My hands are clinched at my side when she turns around. She's walking toward me, looking at the ground. When she see's me, she stops completely in her tracks.

"Easton? What are you doing here?" she says shocked, like I expected she'd be.

I want to tell her I had all night to think. One sleepless night and I realize how stupid I've been with her heart, with our lives, with us. I want to tell her that I won't get in the way of her future and that I'm gonna become the man she sees. The singer and songwriter I dream of becoming. I want to tell her I feel all the ambition that she does for my future. My bones ache to tell her exactly what I practiced saying in the mirror before I drove here.

I've never been happier to get a text from Walter. He told me to be here at the Delta entrance. He told me to apologize and hug her and tell her exactly how I feel. He told me to let her go, but not without saying everything I need to say first.

"Walter told me you'd be here."

"Did he?" She looks behind her like Walter might still be there, even though we both know he's long gone. "What else did he say?" She asks taking a couple steps closer.

"He said I should apologize and tell you exactly how I feel."

She's only two or so feet from me. I want to close the distance and hug her, but I can't yet. "I'm sorry," I blurt out. "You're right. I can't just drop my life to follow you. That isn't fair to either of us… *shit*." I can't say the things I've practiced. It's too much. There's too much to say.

I try my best to piece it all together. "Tate, I love you. I always have and I think I always will. When you left last time and didn't come back, I was shattered. I thought nothing could feel worse than losing my best friend. But this, watching you get on a plane and not knowing if I'm ever gonna see you again, or, or kiss you again? I'm not watching my best friend leave this time, I'm watching the love of my life leave me."

"Easton," she says eyes heavy, but she doesn't look like she's gonna cry. I'm the one about to cry this time.

I try to push my words out into the air before she can say anything else. "It might have just been a week, but we've been in the plan for as long as I can remember. And when you didn't come back, I really thought I could finally forget you, but I realized… I'd be an idiot to think I could ever forget you. It's always been you. And no matter how far apart our lives take us, it's always gonna be you. I'm not asking you to choose me or to choose at all. All I'm saying is that I don't think I'm capable of truthfully, honestly choosing anyone other than you," I say.

There's nothing more I can say. I want her to stay. My body feels like it's giving out on me. My throat is on fire, my eyes are burning, and the tears I so badly want to suck back into my body are welling up in my eyes.

She takes two big steps toward me, leaving no space between us. She grabs my face with her soft little hands.

She doesn't have to make me look at her because I'm always looking at her. She kisses my lips, softly. It's so gentle it hurts. She pulls away, resting her hand on my chest.

"I need you to choose you."

Her hand drops to mine, grabbing it like she doesn't want to let go. She backs away and I hold onto her hand for as long as she'll let me. I hold on so long that our arms are extended and only our middle and pointer fingers are intertwined.

And then, she lets go.

I'm shaking my head, back and forth, tears dripping onto my shirt.

That's not how I saw this. Despite what Walter said, I wanted her to choose me. I wanted her to choose us. I wanted what I said to be good enough.

But she's gone, out of my grasp.

I wanted to hold her tight when she kissed me and tell her I'm done losing her. Anchoring her here with me. Begging her to stay.

I'd lean in, our foreheads touching. I'd tell her she feels like home to me. I'd cover her with a truth to combat every lie in her head. My words softer than anything I've ever said.

"Every girl I've ever dated," I'd whisper, "I compare them to you. They aren't as funny—" I'd kiss her right cheek.

"Not as beautiful—" left cheek. "Not as freckled—" her forehead. "Not as kind—" the back of her right hand. "Not as loyal—" her palm.

"Not as nerdy—" the back of her left hand. "Not as trustworthy—" her left palm. "Not as honest—" the tip of her perfect nose. "Not as goofy—" her chin. "Not as sweet—" her soft lips. "Not as ambitious—" her perfect lips. "Not as… YOU." I'd punch every word with a kiss. Her face, her hands, her mouth. Her tears would mix with mine — salt on salt. Love on love.

And when she'd say my name, it'd be like a prayer. I'd tell her, "I tried to forget you; I tried to replace you. I tried to date someone like you, but no one is you, Tate Knightly. I've tried everything. And it all sucked because none of them were you. *I finally have you.* Don't take that from me. Please," I'd beg.

I wouldn't hide my fear, and she'd see it. She'd see the boy she grew up with. She'd see the man I've become.

"I want you. I have only ever wanted you," I'd tell her and she'd trust me.

Her eyes would answer *yes* before her lips do.

"I love you," she'd choke out. "I really love you. And it terrifies me, but I do. I only want you too," She'd say.

My smile hurts my cheeks. I'm so happy I can't breathe. I'd pull her into me, and I'd take her home. We'd live out the summer we were suppose to always have. We'd make up for the five years of silence…all the lost time, lost moments and lost kisses.

But none of that happens because she's already gone. She let go of my hand and walked into the airport.

She's gone.

She left me here.

And the worst part is that even though I want to be mad at her — even though I want to yell and scream and hate her for choosing this… I know that she made the right choice.

I hate that I know she's always deserved better than me.

Someone that fights like hell for their dreams.

That someone isn't me.
Yet.

29

Departure

TATE

I don't believe in signs. But if I did, I got one. As if it was meant to be, right after I walked through TSA I got a phone call from an unknown number. I almost silenced it and turned my phone off all together, but the unknown number makes me curious, so, I answer.

"Hi, is this Tate?" The voice says over the phone. His voice is deep and raspy and has a slight accent. It sounds vaguely familiar, but I can't quite place where the voice is from.

"Yes, she's speaking. Who's this?"

"This is Mark. Mark Simone. I'm the head beach volleyball coach at Pepperdine University, located in Malibu, California. I gave you my card at the tournament last week," he informs me.

Oh, that's where I know the voice from. His accent is Brazilian. I almost lose the gum in my mouth from how wide it's hanging. "Yes, oh wow, hi!" I say trying to sound less shocked than I am. I fail terribly.

"Do you have a moment to talk?" he asks.

Yes, of course I do!!

I stop in my tracks immediately and set my bags down. I can't keep walking with my backpack, suitcase, and water bottle. I need to pace around for this conversation. "Yes, I'm at the airport," I say. "Sorry if it's a little loud."

"No worries. I'm reaching out to let you know how much I enjoyed watching you play this past tournament. I love your spunk and your style of play. It's unique. It's different."

"Thank you sir, that's so kind," I say, truly flattered. I can feel my cheeks turn pink.

"Tate, I think you would be a perfect fit for our team.

You're exactly what we've been looking for. We would love to have someone with your confidence and ability on our team.

Holy shit. Holy shit.

Never in my life have I believed in signs or confirmation occurrences until now. The second I step into the airport I get this call. I've never felt more confident in my decision than I do right now.

I can't believe what I'm hearing. Words struggle to form but I manage to mumble out, "Oh, that's that's—"

He interrupts. "You don't need to make a decision right now. Especially since you haven't seen our campus or our courts. I know you have other options. Based on the conversations I've had, you're highly sought after. I knew I would need to reach out quickly to insure we would even have a chance with you. All that to say, I would love to get you out here in California for a visit and then you can decide if Malibu feels like home to you or not. How does that sound?"

I didn't think after getting second last week anyone was going to reach out, and now I'm being offered a spot at one of the most prestigious beach volleyball programs in the nation. Did he really say I'm highly sought after… it makes me wonder who else wants me too? I didn't realize how important all of this was to me.

"That sounds perfect," I tell him, before I have any real time to think about it. "When can I come?" I ask.

"I can book a flight for today, if you'd like. I know you said you're at the airport. If you'd be willing to switch up your plans, we'd love to have you," he says.

"Yes, I'll be there." I sound entirely too eager, but it's too late to change my tone.

He chuckles over the phone, "Perfect, I'll text your flight information as soon as I have it. Thank you for your time, Miss Knightly. See you soon."

He hangs up, and just like that, everything changes.

My flight. My plans. My future.

* * *

The gate smells like burnt coffee and old carpet cleaner. The stale airport air is heavy with the sounds of too many *goodbyes* and not enough *hellos*. I stand in line with my carry-on slung over my shoulder, hugging my elbows trying to contain my excitement.

I see couples telling each other goodbye, kissing each other, and holding each other for just a second longer. I can't smile at them the way I use to, knowing what I'm leaving behind here in Florida. But it doesn't make me feel as sick as I thought it would. Not when I have a university and a possible scholarship on the other end of this plane ride. I avert my eyes and focus on the flight attendant in front of me as I hand her my ticket.

Something in me shifts.

I can't really decipher my feelings right now. I'm excited for what's next, but there's a little piece of me grieving what I'm leaving. I take a big, deep breath and settle with the idea that I will leave that piece of my heart here. I will leave that chunk of my heart that beats for

Easton Mills here in the Orlando Airport terminal. It will drag me down if I take it, so I kiss it goodbye like I tried to do five years ago. This time with no regrets.

My phone is tucked in my pocket, dark and quiet. After I got off the phone with my my mom and Walter, I silenced it.

She wasn't thrilled to hear I was leaving but I could hear in her voice that she understood, like she always does. I was thankful to have such an understanding mom in moments like these. She was thrilled to hear about the offer from Pepperdine, so I think that helped with the whole *leaving* part. She might not agree with what's going on exactly, but she trusts me and supports me. Not every girl can say she has that in her life. I was one of the lucky ones. I told her not to leave early. She loves the summer, and she loves being with Jessie, so she deserves to stay and she promised me she would.

I called Walter to thank him for the flight, but informed him I'd be changing it and heading out to California. To which he replied, "That quick huh?" But I know he wasn't really surprised. He was proud. I secretly hoped he'd tell Easton, and because of that secret hope, I silenced my phone. Because even though I just left him, I know that Easton would text me to congratulate me or even worse, maybe call. I can't handle that. Not right now. I need time to form a piece of my heart that beats just for me and a part of me that beats for the friendship I will eventually have with Easton. But I can't have that until I heal from leaving the piece of my heart that loves him here. Right now, I'm broken and bleeding. I need a band-aid and some distance. I think California can be both.

But in time, I'll be able to talk to Easton and not openly bleed on the floor. Today is not that day though. So, I make sure my phone is silenced before I stuff it into my backpack as I finally find my seat on the plane.

When I open the front pocket of my backpack I see something that doesn't belong. A brown envelope that's a bit crinkled. It's folded over in the middle, made to fit that small pocket of my backpack it was in. It's old, like it's been stuffed in a drawer for years.

There's no name is on it.

Just this: For if we ever get her

The words tilt downhill in Easton's sloppy cursive; the kind the Jessie taught him as a kid when he was still homeschooled.

I trace the letters with my thumb. I know I shouldn't open it. I don't even know where it came from. I'm opening it before I can think of how it ended up in my backpack. I slide my finger under the flap and tug the paper free. It's notebook paper — lined, frayed at the edges. I recognize the way he loops his g's and crosses his t's too high.

Going against all the thoughts in my head and the bleeding of my still broken heart, I read it.

Tate Knightly,

I don't know if I'll ever be enough for you. I think about that a lot. I always have. How you are gonna leave here someday and do everything you say you will. And it finally happened. You didn't come back. I'm happy you didn't if it means you'll get to be everything we talked about on the front porch as kids.

That's all I've ever wanted.

Movies always talk about how you don't realize how much you appreciate something until it s gone. I didn't think that was true until now. I didn't realize how much I looked forward to having you in this house every summer until you weren't anymore.

It's so empty without your smile. And a lot less happy without your laugh.

I miss you.

I always do. But this time it feels like I'll miss you forever.

Part of me always knew this day would come. I always knew I'd have to say goodbye.

So, I'm writing this to you and my future self, in hopes that I can open this one day with you sitting in front of me.

I pull out a second paper, from right behind the one I'm reading. This one is addressed to him, but I read it anyway.

Hey, Easton.

How you doing man?

If you're opening this, then well, you're probably over the moon. How could you not be with Tate Knightly sitting in front of you. I bet she's even more beautiful now than she was when I m writing this. But her eyes, they'll be the same. Pots of honey.

This is your reality check. OK?

I don t know what you did to get her to come back or why she's there with you but listen to me when I say, DO NOT SCREW THIS UP.

She is your best friend. Don t ever forget that. To help you with that... here is a list of rules you will need to follow in order to be what she needs.

1. Don't ever hold her back. Her dreams are big. Be glad she let's you be part of them.
2. Don't ever stop making her laugh. She loves to laugh so hard her belly hurts.
3. Give her the life she deserves. Work as hard as you can to ensure that she can have everything she's ever dreamed. She deserves that.
4. Don't ever let her lose her love for Marvel & Star Wars. Could

you even imagine. Yikes. She'll thank you for this one.

5. Listen to her. She always has the best advice.

6. Kiss her damn well. Like so well she forgets her name.

7. Don't ever stop loving her like she's your best friend!!!

If you get the joy of being with the most epic girl we've ever met, then you better not be stupid enough to let her go. Our heart can't handle that twice.

If you're reading this then you must've done something right. So yeah, maybe just keep doing that.

From Easton

I flip to the last page, and it reads:

TK,

Even if it hasn't felt like it. It's always been you.

It will always be you.

Your other half, Easton

07/21/2019

My eyes blur when I'm done. Tears threatening to fall down my cheek. I fold it back along the old creases, put it back in the envelope and press it to my chest for a heartbeat and take a deep breath.

I can't believe he wrote this five years ago. I can't believe he felt this way for me all those summers ago.

It floods my brain how much time we lost over those years, both secretly desiring the other. I feel like I'm drowning in the thought of what could have been. If only it had been different.

If only I had known. I wish I would've known.

The letter was written exactly how he talks. Thought out, but sort of purposefully sporadic. Jumping from one thought to another, but somehow each puzzle piece fits together, and I don't know how. They just do. His brain works that way. It's one of the things I love about him. *Oh. Love.*

The butterflies in my stomach have multiplied and won't stay still.

I don't feel guilt like I think I should. I'm afraid I'll forget him. That by leaving that piece of my heart here, I'll forget the person it beats for.

Easton Mills, the boy who would've moved mountains if I'd asked him to. And I'm the girl who didn't ask. I'm the girl who left. Again.

I keep replaying it in my head — his bedroom, his hands on my face, that grin when I finally said *I love you.* The way his laugh echoed through the apartment, the way his skin felt against mine, the way he kissed me in the kitchen, the way he said *I love you,* the way he looked when I let go of him — It's all burned into my brain.

Gosh, I meant all of it. Every word. Every action. Every moment. Every piece of it.

But some things love can't fix. Not yet.

I think about Lila, barefoot in her room, messing with the edge of that garbage bag while we made a mess of apologies we should've made years ago. Her voice when she said, *the greatest things aren't ever things we expect. They're things we hope for, but that's what makes them special. There's no guarantee that we'll get them in the end. You just have to hope.*

It rings in my ears.

Maybe she's right.

I'll leave that piece of my heart here with him, and if it's right, then in time that piece of my heart will find me again. I have to hope.

I'm ready for him. But my life isn't. And neither is his.

It's better for both of us this way.

These chapters have to play out before we can have our chapter again. I hope we're lucky enough to share pages in the same chapter again.

I sink down into it my seat, tucking my knees to my chest as the rest of the plane hums with strangers and overhead bins and the pilot's voice over the loud speaker. I put the letter back in my backpack.

I slide my headphones on and put on the only song I can think of right now, *Kirby Girl* by the *Backseat Lovers*. I turn the volume all the way up, attempting to drown out any thoughts left in my head.

I love this song. Before this summer, I had never heard it. It was something special, but it wasn't as special as when Easton sang it that night on stage. I guess for now, this will have to do.

I press my forehead against the glass.

I love him.

I do.

Maybe the best kind of love is the kind that can wait.

The engine roars. *Here we go.*

My future awaits. We depart and as the ground falls away beneath me, a thought lands heavy in my gut — an anchor and a lifeline all at once.

Gosh, I hope I don't have to wait another five years for us to be ready.

30

Epilogue

A sneak peak at — *The Past 5 Years*

TATE

The first time I tried on a wedding dress I was twelve, in Jessie's closest. Easton was sitting cross-legged on the ugly green carpet of their old house. He was pretending to study his brand new phone, but he was really waiting for me to step out from behind the closet door and twirl around for him. "You look ridiculous," he said when he saw me. But his smile told me he didn't mean it. His smile told me he was already storing away that version of me, just in case.

That was ten years ago.

Today, under the soft, white glow of the bridal showroom lights and the swish of satin smoothing across my skin, he's nowhere to be found.

He hasn't been anywhere near me in five years.

"Tate? Earth to Tate?"

I blink, pulling myself back to now. Back to the woman kneeling at my hem with a mouthful of pins. The consultant beams up at me like we're co-conspirators in some fairytale.

"Sorry", I say, voice too soft in the mirror filled room. "What did you say?"

"You look beautiful," she repeats, tilting her head like she's imagining the veil and the flowers and the man at the end of the aisle, who isn't Easton Mills.

I look at myself. Really look. The dress is simple. Classic with a little bit of lace, and a little bit of silk. Nothing wild. No plunging neckline, no beads that catch the light like a disco ball. It fits me the way I always wanted a wedding dress to fit me. It's the perfect dress. I love it. I feel beautiful in it. My fiancé will love it.

My fiancé — the word still sticks in my throat sometimes. He's kind and he's very, very handsome. He's six foot five, tan, with piercing blue eyes. He has strong shoulders and a solid sculpted frame. He makes good coffee and is the head of a local non-profit in LA county that teaches little kids lifeguard safety. He loves me in the way that feels like fresh sheets after you shave — perfect.

You couldn't ask for much better.

He just isn't Easton.

My college roommate Gwen introduced us. She thought we'd be perfect for each other because we both loved superheroes and alt rock music. We hit it off, but it wasn't so shocking. Gwen told me she met the most perfect specimen of a man at the beach. Total surfer vibes with a little bit of oddball. She planned a double date for us my sophomore year at Pepperdine. It was at a country western bar through the canyon. He was tall and had shaggy beach blonde curls. He wore a cowboy hat that smushed his curls to the side of his face and boots that made him look like someone I didn't know. When he turned around, I was met with deep blue ocean eyes that I had looked into before, lips that I had tasted, a neck I had wrapped my arms around, and hands that once held me in one of my darkest moments.

When our eyes met, he didn't even flinch. He looked me up and down, tilted his head and saluted me like an army general. And without thinking, I did it back.

Walter Hughes.

We danced the night away, had a couple drinks, and he took me to the beach. We didn't talk about that summer or the Mills or Easton. We both knew to avoid the elephant in the room. We texted almost every day for about four months after that summer we first met, but I ended up ghosting him. I needed to let him go to fully heal from that summer. He understood...which only made him that much hotter. A tall, sexy man, with perfect beach boy hair and rock hard abs that respected my boundaries... and I chose to stay away from him... willingly.

By the humor of God alone, somehow Walter ended up about an hour away from me at USC. He was pursuing an entrepreneurship degree and doing music on the weekends with his band, *The West Coast Fakers*. He went to class most days, except for when the surf was good.

When I saw him that night in the bar, I almost couldn't believe my eyes. He was stronger than the last time I saw him, like maybe he did more than just shred waves as a workout. His biceps looked like they were sculpted by an ancient artist, and he was the tannest I'd ever seen him. His curls were blonder somehow, like the sun kissed his head.

We were inseparable from that night on.

That night at the beach it took everything in me to not let him kiss me. I had kissed a boy or two or three, in the time I'd spent away from Florida. It was mainly to help rid my brain of everything that happened that summer, but nothing helped. Nothing really worked. I hadn't dated anybody, because I didn't have the time or the want to.

When Walter and I danced in the sand that night on the beach, I leaned my head against his chest and let my feet move to the rhythm of his heart. We danced like that for a while and it was nice. There was no expectation in the air. I knew he wasn't gonna try to kiss me, even though his eyes had already undressed me and kissed every inch of my body more than once that night. Even though his eyes deceived him, I knew he was only going to dance with me.

As we watched the moonlight dance across the water, he told me about the past two years and all the things I'd missed. His hand sat so close to mine in the sand, I was positive he was going to grab it… but he never did. He rattled on and on about all the things he was doing now. He smiled so big when he talked about the guys in his band and how they met. He said USC was a very different experience from what he expected. He told me he doesn't really go home anymore, and I didn't ask why.

There were nights when I couldn't fall asleep, and I'd often wonder if Walter ever told Easton about what happened between us that night before the airport. That could easily be the reason Walter doesn't go back to Florida anymore. A confrontation with Easton Mills kept me out of Florida for five years… I have a feeling this would hurt Easton a lot more than anything that happened back then. I didn't ask him if I'm the reason he doesn't go back because I didn't want to make the moment about me. I didn't want to talk about Easton and I'm not even sure I wanted to know the answer to the question anyway.

He said the gas prices were hard to get used to, so he sold his truck and used the extra cash to buy a camera. He does senior photo shoots and sorority events and things like that whenever he has the time. His eyes lit up when he mentioned the camera, like it was a newfound love of his. I could've listened to him talk til the sun came up.

He asked me questions about college and life. It was refreshing. I hadn't had a conversation like that in a while. One that had ebbs and flows like the ocean. There was never a dull moment. Even in the silence, which never last long, there was a peace in the air I was familiar with. It was comforting, like your mom's hug after a breakup or your own laugh after a good cry.

I didn't realize I had missed him like that. But I did.

And for that reason, although every fiber of my being wanted to, I didn't kiss him. The ball was in my court, and I didn't play. I sat the ball down and walked away, again. I was starting to think I had an issue of leaving when things got good.

When the night came to an end, Walter ended up sleeping on the couch at my place. His friends assumed he had a ride because he left the bar with me, so they went back to USC and didn't want to pick him up in the middle of the night. When I woke up the next morning, he had coffee made, the exact way I liked it… although I don't remember ever telling him how I liked my coffee. It had two splashes of cream and entirely too much sugar. He made us chocolate chip pancakes and flipped them shirtless in my kitchen.

I ate the pancakes with him, after I politely offered him his shirt. I don't need the temptation of his washboard abs. His smile was enough to make my stomach turn, and he'd flash it at me every 4.5 seconds. After we ate the pancakes and we drank our coffee, I kindly asked him to leave. I couldn't take much more of his presence without losing the battle between my heart and my brain. My brain is not putting up much of a fight.

He left as soon as his friend swung by my place. It wasn't until his friend pulled up in a convertible that I remembered Walter came from money. Nothing about him screamed that he was rich, but he was. He didn't ask to keep in contact with me. He didn't call, text, or DM me. He didn't even come to that bar again. He just left me alone. Which I guess is the vibe you would assume in return for kicking him out of my house, not kissing him and making him sleep on the couch… but I had secretly hoped he'd ask to see me again. So when he didn't, I sat with the realization that I WANTED HIM TO.

But, none-the-less… I did nothing about it.

One week later I got an envelope in the mail. Inside there was a picture with a note scribbled on the back. The picture was mostly dark, except for what the flash exposed…it was of me, mid-laugh, standing on the beach. My hair was slightly in my face, and my hand is waving out in front of me, begging him not to take a picture, but clearly, he did.

I turned the picture around; on the back he drew out what looked like his version of a postcard.

It said:

Thanks for letting me crash and for letting me make you pancakes. And obviously, thank you for eating them. I hope you like the picture… it took a lot for me to part with it.

-Walt

The black ink was smudged in a place or two from where his hand ran over the words as he wrote it. It smelled like him, or like his cologne rather. I couldn't help but sniff it. Ugh, I was pathetic. I was pathetic, but I liked him. I was pathetically in like with a surfer boy named, Walter. People don't sniff the paper of a handmade postcard from a boy they don't like.

I had forgotten his persistence in taking a picture with his camera that night on the beach. I had forgotten he even had his camera with him. But I guess he does take it everywhere.

The date marked on the back is *03/18*…Easton's birthday. I ignore that minor detail and push past it, because it's also the day Walter woke up at my place and made me pancakes. He wrote me a letter that day and sent it.

I hoped he still liked me.

I wrote him back a short letter telling him he was silly for communicating to me "basically by pigeon", but secretly I admired it. He sent me a homemade postcard every week for fifty-two weeks, with the exception of an extra one or two if something crazy happened, like a big show he had that weekend that he couldn't wait a couple extra days to tell me about. I loved the pictures. Especially the one's with him in them. Those one's were few and far between, but those were my favorite, because I loved seeing his smile. I'd hang them on the wall by my mirror. Just so I could catch a glimpse of him when I passed by.

After the 52 weeks he showed up the gated entrance to Pepperdine. He waited there for me to get done with class. He was holding yellow tulips and a Starbucks chai tea latte. It was then that I really fell.

He yearned for me. It was all over his face. The way his eyes were filled with hope and his smile full of joy. The way he waited and wished that I would ask him to get in the car with me. But when I invited him in, he pointed to a beat-up yellow Ford parked on the corner and said, "I had to save up. Can't take a beautiful girl on a date without a car."

My cheeks hadn't blushed like that in months, maybe years.

I parked my car next to his and got in his beat-up yellow truck. He told me when I sat in the passenger's seat, how he told his parents he wanted to be cut off from their finances. He wanted to make a man of himself without their help. They agreed, even though they wished he would just take the allowance they offered him. They negotiated and settled on paying for his tuition. Everything else would be Walter's responsibility. That was the best deal Walter was gonna get from his loving parents, so he took it. He had that conversation the night after the beach with me. He didn't say it, but I knew it was to prove that he could handle himself... so that maybe he could take care of me.

That is, if I ever let him.

He spent a year saving up to buy that beat up truck. He spent a year pursuing me with homemade postcards, waiting for the right time to take me on a date. A real one.

How could I say no to that?

So, I didn't. I said yes, and he just kept getting better with time. Like fine wine, he remained perfect and just got sweeter and more adventurous and more loving. But he never smothered me. He never crowed my space. He let me be me.

Every day I swear I fell in love with him more.

So now, two and a half years later from that day, I'm trying on wedding dresses and I'm happy to marry him.

Ecstatic. Over-joyed. Blessed.

"Is it the one?" The consultant asks me, hands hovering near the zipper like she's waiting for my *yes* to secure the sale.

I smooth my palms over my waist, the satin cool under my fingertips. "Yeah," I say, my voice steady, a little older than it used to be. "It's the one." I mean it, mostly.

But somewhere, buried under five years of distance and growing up and pretending that first loves don't have a secret place in your heart. There's still this soft, traitorous spark in the back of my mind.

The smallest part of me wonders if Easton Mills would think I looked *ridiculous*.

Or if he'd just smile that same perfect smile and say *beautiful*, like it was the simplest truth in the world.

Unfortunately, it's just not that simple anymore.

31

Acknowledgments

This is my first novel. My first pancake. The start of what I hope and dream will be a bookshelf full of more stories. I would've never known I was capable of writing a novel at all, let alone while in college playing a D1 sport and just trying to stay afloat, if it weren't for my mama, Robyn Campbell. So, the first thank you, goes to my mom, for believing in me when I couldn't even believe in myself. I'm a lucky girl to have both a best friend and a mom in the same person. Thank you for always being my first read, first editor, and first fan. I love you forever.

The next *thank you* goes to my nana, Rebecca Kuntz. I've never met a woman who loves to read more than she does. Every time she reads my pages she says, "I couldn't put it down sweetie! So good!!" She's the definition of a *reader* and I'm blessed to have a forever fan in her. We share a love for books and now she gets to hold my book in her hands and read it. WOW, isn't that crazy.

(I wrote the Dedication and the above paragraph about my nana two weeks before she passed away suddenly. Although she didn't get to hold it... she did get to read it. I'm forever grateful for that. I will miss her forever. I will keep her spirit and love for reading alive with my books and my love for writing. Every book I write is for her.) I love you, Nana!

The next *thank you* goes to my dad, Ian Campbell, for being my reading buddy and one of my first readers. Although we don't often read the same authors or genres, I'm a happy camper when he reads my pages. I love his feedback and his honesty.

Another *thank you* goes to one of my besties, Lillie Veer, for always being willing to read whatever I send her. Thank you for listening to me talk on and on about fictional characters and their "lives".

To the people who read this book and see a piece of themselves in it — I thought of you, but take it with a grain of salt. If it's good, then it's true. If it's bad, then I probably made it up. Don't hate me. I love you, that's why I put you in my story. Thank you for your inspiration and presence in my life.

About the Author

Gracey James— A young creative from Dallas, TX. She discovered her passion for storytelling during her career as a D1 beach volleyball athlete, first at Pepperdine University and then LSU, where she studied Sports Administration. Geaux tigers!

As a kid, Gracey James devoured books, rewatched her favorite movies and TV shows. She spent hours getting lost in the worlds other people created. As she grew up, she realized she wanted to build worlds of her own.

When she isn't drafting novels, you can find her developing screenplays, acting in and directing short film projects, writing songs, recording music and just hanging out with her family. No matter the medium, Gracey James is happiest when she's creating!

You can connect with me on:

🌐 https://www.instagram.com/graceyyjamess

Also by Gracey James

Coming soon!!!

Half of Me

Lakelyn is confident in the quiet ways. Artsy. Observant. The kind of girl who feels deeply but keeps most of it to herself. Her world is rich with creativity and emotion, even if her love life has stayed almost entirely still—paused somewhere between longing and caution.

Eli is the opposite. An overachiever who rarely stops to think. Charismatic, driven, and constantly moving forward, even when he's running from himself. His love life is messy, public, and always a little out of control—proof that it's easier to chase connection than to understand it.

They couldn't be more different.

The only thing they truly share is the fact that they're twins.

But when the balance between them starts to shift—when choices are made, lines are crossed, and secrets begin to surface—their bond is tested in ways neither of them are prepared for. What was once instinctive becomes fragile. What felt permanent starts to crack.

Because when the person who has always felt like half of you begins to change, you're forced to ask a terrifying question:

Who are you without them?

Half of Me is a haunting, emotional story about identity, tangled love, and the quiet unraveling of a bond you never thought could break.

www.ingramcontent.com/pod-product-compliance
Lightning Source LLC
Chambersburg PA
CBHW050031120726
47903CB00006B/1989